Genesis

Genesis

A NOVEL

DELON NICOLE STARKEY

COPYRIGHT

To my family: I am so incredibly thankful for the way you raised me. You showed me faith, love, hope, and joy. You are the reason I keep on living. I love you. Because of you, I never gave up hope, even in my darkest days.

Readers: To those who are still fighting for one more day. You're here now, and that is no accident. You are not defined by your past mistakes. There is still hope, and love will find a way.

ALSO BY DELON NICOLE STARKEY:

It Crescendos A Poetry Collection: The Oklahoma Years

The House on Monarch Street

TRIGGER WARNINGS

This story contains strong elements that may be triggering for some. I won't mention them here as they contain <u>spoilers,</u> so please keep that in mind if you decide to review the warnings ahead of time. If you are not easily triggered, then please carry on.

Life is full of pain, trauma, and grief. But know that there is still hope. This novel is a work of fiction but depicts real-life trauma. I hope this story will meet you wherever you are in your story.

You are not alone.

See page 281 if you'd like to review the trigger warnings ahead of time. It contains spoilers.

ACKNOWLEDGMENTS

First of all, I have to thank my Heavenly Father for getting me this far. I wouldn't have accomplished any of this without His endless love, mercy, and grace poured over my life. Thank you, forever.

Secondly, my family. For all your encouragement, kind words, and continued support throughout this entire thing. You didn't even know what this book was going to be about when I wrote it, because it didn't matter. You just said keep going, and I did exactly that. Thank you for pushing me to never give up, even when my dreams are tough and time-consuming. This also includes my Hubby Bear. Yes, you. You may never read the things I write, but you inspire me every single day. Love you!

Third, thank you to all my friends, all my readers, my ARC team, as well as my Hype team. Seriously, you guys are awesome. Thank you for taking yet another chance on me. I am forever grateful for your enthusiasm, encouragement, and support behind the scenes. I see you and appreciate you more than I can say here on paper.

Finally, a big big thanks to Stacy, my editor. You guys, she is not just an editor. She is magic. She makes the words come to life. She is fun, energetic, kind, caring, and compassionate. In short, she's amazing at what she does. My story would not look like this without you. I owe you big time. Thank you.

And a big thanks to YOU if this is your first time reading anything of mine. Thank you for taking the time to dive into this story that I poured my heart and soul into. It's spoken to me in a thousand different ways, I hope it speaks to your heart in a thousand more.

All My Love,

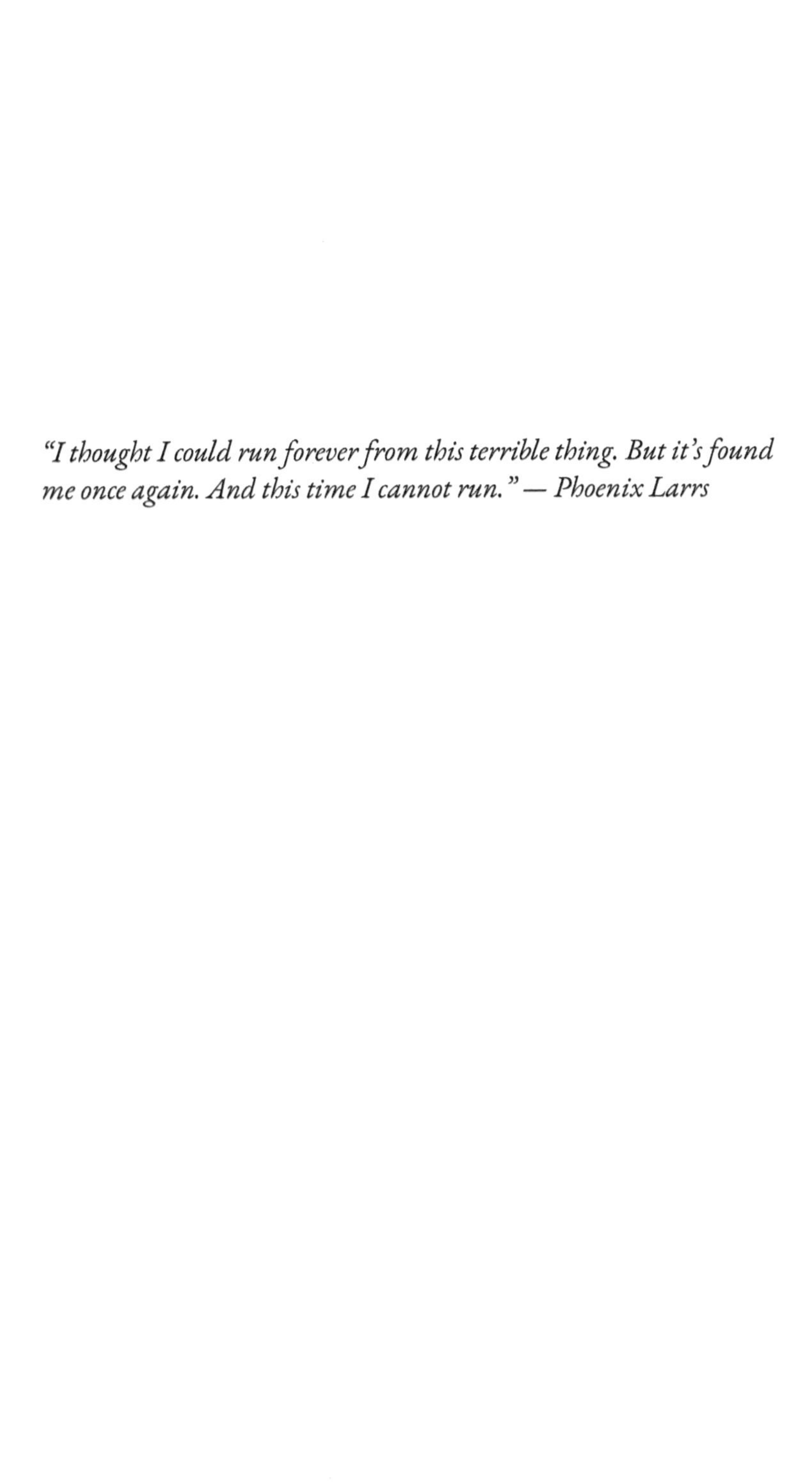

"I thought I could run forever from this terrible thing. But it's found me once again. And this time I cannot run." — Phoenix Larrs

PROLOGUE

New Beginnings

I wake up in a hospital bed. I'm surrounded by whirring machines and constant beeps. I have no idea how I got here or why I'm here.

Why am I here?

The room is dark save for the soft glow of glistening snow outside. I'm mesmerized by the steady fall of the snowflakes coating the cars in the parking lot. I watch them fall to the earth one by one.

Mom used to tell me that snow is a sign of new beginnings. Only for me, it won't be—it can't. For me, this is the beginning of the end. Reality sets in as cold as the snow outside the window. I am here alone. There is nobody here to hold my hand and reassure me that everything will be alright. Because I'm not sure that's the truth anymore. I'm not alright. The people I care about the most aren't here, and it's all my fault. I did this.

This was supposed to be the year that everything changed.

Changed for the better. That *I* would be better. I've been working so hard to leave the broken pieces of me behind and face the future. But that's a lot of pressure for one person to take on. I'm doing the best I can.

I suddenly remember the night before. The broken glass. My entire world going black. And here I am, alone in a hospital room. Some things can be fixed, but the mistakes I've made cannot.

I should just come out and say it, the real truth I've been running from. I've been running for so long, and I can't do it anymore. I can't outrun myself.

I have nowhere left to hide. Nowhere to run. I have to face this. I am through running. I don't like making promises because they are often broken. But I'm promising myself something right now: No matter what life throws at me from here on, I won't run away. I will choose to stay.

I'm not going anywhere. Not if I can help it.

Now: September 13th

My alarm goes off promptly at six a.m. The alarm isn't a loud or annoying tune like they often use in the movies. Rather, it's a soft instrumental piece that reminds me of something Snow White might use in her little brown cottage in the woods.

I never hit snooze. I let it sound no more than three notes before I shut the alarm off. I'm out of bed immediately. No point in wasting the day. I quickly use the restroom and come back to make my bed. I never used to be this anal about getting ready in the mornings, but now it's become one of the better parts of who I am. I *need* this routine to feel alive. To breathe a little easier. To make it through yet another day.

Next, I quickly rinse off in the shower. I used to be lazy and showered only at night out of necessity. Showering in the morning not only helps wake me up, but it's a shock to my entire system. It shocks me back to life, and afterward, I feel more alert than ever.

It's why I now prefer lukewarm water over water that turns my skin pink.

After I've dried off and dressed for the day, I head into the kitchen to pour myself a steaming cup of coffee. It's always ready and waiting by the time I'm out of the shower thanks to my dad. He's an early riser too, but doesn't get out of bed as quickly as I do every morning. There was a time when the roles were reversed. He'd be gone every morning for work before I'd even made it out of bed. Now, I'm usually the first.

He's already sitting in his cozy chair by the window, reading the paper while taking slow sips from his coffee mug. Every morning, without change, I can always expect to find him here. It's both comforting and sad at the same time. I know that he does all of this so that he can keep an eye on me. And while I appreciate his concern, I don't need it. I'm a grown woman now. I'm not his baby girl anymore, I'm thirty-two. Yes, I can't say I blame him. I *chose* to stay when I could have left. Only I can't leave him. It's not that simple.

He doesn't glance over at me as I pour myself a cup. I add a splash of creamer and walk over to the kitchen table to join him. The chair that he's sitting in used to be in the living room. For the longest time, neither of us could bear to sit in it. It'd been Mom's favorite chair. After she was gone, it sat empty in the corner of the living room.

Then, one day I decided to become a morning person. I set my alarm and woke up early. I came in here to find the table shoved to the side and Mom's chair pushed up against the window. He didn't ask me why I was already up, and I didn't ask him why her chair was in the kitchen. Sometimes we simply didn't have answers for why we chose to do some of the things we did after Mom left us. There was a silent understanding between us in that regard.

Some things just were. And that's how it's been for the last sixteen years.

I wake up to the smell of pancakes. Not just any pancakes though. Mom's homemade butterscotch maple pancakes. She's made them for me for as long as I can remember. They were one of the first foods she gave me when I was a baby.

Of course, I never minded because they are delicious. It's already after seven, and if I don't hurry I won't have time to eat them before school. I throw on some clothes that I think are clean and rush into the kitchen.

Mom is right where I expect her to be. She's already sitting at the table with a big ooey, gooey bite in her mouth. There's a plate next to hers stacked high with pancakes waiting for me to dig into. Dad's already long gone for work. He wakes up earlier than both of us and is long gone before we have breakfast.

But that's okay because this is my tradition with Mom anyway. She does this every year on my birthday. And today is my sweet sixteen. She attempts to pull out my chair for me with her foot but misses, completely kicking the chair over. It startles me, and I jump back, nearly dodging the impact.

Mom lets out a small laugh at first, and then it echoes inside her entire petite frame, rattling her from the inside out. Pure joy. Pure amusement at the scene in front of her. Her laughter spills out everywhere, and it's contagious. I find myself laughing too. Full-on belly-clenching laughter.

We are both laughing until the pancakes grow cold and tears are streaming down our faces. We don't stop laughing until we hear a loud, blaring sound outside. Our eyes lock, and I become a sped-up version of myself. I yank a pancake dripping in syrup off the plate and shove it as quickly as I can into my mouth. Mom nearly knocks over her chair in her haste to search for my backpack.

We work amazingly well together in the morning chaos. We are reckless and messy, and she's shoving me out the door before either of us has even spoken a word to each other. My backpack is thrust over my shoulders and fingers are swiping at my mouth, catching the remaining drips from the sticky, sweet syrup. The bus honks at us again and we both stifle a giggle. Before I can dart off in its direction she grabs my face in between her sticky fingers and kisses me on my nose.

Most of my birthdays start like this. Rushed, sticky, and sweet. These are the mornings I love the most. The mornings I wouldn't change for the world.

Now: September 13th

How'd you sleep, Sweet P?" Dad asks me when he finally looks up at me from over his paper. He always looks so tired these days. He works from home and is done no later than four every day, but the dark circles underneath his eyes are always present.

He doesn't openly talk to me about his exhaustion, but if I had to guess, I'd say it has to do with Mom leaving us sixteen years ago. I don't ask him about it because I'm pretty sure he'd deny it and chalk it up to his workload. He does stress about work a lot, but I doubt that's it.

Ever since she left, I don't think he's been able to sleep properly. I'm sure I'd feel the same way if I'd slept next to the same person for well over a decade and suddenly had to learn how to sleep on my own again. I can only imagine what that might be like because I've never had anything like that with someone else.

I pull out a chair at the small table, wood scraping against the rough wood of our floors, and sit down. I wrap my hands around my mug and stare down into my coffee. "Fine," I say flatly, and take a sip. Without looking up he shuffles his newspaper and turns to another page.

Dad and I talk, but more out of necessity than for conversation. It's like we have to speak to one another because we are in each other's space often, not because we have real things to talk about. At least I think that's what we both believe.

Our talks are nothing like the ones Mom and I used to have, giggling like teenage girls and gossiping about which boys we thought were cute. I had been a teenager at the time, while Mom pretended to be one.

There was one time when I'd brought home one of my yearbooks, and we'd sprawled out on my bed flipping through it page by page, laughing and making up stories about my classmates. I'd point to a football jock and she'd tell me his entire, made-up life saga. And then we'd gush over which boys we thought were dreamy and which ones we predicted might be single forever.

Thinking about it now, it was probably an immature thing to do. But I loved her for it. I didn't have any siblings. It's always just been me and my parents. The fact that she had been willing to do something as small as gushing over a high school yearbook with me had meant so much. I couldn't name a single person I knew at my school who would have wanted to do that very thing. Yet she didn't even have to think twice, she just did it. I loved and hated that aspect of my mom. She rarely thought twice about things, she just did them.

We both finish our coffee before either of us speaks again. I break the silence this time.

"I think I'm going to work in the study today."

He's wearing his thick, black-rimmed reading glasses. He doesn't wear them when he's working, but always uses them whenever he's studying the newspaper. He looks at me with his pale, tired gray eyes and nods.

We both work from home. He owns a large accounting firm, and I'm an author. Usually, I'll work in my room. I've set up an office space in the corner, complete with a desk, bookshelves, and pull-out filing cabinets with drawers. Dad, on the other hand, is what I like to refer to as a migrating worker. He doesn't like to work in one spot. He'll always start in his study, but he never remains there. As the hours tick by he'll move to the living room and work on the couch with his laptop perched over his lap, and a headset propped up next to him.

Other times he'll work in his bedroom or downstairs in our half-finished basement, and on warm days I'll find him sitting outside on the porch swing typing away. For the first half of my life Dad had always worked outside the home—your typical eight to five, only he'd leave before seven and not return home until close to six. The second half of my life he's been here, with me. If only it hadn't taken something traumatic to bring him closer to me. Funny how life works out that way.

There were a few years right after Mom left when we'd become close. It hadn't always been that way, but something about losing one parent brings you closer to the other. We were all we had, and for a time, we'd both needed one another, in the same sort of way that you need water and air to survive. It wasn't until I'd started classes for college and Dad had picked up more complicated cases at work that we started pulling apart again. As if we hadn't really been attached to begin with, and our rope was beginning to fray.

Eventually, we stopped relying on each other as much. I'd become an official adult and stayed busy with my studies and writing. He poured all his time into work, and when he wasn't working, he was watching TV or reading the paper. We existed together but didn't really need each other anymore. Not like we did before.

On the days that I request the study, he knows I'm in the middle of either starting or finishing something big. Currently, I'm in the middle of finishing a big project. And by project, I mean story. I am mere chapters away from completing my current novel.

Today, I need the study to focus. I need the space, I need the quiet, I need the one room in the house that doesn't make me think about Mom.

Gathering his newspaper, his eyes don't meet mine this time. I know he hasn't been sleeping well because I'll wake up in the night and hear him puttering around in the kitchen or the laugh track of a sitcom on the television. But I can usually fall back to sleep within a few minutes, and he always acts normal the next morning, as though he hadn't been awake for most of the night.

"That's great, P. Are you getting close to being done with this one? Remind me what it's about?"

There he goes again, calling me P. Short for my real name, Phoenix. I haven't gone by that name in years. My pen name is Nicki Larrs. It's close enough to the real thing without having to *be* the real thing. My birth name is a name that I no longer care to be associated with anymore. Yet, he still insists on calling me by the shortened version of it.

I choose to let it go. I don't feel like fighting him on the issue right now. It's something we can discuss later, or not. It will most likely be the latter.

"Yes, I am. I have a couple of chapters to wrap up and then it'll be ready to send off to Wendy for edits. This is the third and final book in my most recent trilogy."

I don't bother elaborating more about my story, despite his request. I get up to pour myself a second cup. I gently push my chair back in, ready to get started.

I can hear him scoot away from the table, and I look away. There's a tugging from within that makes my chest ache when he walks away. It's nothing new, this is how we exist on any given day. But some days, like this one, it strikes me harder.

I feel a small tug on my arm, and I force my eyes to meet his. My worn and tired father, whom I've grown a little closer to over the years. Not by a lot, but a little. I wonder if he feels the same little tugs that I do from time to time. Almost as though we know we belong here together, yet we are both too set in our ways to be the first one to bend.

His eyes crinkle and a soft smile forms on his lips, "Happy Birthday, P."

Today seems like an ordinary day to me. There's nothing significant about it, other than the fact that yesterday I was thirty-one, and today I am not.

I swallow the lump in my throat. I want to say a lot of things, like: *Does it even cross your mind to try and make pancakes like Mom used to? Are we doing anything special later? Do you see her when you look at me?* Instead, I say nothing at all.

I spend the rest of the day typing away at my computer until my fingers are cramped and my hands are sore. Pouring out my heart and soul on paper. Because in real life, I could never say any of these things out loud.

4

Then: September 16th

It's Monday and Mom refuses to get out of bed. This has only happened a few times before. She's been trying a new medication. I was tempted to ask her what it was for but didn't want to make her angry so I stayed quiet.

I nudge her shoulder for a third time, but she still doesn't make any effort to get up. Instead, she waves her arm lazily in circles above her head as though trying to shoo a fly. In this case, *I* am the fly.

"Mom, I'm going to be late for school. Can you *please* get out of bed?" There's an urgency in my voice I don't recognize. Fear? Panic? Maybe both.

She sighs softly and, without turning around, feels for my hand. I find hers first and hold tight. It scares me a little when she gets like this, but she must just be tired. She doesn't work, and to be honest, I'm not sure what she does all day while I'm in school, but her exhaustion is evident.

"Don't worry about your mama, darling. I'm fine. I didn't sleep great last night, and I'm moving a little slower this morning. Can you make yourself some toast?" She's squeezing my hand with a force I didn't think she had.

Even though she can't see me, I nod my head. I'm not sure what to say to her right now, but I want to be understanding. I want to be whatever she needs me to be.

Clearing my throat, I muster, "Yes. I can make some toast. Are you sure you're alright?"

A groan escapes her lips as she rolls over onto her back, and her big, brown eyes that mirror mine hold me steady. She's always been good at that. Grounding me when I need it.

We look a lot alike. Besides our brown eyes, our dark hair matches perfectly in color. The main difference is that hers falls in careless waves past her shoulders, while mine hangs as straight as a picture on the wall.

I share my dad's dimples and freckles that cross over the bridge of my nose. Mom is a couple of inches taller than Dad. If he didn't occasionally make an appearance with us in public you'd never recognize us as a family. I like to think that maybe God had a sense of humor when he created us. Especially me, with my board-straight hair and sprinkled freckles dotted in various places across my body like a map.

Mom's brows furrow, and I can tell she's studying me closely. Still holding my hand, she squeezes once more and then closes her eyes. I wait another moment for her to say something else to me. Reminding me about the toast, or making sure I brushed my teeth before heading out the door. Instead, she remains silent and still.

From the soft rise and fall of her chest, it's obvious she's drifting back to sleep. Her grip loosens and her fingers fall to her side. I lean down and softly kiss her on the cheek. She smells like her shampoo—honey and vanilla.

I've never loved anybody as much as I love my Mom. I hope she knows that. I hope as she drifts off to sleep in whatever world she's in right now, that she knows even a fraction of my love that runs deep and wide for her.

Now: September 16th

There's a long mirror propped into the corner of my room in my office nook. It used to be Mom's, and it's one of the few things of her's I'd kept. Dad kept her favorite chair, but not much else of her exists in the house anymore beyond that.

For six months, the ghost of her lingered in the house. Her presence could be felt in every room. I think Dad and I were frozen in time. A small part of me thought maybe, just maybe, I'd see her walk back through the front door. After all, she was notorious for leaving, and she always returned.

Eventually, piece by piece, every little trace of her had been erased. As if she never existed in the first place. Now, all we have left are the memories, a few pieces of furniture, and a journal she'd given me ages ago that I can't bring myself to look at.

I'm jerked out of my daydreaming by the sound of soft, instrumental music playing. It takes me a moment to register the familiarity of the tune. Oh, right, my phone is ringing. Someone is calling me.

Before I even glance at the caller ID I know who it is. I say her name without missing a beat.

"Wendy. Hi," I say in a rushed huff.

She lets loose a laugh on the other end. There are only a handful of people who even have my cell phone number. Wendy, my editor/agent, and Janie, my publisher. Dad has it too, of course, but I don't expect any calls to come from him.

Our relationship may seem a bit odd, but somehow it works for us. He gives me the space I need, and I give him his. I've come to realize that time on this planet is far too short, and I'd rather remain here, where it's safe, than somewhere else completely out of my control. I do love my dad, I just think sometimes we aren't quite sure how to express that love to one another.

Wendy and I have worked together for ten years. I wrote and published my first book a few years after I graduated college. It wasn't much but helped dip my feet into the water. It was a crime novella I'd started writing right after I graduated high school and hadn't picked up again until years later, after completing a few college writing courses.

The novella, *Murder at Midnight*, hadn't won anything in the writing competition I'd entered, but Wendy, one of the judges, wrote to me personally after the winners had been selected and encouraged me to keep writing. She said I wasn't quite there yet but knew someday I would be. She'd given me her email address and told me to reach out to her after I'd written my next novel. I'd kept it on a Post-It note stuck to a corner of my desk as a reminder. I'd doubted her then, but she hadn't been wrong. She'd somehow been able to see past the first, awkward story I'd written and recognize the author I'd grow to be.

A year later I wrote my first, full-length novel, *Life in the Dark*, about a blind teenage girl who finds love and hope despite living in a world of darkness. It was a genre I had never written before, but something had drawn me to it. Like a moth to a flame.

I came in third place this time, and Wendy reached out to me immediately, practically pleading with me to allow her to be my editor and agent. And the rest is history. Ten years later, and with twenty-five novels on the shelves, it's safe to say that Wendy is my closest friend.

Besides my dad, I don't have anyone else.

Wendy is shuffling what sounds like a stack of papers or something in the background. "Hi, Nicki. Did I catch you at a good time?"

I have nothing but time these days. When I'm not pouring myself completely into my writing, which is pretty much all the time, I pick up a book and read. Write, read, write, read, repeat.

"Now is good," I say.

Wendy is someone I can be straight with. I'm often short and to the point, but she doesn't seem to mind. Wendy is a bit of a talker, and if I don't shoot her straight she's likely to launch into a twenty-minute story that I'd rather not have to listen to. *No offense, Wendy.*

She softly smacks her lips and I can picture her wedging the phone between her shoulder and chin, as she often does whenever she has to take a call when we're together. Unlike mine, her phone rings a lot. She has a very busy career, and she's always putting out fires, planning events, and handling whatever else she has on her plate.

"Okay, perfect. So, first of all, happiest of happy birthdays! I'm bringing you a cake later. Don't say no! And, secondly… your latest masterpiece. Oh my, just wow. Absolute perfection. It's the perfect ending to *The Honey Sisters* trilogy. I think that's the fastest I've ever read one of your books! The moment you sent it to me I started reading it, and I couldn't put it down. And yes, I cried at the end! I was telling Rick last night—"

I cut her short. I have to or she will spin into a long-drawn-out tale about what her husband thinks about my novel. I know she means well, but right now I'd rather her just say what she's called me to say.

"Thank you, Wendy. Really. That means a lot. I'm glad that you enjoyed it. Was there something else you needed to tell me?"

"Oh, yes! Sorry, I should know by now that you hate when I start rambling, which I seem to do all the time. I'm doing it again, aren't I?"

It's hard to tell if she's rambling because she's nervous to tell me something, or if she's talking fast because she's excited. Either way, I need to help her slow down a bit or she'll never get it out.

"Relax, it's okay. I'm not that scary am I?" I force out a laugh and sit down gently on the edge of my bed. The mattress is several years old, and the springs squeak underneath me when I sit.

She laughs again. Her laugh is quaint and petite, like herself. Her hair is darker than mine, almost a violet-blue-black color that never goes past the edge of her chin. She's no more than five feet tall and bounces lightly when she walks. Opposite of my five-foot-six frame with long, lanky legs. My mom used to teasingly call me Spider-Girl because of my spider legs.

"No, no, of course not. I'm being silly. It's good news, don't worry. You may not think it at first, but it is good. I promise." She pauses for a second too long, making me question if it is good news after all. I wait with bated breath, allowing her the chance to finally spit it out.

"I'vebookedyouforasigningnextmonth." It comes out in such a rush all of her words run into one another.

Wait, what did she say? If she said what I think she said, there's no way I'm agreeing to this. No way.

"Wendy, slow down. What did you just say?"

She sighs and repeats herself, slowly this time.

"You have a signing next month. At the new Books and Beyond store that just opened up downtown. Believe it or not, they reached out to *me,* begging me to set you up with an in-person signing! Once a month they pick an author to spotlight, and they would love for you to be their first! I know your newest book won't be released for a few more months, but it's still a great opportunity to introduce them to the first two books of *The Honey Sisters* trilogy, and people can always sign up for pre-orders. I know what you're thinking right now, but this is going to be a great thing for you, Nicki. You'll see."

She probably does know what I'm thinking. *No way!* But she's wrong about the other thing. This will not be a great thing for me. I haven't gone to a public book signing in *years*. I simply don't do them, and she knows this about me. Why does she suddenly expect me to be okay with the idea *now*?

I still haven't responded, and she begins nervously shuffling something again. Did she expect me to jump for joy and say *Yes, thank you so much, Wendy. Let's get started campaigning for this event right away!*

"I'm not doing it. You'll need to call them back and cancel," I say flatly, twirling a piece of my hair around my finger.

She lets loose a long sigh. We've gone through this before. She knows why I don't want to do this. At least part of it.

"Look. I had a feeling this is how you'd take the news, but I think it's important for you to get back out there. Your books are selling, yes. You're still making the charts and your fans love you. But they also want to *see* you. People can't connect with you behind a screen. Not really. Please say you'll at least think about this."

Wendy isn't usually one to push my buttons, but when she's determined to change my mind about something, she's adamant about it.

I don't want to give in and tell her yes, but if I at least give her something, maybe she'll leave it alone for the time being. I'll call the bookstore myself and cancel if I have to. I'm not doing this. No matter how badly she may try and convince me otherwise.

"Okay, sure. Fine," I say to get her off my back.

"Sure, as in you'll think about it? Fine, as in you agree with me?" She sounds hopeful. Too hopeful.

"I'm not agreeing to anything, but I'll think about it."

She squeals into the phone, a little too loudly.

"Oh, yes, of course! Okay, I'll check back in with you in a couple of days so if you say yes we can get this ball rolling."

I thank Wendy and we say our goodbyes.

As much as she'd like to believe I'm ready to meet the public again, she has no clue how terrible of an idea that is. I won't tell her no today, but it'll come soon. Today, we can both dream about the idea of what *could be*.

6

Then: October 10th

Phoenix, you're needed in the front office. Your mom is here to pick you up," says Mrs. Goode from the front of the classroom.

My cheeks burn when she calls me out in front of everyone. I quickly gather up my things and head to my locker.

My mom is here. Why would she be here? I always take the bus. It's only one-thirty, and school doesn't get out for another hour and a half. Is she ok? Did something happen to Dad? Are we moving and she's picking me up early to go home and pack?

So many questions are running through my mind right now, and I do my best to shove them away as I make my way as quickly as I can to the parking lot. I'd stopped by the front office first, but apparently, Mom had already signed me out and was waiting for me outside.

As soon as I climb into her cute little red Coupe, I turn to face my mother.

"Mom, why are we leaving? Did something happen with Dad? Are you okay?" I ask, full of concern.

Music comes pouring out of the speakers the moment she turns on the car, and it's so loud I immediately cover my ears with my hands. Her lips are moving as though she doesn't even notice the noise and is trying to speak to me through the music.

I reach over and turn the volume dial to mute. I repeat my question. Her eyes don't seem to be filled with worry though, they flash with something else. Excitement. Exhilaration. And something unknown. They are always mixed with something I can never quite name.

She apologizes and gently squeezes my shoulder. "Nothing is wrong, P! I thought it might be fun to have a girls' day! We never get to have a day just for us anymore."

I'm not sure what she's talking about. We spend way more time together than I do with Dad, but I don't feel like now is the time to correct her.

"But I wasn't out of school yet. I still have a few classes left, and then we can have a girls' day," I try, but she lets go of my hand and waves her own in the air like she's waving my concerns away. After all, she gets to make the rules. I'm supposed to follow them.

"Oh, stop it, you're ruining the fun! Come on. We never get to do this. You and me, just us girls. Please," she begs.

I've never heard her beg me for anything. I should say yes, at least this once. What harm could it do?

I shrug my shoulders and fasten my seatbelt. She slaps the steering wheel and lets out a loud whoop, zipping out of the school parking lot.

WE SPEND the rest of the day playing hooky. First, we stop at one of our favorite, local ice cream shops, Dreams of Ice. We talk the entire time. She's always been a great listener. Between bites, we discuss the most random things. She tells me about the different kinds of places she'd like to visit someday and how she'd want some kind of souvenir from each. I tell her about these stories I get in my head sometimes, but how I've always been too afraid to write any of them down.

At this, she leaps out of her seat. Thankfully, no chairs crash to the ground this time, and she rushes me out the doors and back to the car. She doesn't tell me where we are going, but stops when we pull up to the nearest gas station, which happens to be Love's.

She hands me a crumpled twenty-dollar bill and tells me to run inside and pick up a set of pens and the prettiest journal I can find. I browse around the convenience store while she fills her car up with gas. She's already waiting for me when I walk back to the car holding a bright pink and purple tie-dyed journal and a set of fine-point pens.

It's a proud moment for her, because when she sees me, she has tears in her eyes as she rushes over and embraces me in a big hug. I don't understand how buying a journal has made her this happy, but I'm grateful for the simple gesture. If something so small and simple can bring her joy, I'd do it again in a heartbeat.

"I'm so proud of you, Spider-Girl. You've got a head full of stories that deserve to be heard. Write your heart out, and let your stories shine. We were meant to create. Don't hide your words away. Write them down, give them a purpose, and then share them. I don't care how you choose to do it, but when you're ready you'll know what to do," she says, her smile wide and her eyes bright.

I don't know exactly what she means by that, but I tuck it away close to my heart. A place I won't soon forget.

After that, we find ourselves hungry again and hit the mall. It's on the outskirts of town and isn't much of anything anymore. Most of the stores have closed over the recent years, leaving only a few still open. Our town simply isn't big enough to support large chain franchises, other than McDonalds.

The food court has three options: Chinese, McDonalds, or a smoothie place. We end up picking Chinese. After we're done eating, we walk around window shopping until our feet are sore. I have no idea what time it is, but I have a feeling Dad will be getting off work soon and we should be heading back.

I nudge her. "Mom, this has been a lot of fun, but shouldn't we start heading back soon? Does Dad know that we did all of this?"

She's looking at pretty dresses on display and turns to look at me. She scowls and folds her arms.

"This was supposed to be *our* day, P. Why are we talking about Dad?" She frowns.

I'm a little dumbfounded at this. Is she being serious or is she joking? Sometimes it's hard to tell.

"I know, and it was. I've had the *best* time with you. I just think we should be getting back home. I have homework," I say.

She turns her attention back to the window.

"I was hoping we could go see a movie, but I guess we'll just go home instead. If that's what you want," she retorts in a tone that sounds similar to a toddler not getting their way.

I don't think she's joking, but she's impossible to read right now. It has been a great afternoon. We've shared a lot of laughs and talked about things we've never mentioned before. But she's not acting like my mom right now, and I need my mom. I want to go home. I don't want to be here anymore.

I tread gently because I don't want to upset her more. "Maybe we can some other time. Just us, or Dad can come too if you want. But I would like to go home now, Mom."

Then, she does something surprising. She's often full of surprises, but this is something she's never done before. She reaches into her purse and tries to hand me her car keys. I'm sixteen but don't have my license yet. I've practiced driving some, but never this far. We are thirty minutes from home.

"If you want to go home so badly, you can drive yourself. You know how to get home, right?" She doesn't face me, her eyes still glued to the dress. The keys jingle in her hand as she holds them out to me. I don't take them from her.

I'm not sure I understand. "Yes, but Mom..." I start. She doesn't let me finish.

"You can drive home since that's where you want to go," she says flatly.

"But what about you? How will you get home?"

She shrugs, as though it's not really a big deal to her. And maybe it isn't. But how could it not be?

"Don't worry about me. I'm going to watch a movie and then I'll come home."

I've seen my Mom in many moods, but never like this. I don't want to leave without her. Should I call Dad? I don't know what to do. I'm hoping to get my license in a few months, but I'm not ready yet. If I get caught...

"Mom... Please. Don't do this."

She turns to face me once more. "Go, P. I'll come in and kiss you goodnight when I get home, okay? I need some time alone."

I don't understand any of this, but I don't argue. I silently say a prayer that she'll change her mind as I'm walking away and come running after me and drive us home.

But she doesn't. Instead, I drive home scared and alone. Dad isn't home yet when I arrive. I attempt to distract myself by preparing dinner. Maybe somehow it'll lure both of my parents back into this tainted space. Music turned up, apron on, I do my best to drown out any hint of loneliness and worry. It's all I can do, and for now, it'll have to be enough.

Now: October 10th

Reluctantly, I've agreed to the book signing. Under a few conditions. It has to be a private event, tickets are required upon arrival, and the number of guests allowed will be set to a max of one hundred. If your name isn't on the list when the doors open, you won't be allowed in the building, period.

At first, Wendy balked and tried to make me loosen the reins. But saying yes to this in the first place was a huge compromise on my part.

I never did officially tell her no, though I'd tried plenty of times. It wasn't until she showed up at my house one afternoon, despite the chilly autumn air, and spent the next half hour running through a slide show she'd prepared herself to try and convince me that the pros outweigh the cons. Her list reminded me of all the lists my mother used to make around the house.

Like I said before, Wendy doesn't easily back down from something. But neither do I. It didn't help that Dad had been home and sat through her presentation and completely sided with Wendy. Thus, it was a losing battle, to which I gave in.

So, here we are, a full month later, with our table set up in the middle of the new bookstore, Books and Beyond. I'm not sure I get the "beyond" reference. Sure, they sell other things besides books... such as journals, calendars, tote bags, candles, etc., but I don't get what is so *beyond* about it.

At my table, Wendy is seated at my right to help greet customers, hand out free stickers and bookmarks, and help me with whatever else I may need. Truly, I don't think I would have even considered doing this if she couldn't come.

I may be the one who wrote the books, but she's done so much for me. I should find a way to let her know how much I appreciate her after the event.

The doors open in five minutes and I can't sit still. I've already had to refill my water bottle twice, thus resulting in multiple trips to the bathroom. Breathe. I *can* do this.

ALL ONE HUNDRED spots were filled. People were lined up at the doors well over an hour before opening time. It amazed me. I had only done one public signing early on in my career. When I'd finally received my first Best Choice Book Award, a local venue had asked me to speak about my book. I was young and terrified, shaking the entire event. I left with pit stains underneath both arms. Needless to say, it was a one-and-done type of deal. The fact that I am even here today is a *very* big deal. It's still hard to believe all these people are here for *me*.

It takes over three hours to get everyone through the line. Some ask me to personalize a message in the books they've brought with them, and somehow I don't mind. I might even enjoy it a little.

I don't notice the cramp in my hand because I'm having such a good time chatting with everyone like we are old friends rather than strangers. I take the time to pose and smile for a picture with each fan. Wendy, or someone else in line, snaps the pictures for us.

By the end, I can't even count the number of books I've signed, the pictures I've posed for, or the hands I've shaken. I can't help but feel both exhausted and on fire. In the best way possible. But I'm not ready to admit this to Wendy yet.

I start to gather what's left on the table to wrap up for the evening when I feel her nudge my side. The slight jab tickles, forcing me to look up. She isn't looking at me though, there's someone else waiting in front of our table.

My gaze follows hers. First, I notice the man. He's tall, at least six foot, and his hair is a little longer than I'm used to seeing on the opposite sex, sweeping just below his ears in a soft curl. His hair is a light brown and his eyes are an intense bluish-green. Teal. But he's not alone.

Standing beside him is a young girl with light, long blonde hair that cascades down her back and the same intense eyes as the man beside her. There's something familiar about her, yet I can't put my finger on what it is. Wendy's kids are a lot younger, and I don't get out enough to recognize many in our small town.

Her smile is kind and innocent. In her arms, she's clutching my novella, *Murder at Midnight.* I didn't think anyone still read that anymore. I wrote that book so long ago that I'd nearly forgotten about it. Until now.

After a few moments of silence, Wendy comes to my rescue, as she often does. "Hi, there! Sorry, we almost missed you. Do you have a book you'd like Nicki to sign?"

The girl doesn't take her eyes off of mine, and it makes me slightly uncomfortable, but I nod my head gently and usher her forward.

"Yes, thank you! That would be great. I'm a big fan of yours. When I told my dad you'd be here, he got us tickets right away!" The girl glances back at the man and then back to us, handing over her copy.

"Well, I'm glad you made it then. I'm happy to be here." I don't realize how robotic I sound until the words come out, and I frown. Embarrassment takes over and my cheeks flush.

This book is well-loved. The edges are bent and faded, and the slightly yellow pages are starting to curl. This is a book that has been read over and over. I carefully open the book. There's already something written inside the front cover. It's a name, and I don't think it sounds like a name that would belong to a young girl: Denver. But then again, who knows? We live in the middle of the Rocky Mountains, and the city of Denver is only a couple of hours from here. Maybe she was born there.

"Are you Denver? Would you like me to make it out to you?" I ask politely.

The girl smiles, and this time the man grins as well. I don't mean to stare, but I can't help myself. His whole face lights up with his smile. It's infectious. His teeth are the perfect white I strive for daily, and a dimple peeks out of his cheek. *Quit staring!*

The man with the perfect smile laughs. His laugh is deep and perfect too. "No, I'm Denver. This is my daughter, Marvel. She borrowed the book from me and never returned it. Make it out to her, please."

So his name is Denver, and that's his daughter. *Daughter.* Wow. I would have thought maybe she was his niece or something. I'm terrible at guessing ages, but he doesn't seem old enough to have a teenage daughter. He looks like he's just a little bit older than me. I can already tell he's way out of my league.

The girl named Marvel—*where did they get their names*—elbows her dad and nods at me.

I write her name into her book and sign my name underneath.

Wendy offers Marvel a few stickers and a couple of bookmarks, which she excitedly accepts.

I think that's it when the man, apparently Denver, asks me something else. "What inspired you to write? Most authors I know only write one genre but not you. You write in many. Why?"

His questions catch me off guard. Some of the other guests tonight came with prepared questions, but nothing like this. I don't know what to say. After all, he came with a worn copy of my *debut* novella. A book I wrote forever ago and thought nobody read anymore. A book that I hadn't ever seen on shelves in stores. How did they even come across this?

The pages are folded and the spine is cracked, as though one of them has read it many times over. But which one? Denver, the handsome man standing before me? Or his daughter, whose eyes lit up the moment she saw me? I tear myself away from my thoughts and back to his question. *What inspired you to write?* More like *who* inspired me to write. But he didn't ask me that, and unfortunately, I don't think Wendy can help me out of this one.

"I... um..." I stutter. I can't find the right words. I reach for my water on the table to buy me a few precious moments, only to realize it's empty.

Marvel's eyes lock with mine and it's a look I recognize all too well. It's a look of worry and concern. A look I'd often given my mother. A look I'd forgotten about until now.

Suddenly, I can't breathe. The walls are tightening around me, and my vision is starting to blur. I hear a soft voice in the background calling out something that sounds a little like my name. But it's not Nicki that my brain hears. It's Phoenix, and the voice sounds a lot like my mother's.

I picture her face hovering above mine for a few moments before it morphs into somebody else's. It's always somebody else that I see. And that's the last thing I remember before everything around me goes black.

Then: October 10th

It's a rare occasion when I cook a meal for my family. I don't do it often, but I enjoy doing it, surprisingly. Mom cooks most of the meals because of Dad's busy work schedule. He's an accounting manager, whatever that might mean. He's always gone before I wake up in the mornings and never gets home before six in the evening.

Mom still hasn't made an appearance. Dad will be home any minute and wonder where she is. I haven't made up my mind yet if I'm going to tell him about our girls' day of playing hooky. He doesn't know I skipped school and drove myself home from the mall across town. He also has no idea that, likely, Mom might still be there if she stayed to watch a movie.

There is no point in trying to call her or send her a text because she doesn't own a phone. She said once that all the people she needed in her life were right here, meaning me and Dad, so what is the point of carrying a device around?

Dad had bought me a phone for my birthday last year. I was nervous when I opened it, waiting for Mom's reaction, but she didn't act bothered by it in the slightest. She didn't act overly excited, but she didn't seem disappointed either. I took that as a good sign.

Tonight I'm making one of her favorite meals, one she taught me how to make a few years ago. It's simple, but the dish takes a lot of time to fully prepare. Timing everything to come out at the same time can be tricky. I'm making meatloaf in the oven, cornbread, green beans cooked with bacon and brown sugar, and a chocolate cake for dessert.

Today has been a lot of fun, other than Mom whining like a child when I said I was ready to go home. She doesn't deserve this kind of treatment, but I still love her despite everything. I want to make this for her. But I also just want her *here*.

I've got flour and bacon grease on my apron, and I haven't stopped moving for the past hour and a half, making sure everything is going to come out at the same time.

Dad is the first to get home. He walks in through the garage. It's early October now and all the leaves have turned. We've already had a few snowfalls, and Mom doesn't enjoy being out in the snow. I wonder who she will end up getting a ride home with. I just hope she makes it home okay. I push away the worry for now and serve Dad a plate of steaming food.

Taking the plate from me and walking over to the table, he looks back at me, beaming. "Thanks, Sweet P. This all looks amazing! Is Jo here?"

Jo is what he always calls Mom, short for Jolene.

His eyes shine with a trace of worry, but he doesn't move from his seat as he shovels in a large bite.

"No, not yet. I'm sure she will be here any minute." I have no idea when she will arrive, but I hope it's soon.

He wipes his mouth with a napkin and nods, as though we've

gone through this routine a hundred times. Only we haven't. She's always home in time for dinner, no matter what.

He pats the chair beside him, indicating that he wants me to come join him. It feels wrong to enjoy this meal I worked so hard on without Mom here, but I decide to sit down anyway. There's enough food that we will all be enjoying its leftovers for the next several days.

Dad and I don't usually talk much during our meals together. Usually, Mom carries the conversation. She always has something new to say. I'm not sure how that's possible since she doesn't have a phone or job, yet she never runs out of things to talk about. Dad and I can only make so much small talk before the conversation runs dry. Bone dry.

He clears his throat and gazes up at me with his steel-gray eyes. "There's something we should talk about, sweetie. Uh, about your mom."

My mind races. What about Mom? Is she okay? Does he have any idea where she is?

I stare down at my plate of food, my appetite suddenly gone. "What do you mean?" I ask.

"Well, have you noticed anything different about her lately?" He asks.

Different about Mom? I don't know. Was I supposed to notice something about her that wasn't there before? What am I missing?

"Well, she hasn't been herself lately," he says after I sit there in silence for a few minutes.

Mom is rarely ever "herself." Some days she's Fun Mom and we skip school and go for ice cream. Other days she's Tired Mom and needs some extra sleep. And then there are days she's Busy Mom and she's everywhere all at once. Everywhere but here, tonight, with us.

Despite whatever "Mom" she is that day, she's still *my* mom, and I can't imagine a world without her. I don't want to think about that. She'll come back home, she always does.

"Just spit it out, Dad. What's wrong with Mom?" I'm getting frustrated and impatient. I'm never that forward with him, but I feel like we aren't getting there fast enough, and I need to know.

He swallows his bite and pauses, eyes staring into mine. But he doesn't look angry. Dad rarely ever gets angry. Sometimes, I wish he would. It would make him seem a little more human and a little less robotic.

"Nothing is wrong with your mom, okay? She just has these episodes sometimes, where she can't control what she does or says. She's started a new medication that we are hoping helps her."

Episodes. I've never heard him call them that before. I don't think he's ever said anything about the way Mom acts. He just loves her anyway, like I do. Like I always will. Maybe it's different for him. Maybe she's different with Dad. I wouldn't know. I hardly ever see them together, even when we're all "together."

When Dad's not working and it's just the two of them, they've always seemed a bit off to me. They might be present in the same house, but it seems like they are two opposing magnets and they can't get too close. If Mom's cooking something in the kitchen, Dad is most likely in the living room watching TV or reading the paper. If Mom's in her favorite chair reading a book, Dad will be somewhere else in the house making himself busy. It's as though they've spent so much time apart they've forgotten how to be around each other. They exist but in opposite directions.

I wish I could remember if they've always been like this or if this is something new. I've only noticed their distance from each other recently. I haven't been paying either one of them close attention if I'm being completely honest. I haven't had a reason to. But Mom's been so up and down lately, it's almost like I can't help but notice the smallest of movements between both parents now.

I don't know what to say. "What kind of medication? Mom's mentioned taking something before. She said they made her sleepy."

He nods as he takes another bite. Mom still hasn't come home.

Worry is starting to creep in. What kind of side effects does this new medication have? *Where is she?*

He doesn't answer my question. Not directly anyway. "Yes, that was the one before. This one should be better, but she just started taking it a few days ago. We'll have to wait and see. Just... you always do a great job with her, Sweet P, but let me know if you notice anything weird, okay?"

He's starting to scare me. What is he not telling me? "Weird how?" I ask.

"Oh, nothing serious. Just, you know, some of the moods she gets in sometimes. She's good to you, right?"

I nod my head. This conversation is making me uncomfortable.

"Okay, then. Good. Let me know, okay? Did she say when she thought she might be getting home?" he asks as he tugs lightly on the collar of his shirt. His neck is red and blotchy as though he's been scratching at it. Is he more worried than he's letting on? What's going on?

I honestly have no idea what to tell him. She's now thirty minutes late.

"I don't know, Dad. She should have been home by now, but she isn't. I'm going to my room," I say, quietly excusing myself to finish what's left on my plate in my room. I'm too numb to cry any tears. I lie in bed awake, waiting for my mother to come back home.

It's nine p.m. when Mom finally walks in through the door. I lay in my darkened room and listen to Dad and Mom talking. I can't hear what they are saying, just the cadence of the talking through the closed door from elsewhere in the house. Ten minutes later the talking turns to shouting. I've never heard either parent raise their voice before. First, it's Dad I hear yelling. Soon after, it's Mom yelling back even louder.

It's not until I hear something shatter that I leap out of bed. I find Mom standing in the living room with broken glass surrounding her. Dad slams a door somewhere else in the house, and Mom stands there frozen and stunned. Someone had taken the glass bowl that sits by the front door that holds our keys and threw it onto the ground.

After I clean up the mess, I pause, considering what I should do next. Dad hasn't come out from wherever he's retreated, and Mom remains frozen in her spot. Her eyes are wide and her hands are trembling at her sides. I gently walk her over to the couch and make a spot for her to sleep. When I start to wrap the blanket around her I bend down to kiss her cheek. Her arms loop around me in a warm embrace.

Like an earthquake, she begins to break. She sobs into my hair as she holds me. I don't let her go until she's calmed herself down.

"He's mad at me. Really mad this time," she chokes out in broken breaths against me.

I don't know what she's talking about, but figure now isn't the best time to ask. Right now she needs me.

I don't want to leave her so I make a spot to sleep in her favorite cozy chair. It's an ugly thing, this chair. I'm pretty sure she told me once that she bought it at a yard sale soon after I was born. It's a light green color covered in flowers of every shape and color. It rocks and reclines, probably part of why she loves it so much. The fabric is worn and frayed, like a loved stuffed animal, and maybe that's exactly what it's like to her. I keep my eyes open as long as I can manage. And like a song on repeat, all I can hear as I close my eyes are the broken cries of the mother I love.

Now: October 10th

Luckily, I'd only blacked out for about thirty seconds. All the times this had happened previously had all been under a minute. Most of them were more like distant dreams I could no longer reach, save for a few that had stuck with me. Once, in an undergrad biology class, it was lab day and we were studying the workings of a pig's lungs. I'd never considered myself squeamish until I walked into class that day and saw a pig carcass on every table.

The teacher demonstrated how a pig's lungs fill up like a balloon and then deflate. It wasn't the inhale that got me, but on that exhale I swear I saw something come out of the pig. While some students gagged, mostly the girls, I blacked out. I quickly came to, my vision fuzzy and my head spinning. The teacher gently ushered me out of the classroom and encouraged me to rest in the commons until class was over.

At that moment I knew for sure that a nursing degree

wouldn't be for me. *Not that I'd been considering nursing, but with current circumstances, the possibility had been ruled out for me.*

There'd been too many occasions similar to this for me to count... but there was one instance in particular that has left a permanent scar on my memory. The pieces I remember about it anyway. The other time was over a decade ago. It'd been so bad that I'd completely shut down. I don't remember blacking out. But the parts that I do remember still haunt me in my sleep. I'm scared one of these days they will suck me under completely.

AFTER THE INCIDENT at the bookstore, Wendy had driven me home. She'd tried to make small talk for the first ten minutes, and eventually gave up and turned on the radio to mask the silence.

I kept my eyes glued on the scenery out the window. Lost in thought. Trying not to think about anything at all. But of course, that was asking for the impossible. When I first started blacking out when I was sixteen, the hospital had tried to put me on medication at the time. Mom refused but hadn't explained her reasoning. She'd been on medication herself but hadn't wanted me relying on anything. But now I'm thinking that she should have told the doctors yes. Maybe this wouldn't keep happening. Especially on days like today, of all days.

We turned a corner nearing my street when I called out abruptly, "Stop!"

Wendy, who is normally an extremely cautious driver, slams on her brakes, and I lurch forward. My arms fly out and slam against the dash, stopping my forward momentum. I huff out a breath and she whispers, "Sorry."

"Here is fine. I'd like to walk the rest of the way home." We are stopped in the middle of the street a few blocks away from my house. I begin to unbuckle when Wendy gently pats my arm.

I glance over in her direction to see her eyes dancing with concern. I get it, I'd be worried too if the roles were reversed, but I don't need her worrying about me. I'm fine. I'd gotten a little overwhelmed today is all. That's the most people I've interacted with in decades. Maybe it'd been too much too soon. I need the fresh air the walk home will give me. Even though the temperature will only be dropping this time of night, I need it right now.

"Nicki, are you okay? It's freezing, almost dark, and I don't want you walking home by yourself. Especially not after you just..." her words trail off.

Her look is full of pity, and I shake my head. I don't want it. I don't want any of it. "I'll be fine, Wendy. I felt better during the drive, and I'm fine now. I'll text you as soon as I make it inside, okay? Stop worrying, I need to clear my head."

I am telling the truth, I do need to clear my head, and I also want to be alone for a bit. The air is crisp, chilly, and just enough to keep my mind awake. Active. Alive.

I can tell she's skeptical, but she lets it go for the time being. "Alright. But if I don't hear from you in the next fifteen or twenty minutes I'm calling you. And if you don't answer I'm calling your dad. And if he doesn't answer—"

I cut her off again. "I will text or call you, Wendy. Thanks again for everything. You were great today." I climb out of her car. She waves, defeated, before slowly driving off.

I know she means well. There are not many people who care about me the way she does, and I appreciate it. But right now, I need the space. I'm not ready to face Dad at home and all his questions about how the event went today.

Mom rarely thought twice about the things she did, she just did them. Kind of like what I'm doing now. I shiver. I'm not sure if it's from my thoughts or from the cold.

I tug my coat closely around me to ward off the cold blast of autumn air and start making my way towards home.

I'VE BEEN WALKING for close to ten minutes now, fully aware that if I'm not home in the next ten Wendy will start to worry. She's the only other person, besides Dad, that knows the truth about my mom. But there's another truth that nobody but me knows, and I plan to keep it that way.

I round the corner, my toes and fingers slightly numb from the cold. The sun has set and street lamps are starting to glow. I pick up my pace when my shoe suddenly catches on a pebble along the path, and I nearly fall. I glance around me to see if anybody else saw me, but it's just me out here. Nobody else is crazy enough to be walking in the bitter autumn wind.

I'm about to keep going when my eyes dart to the house on my left. A single light is left on in the kitchen. All around it, houses flicker to life with families eating dinner or getting their little ones ready for bed. I can almost hear the echo of laughter coming from within, a time I'm remembering from long ago. I don't hear anything now, and I don't see any movement from within, but I remember.

How could I forget?

The grass is neatly trimmed, and there's a tire swing hanging from the big tree in front. I don't remember there being a swing before. But there's one now. I can't help but wonder about the family that lives here now and what they are like.

Do they know?

The wind has picked up and my arms are dotted with goose-bumps. I should get going. I don't have time to linger here, but I can't help it.

But then I see it. The small, metal cross hanging from one of the tree's branches, dancing in the breeze. Maybe the family is religious, but I wonder if it's a symbol for something else. In the distance, I hear the sudden screech of tires on asphalt and my entire body freezes in place. My eyes blur from the cold, and I have to will myself to keep moving. *Run!*

I take off running and don't stop until I make it home.

I'm out of breath and exhausted when I get inside. Luckily, I don't see Dad as I make my way to my room to shower and sleep. I don't have the energy to answer questions about the signing event right now.

As promised, I send Wendy a quick text letting her know I made it safely. Safe and sound. Only sometimes I don't think I deserve to be.

Then: October 24th

Mom is sitting at the kitchen table with a heaping plate of cookies when I get home from school today. Since she started her new medication, she seems to be in better spirits. I still have no idea what they are giving her, but as long as it's working and she's happy, it doesn't matter.

So seeing her with freshly baked marshmallow oatmeal cookies doesn't surprise me. While reading and writing are my top love languages, hers, hands down, is baking. I shove a cookie into my mouth, and she motions for me to join her. I set down my backpack and wipe the crumbs from my lips.

Instead of grabbing a cookie, she reaches for my hand and holds it softly in hers. "How was your day Sweet P?" she asks.

Her eyes are bright today, shiny like a penny. I like seeing Mom like this. "It was pretty good. We have a field trip coming up. It's a tour of the local university to introduce us to college and get us thinking about where we might want to go someday."

I usually avoid the "college talk" altogether, as it can be a sensitive topic for Mom. She had plans to graduate from college, but had gotten pregnant with me her freshman year and dropped out. She never tried to go back and finish. She told me once that being a mom means more to her, and for the most part I believe her, but some days I can't help but wonder who she'd be if she had continued her education.

She pats my hand and nods her head. "That sounds fun, honey. Just remember you don't have to pick the one you're visiting. Jot down your favorites and make a pros and cons list. That's what I always do. And then I pick the best option!"

She giggles at an unspoken joke. "Better than doing eeny-meeny-miny-moe!" She laughs again and finally pops a cookie into her mouth.

"That's a good idea, Mom. I'll do that, thanks." I reach for another cookie. I know I shouldn't eat too many before dinner, but at least one more won't hurt.

Her copper eyes flicker with something else and her spine straightens. For a moment I think Dad is home and he's just come in the door, because she's staring off somewhere behind me. I turn in my chair, but nobody is there. She blinks and she's back with me. It was like she'd thought of something and then it'd vanished into thin air.

"I actually have something to talk to you about." She offers me another cookie, and I gladly accept the offer. *Okay, this one will be my last.*

"It's about your dad, honey. He told me he wants a divorce."

I freeze and the cookie goes dry in my mouth. Suddenly, I crave water or a tall glass of milk. Did she say *divorce?*

Forcing it down, I manage, "What do you mean? Did he say why?"

She takes my hand in hers again and, this time, stares at our interlocked fingers as though they are the only thing providing her with stability. How is she so calm right now? Here I am already freaking out, and she's sitting here with a plate of cookies holding my hand. I should be the one providing her comfort, not the other way around.

"He just said it's all getting to be too much," she says. When I don't immediately respond she adds, "And by that, he means *I'm too much.*"

Sure, Mom isn't perfect. She has her really good days and her really bad days. But she's been better the past several days. I've seen it with my own eyes, and I'm sure Dad has paid attention too. How could he not? He told me to let him know if she was different towards me, and she's been nothing but amazing. I don't understand why he's doing this. I don't understand at all.

I stand up quickly, almost knocking over my chair in the process. I'm angry. How could Dad do this to her? To us? He's just giving up? Is she giving in too?

"Mom, he can't divorce you. That makes no sense." I don't bother hiding the frustration in my tone.

Her eyes soften, while mine harden.

"I'm sorry, Spider-Girl, but he can. He's already handed me the papers," she says, defeated.

He's already handed me the papers.

Now, I'm fuming. He can't do this. He didn't even try talking to me about this. He never talks to me about anything!

"Don't sign them!" I demand. It's not her I'm angry at, but she flinches back into her chair at the blow.

"I haven't signed anything yet. But I think he's done this time. I mean, he's threatened it before, but this time he's serious. This time he brought papers, and he's never done that."

What does she mean *before*? I can't stand to be here any longer. I don't know how to comfort her when it feels like she's already waving her white flag high into the air. Do whatever pleases Dad, because apparently, he gets to call the shots. That's not fair.

"I need some air. I can't face Dad when he comes home. Tell him whatever you want. I'll be back in a bit." I grab a water bottle from the fridge and her car keys off the small table by the front door (The bowl hasn't been replaced since their last fight). I still haven't gotten my permit yet, but that didn't stop her from throwing her keys at me before. Today, she doesn't have to force me to drive. I take her car and do just that. I drive.

Now: October 24th

Ever since the bookstore incident, Wendy has not stopped checking in with me. At least once or twice a day she will send a personal text regarding my well-being. Sometimes it's a long string of emojis. Other times it's song lyrics, or she will send me a link to go and listen to an uplifting song.

And sometimes it's a simple:

WENDY

Hope you're doing something that brings you joy today.

Or even:

WENDY

Are you in the mood for a free coffee? Say the word and it can be at your door in half an hour.

I know, without a doubt, that she one hundred percent means

it. Most of her texts just receive a thumbs-up emoji in return, or I'll simply "like" the message. She knows better than to call me unless it's work-related.

Today's text, however, is different from the rest. Today's is a picture of some type of brochure. I'm not sure what it is but, instead of opening the text, I set down my phone and pick back up the novel I started reading a few hours ago. It's a thriller from one of my favorite authors, and I haven't been able to put it down.

I don't even make it through a full page when my phone pings. Of course, it's Wendy again.

Her text reads:

WENDY

Just hear me out, okay? It's a support group for people that have been in a similar situation, and it's close to you. Like ten minutes tops. I can even take you. I will take you. They meet once a month, so it's not a big commitment or anything. I have a friend who's been going there after she lost her husband...

There's more, but I don't read the rest. I turn my phone on silent and put it down. *Similar situation,* she says, as though she even knows half of the story. Nobody knows the full picture but me, and I intend to keep it that way. I pick my book back up and don't check my phone again until I've finished the chapter. Knowing how relentless Wendy can be at times, I tap the screen on my phone. Sure enough, a new message has come through.

WENDY

I know it wasn't right of me to push you for the book signing. I've apologized a thousand times, and I'll say it again if you want me to. But please just consider going to this. Even if you only go once and decide it's not for you, that's fine. You also might find that it's good for you.

WENDY

Anyways, they meet on the third Thursday of each month at 7 p.m. That gives you plenty of time to think it over. Say the word and I'll come get you. I'll even bring that free coffee I promised earlier.

I crack a smile. Of course, I don't want to go. I didn't want to do the signing in the first place, and it turned out to be a mistake. Going to a group where people talk about grief and loss could be an even bigger mistake. It sounds horrible. I shudder at the thought.

Yet, there's a small part of me that believes she might be right. After all, there's no harm in going *once*. I'll show up for her sake and cross it off my list.

Been there, done that kind of thing.

I shoot her a thumbs-up emoji and say:

ME

ME

Sure, I'll think about it. Better make that coffee a large if I say yes.

WENDY

💚💚💚💚💚

I can almost see her whooping to herself in her room as she replies with a bunch of heart emojis. A maybe in her book might as well be a big, fat yes.

I'm in trouble, and I haven't even agreed to anything yet.

Then: October 24th

When I'd first turned fifteen Dad had been quick to offer to teach me how to drive. Mom wanted to be the one to practice with me, but eventually gave in, as if she understood how little time Dad and I spent with one another. So on my fifteenth birthday, a year ago, Dad took me out for my first drive.

I'd been nervous but eager to get behind the wheel. Several people at school already had cars just "waiting" to legally drive them. I'm pretty sure most of my classmates were already driving around our small, rocky town of Atlas Creek.

Driving came easily for me. Which was a relief to both parents, because learning to drive around curving roads and thick snow in the winter isn't for everyone. None of it seems to phase me. Mom never practices with me, it's always been Dad. It's the one thing we do together, and I enjoy it. He promised as soon as I pass my driver's test that he'll get me a car of my own. Mom never says much whenever I mention it, so I mostly just discuss it with Dad.

It wouldn't be anything fancy, but it'd be a lot safer than Mom's little red Coupe that she's had since she'd turned sixteen. Needless to say, it's a bit dated. Whenever Dad is home, we always go out in his 4-wheel drive Jeep Wrangler. I have a feeling he plans to get me something similar.

But he's the last person I want to think about right now. I want to think about anything else. College, cute boys in my class (there aren't many), books, or puppies. I am not an animal person, but right now thinking about puppies sounds nice.

Today though, I don't have the option to choose a vehicle. Despite being sixteen, I don't have my license yet. There is only Mom's car, and despite the warning flags that my brain is trying to signal my way, I ignore them and pull out onto the street. I don't plan to drive very far, just long enough to blow off some steam, and then I'll circle back home.

I drive slowly, not because I don't feel comfortable in her tiny car, but because the color red on a Mini Coupe doesn't exactly "blend in." Especially around here. Nobody around here has a car like this. Mom's too proud to give it up, and frankly, I'm not sure we can afford to own new cars.

I'm not sure which way Dad comes home, but I'll do my best to avoid him and try not to worry about it too much. Maybe I'll even beat him home and won't have anything to worry about. Mom can just tell him what she told me, and he'll understand why I needed to get out. After all, he's the one to blame. If I'm late for dinner, I can just eat the leftovers in my room. Mom always makes plenty.

I stop at the stop sign and turn left this time. Every other street I go right, then I make a left, then another right. I know every single street and recognize a handful of our neighbors, so I won't have any trouble making my way back home. I didn't think to check the forecast, but there's not currently any snow on the ground. Besides, the skies appear to be clear—not a cloud in sight.

I'm nearing the next street when I notice someone coming

outside towards me. It's a young girl heading to the mailbox to check the mail. She sees me paused in the road and smiles a crooked, questioning grin at me, asking "do I know you" with her expression alone.

She's not anyone I recognize. She walks over to her mailbox, it's bright red and matches the car I'm driving. I shouldn't be so mesmerized by this stranger, yet I can't seem to put my foot on the gas to move. Nobody is behind me yet, and I bring my hand up slowly to wave to her. She surprises me by waving back, the other hand full of today's mail. Then, in the blink of an eye, she's gone. She vanishes into the house full of lights, and from the tiny sliver of my cracked open window, I can hear talking and laughter.

She didn't close the front door all the way, and I eased my foot on the gas, slowly inching forward. Before I head back home, I notice a guy appear in the doorway. He's older than the girl but doesn't look old enough to be her dad. He sees me staring from across the street, and before I can duck my head down and drive away, he smiles the same smile as the girl. He slowly closes the front door, cutting me off from the warmth within.

My heart aches with a longing to hear echoes of laughter sneaking out the cracks of an open front door. *Our front door.* But I don't return home to illuminated windows or laughter creeping beneath the cracks. I return to silence. Which I suppose is better than my parents fighting again, but the silence does something to me.

It leaves me feeling hollow, like broken promises and unsigned papers titled *Divorce.*

With Mom's car parked next to Dad's in the garage, I make my way through the stillness of our home. I don't pass either parent on my way to my room, and I go to bed without eating dinner.

I close my eyes and dream about the family I wish were mine.

Now: November 21st

Wendy finds a place to park and hands me the coffee she had promised, a grande honey lavender with whipped cream on top. I can't complain. Not about the coffee anyway. The real complaints might come later tonight. After I make it through the next hour.

It's just one hour. I can do this.

Wendy has her sympathetic eyes on, like she's proud that I agreed to come here, but also doesn't want to push me too far. I love and hate her right now. But mostly, I love her. I thank her again for the coffee and step out of her car. She tells me she will wait in the parking lot since it's only an hour. She's already turned on her Kindle and has started to read a book. I don't ask if it's a personal read or if she's working right now. It doesn't matter.

I glance up toward the building where the meeting is being held. To be honest, it looks like it used to be open for business but has since shut down. The windows are darkened so I can't peek in, and there are no signs indicating that we are even at the right place. I glance back toward Wendy's car, but her windows are too tinted to see inside.

Sure enough, when I get right up to the glass doors at the front there's a small sign taped on the inside that reads:

WELCOME TO GRIEVE AND GROW! A GRIEF SUPPORT GROUP THAT MEETS ONCE A MONTH, EVERY THIRD THURSDAY 7–8 P.M. AGES 18+ WELCOME.

Hand hesitating on the door for a split second, I consider dodging around the corner and finding some other shop I can wander around for an hour when I feel someone pulling the door open from the inside. Guess that answers that. Any hope of escaping is quickly dashed when I realize who is holding the door open for me.

It's Denver. The guy with teal eyes and perfect teeth from Books and Beyond. You've got to be kidding me. What is *he* doing here? There's a flicker of recognition and sincerity in his eyes. I don't know what he's doing here, but he could easily be wondering the same about me.

A slow smile forms across his lips, and he motions with his other hand to come on in, as though this isn't his first time like it is mine. His shoulders seem to be relaxed, and his eyes don't crinkle with worry like I'm positive mine are doing right now. He lets the door close on its own behind us as he shows me into a large room set up with folding chairs in a circle. He doesn't sit right away but motions for me to have a seat. I watch as the people in the room flock toward him in greeting. He's someone they seem to know well. He's not a newcomer like me. Here he's well-known, familiar —a regular. I am the stranger, the observer, the new-kid.

I am mesmerized by his presence, in how he carries himself, and how he talks to people in a way that I cannot. I'm jealous of the ease in which he talks to everyone. *What is he doing here? Is he here for a similar reason to mine?* I fold my hands into my lap and wait to see what happens next.

WE GET STARTED WITH AN ICEBREAKER. We have to go around the circle saying our names and a fun fact about ourselves. It makes me feel like I'm back in elementary school and we are in circle time, listening to the teacher read aloud a book in a high-pitched animated voice.

To my relief, this is nothing like that.

There are twenty-six of us in the circle. Sam is the leader of the group. She's older than me, roughly about my dad's age, with short, white-gray hair cut close to her scalp. Something about her is motherly. She has big, brown eyes that remind me a little of my mother, and I have to fight the urge to excuse myself to the bathroom and sneak out.

Denver and I don't sit next to each other, but our chairs face each other in a large circle. I can feel his eyes on me. I immediately dodge his glance. To my left is a woman who looks to be in her early fifties, and I wonder if she's the friend Wendy had mentioned who'd lost her husband. On my right is a heavy-set man who sits hunched over in his chair and is making strong eye contact with the ground. I haven't seen him glance up once. *I don't want to be here either, buddy.*

There's a long counter in the back of the room that has a Keurig and coffee display in one corner, along with tea, water, and finger food snacks in the other. I'm too nervous to get up and make myself a plate of food. Besides, I have only taken a few sips from the large coffee I'd insisted on Wendy bribing me with to come here in the first place.

The lady on my left is named Susan, and she travels to Florida every summer with her oldest daughter. My hands tremble when it's my turn to state my name and share something interesting about myself.

This question should be a simple one, but it's not.

Hi, my name is Phoenix, but nobody calls me that anymore. Except my dad still calls me P. But don't call me that. Please just call me Nicki.

Hi, my name is Nicki, though that isn't my real name, I prefer not to go by my real name anymore because it's the name my mom gave me and she's not...

I'm quickly pulled out of my thoughts when I feel someone nudge me in the side. It's Susan.

"Oh, um, right. Hi." A few laugh, a few shift awkwardly in their seats, and someone to the right of me actually snorts. Doubt immediately starts to creep in and my hard exterior cracks a little.

Sam waves them off and is gifted with immediate silence. To have that kind of power over an entire room of adults is something. If only I had that same effect now.

"It's okay to be a little nervous your first time here. We were all new at some point." Several heads nod in agreement at this.

I find my head starting to lightly bob along with them, as though I'm a dog saying *yes please* to a treat. Until my eyes meet Denver's again. I find myself staring at the ground, like my neighbor beside me.

I start again. "I'm Nicki. I'm an author, but I also really enjoy reading. And I can cook a mean meatloaf." The last part gets a few more laughs, and Sam nods in approval. Guess my response this time is better.

I relax in my chair and reach for my iced coffee when I feel everyone's eyes lingering on me. *And his eyes.* I said what I needed to say so why aren't they moving on to the guy still staring at the floor beside me? Even he understands I'm not *that* interesting.

"You don't have to share if you don't want to, but most of us here have been attending Grieve and Grow for a while now. Why are you here today, Nicki?" Sam asks.

I am not expecting her to ask this, especially not on my first night here. She did say I don't have to say anything, and I certainly don't want to share. I came close to chickening out of the whole thing tonight and not coming at all. I don't get sick often, but it wouldn't have been that out of the blue if I'd have come down with something. But I couldn't use that excuse because Wendy would know. She has a canny ability of seeing right through people's lies. And if I'm being completely honest, I'm not sure why I agreed, once again, to show up to something I did not choose.

But everyone is expecting me to say something. There's soft music playing in the background to break up the silence, but all eyes and ears wait in anticipation for me to offer them *something*.

I can't. Instead, I surprise myself and do what I'd promised myself I wouldn't do. I excuse myself and leave the room with all eyes trailing after me. There are still at least thirty minutes left, and I can't risk walking out of the building and Wendy seeing me. So, instead, I use the restroom to kill a few minutes. Once I compose myself, I find my way back to the door I'd walked out of only moments ago. Only now, I'm standing as close to the door as possible without being seen or heard through the tiny rectangle glass so I can listen to the meeting.

I didn't think I was gone that long, but the person speaking now is a voice I recognize. It's Denver's. I wonder how long he's been coming here and why he started coming in the first place. Does anyone really want to be here or do they come because they feel like they should? Out of obligation. To heal from something tragic. Something that has left permanent scars along their heart. Or someone like me who has made the worst mistake possible and doesn't know if I'll ever be able to forgive myself for it?

Denver's voice is as smooth as a waterfall. Like water cascading down the mountainside in the summertime. He's saying something about how he comes here every year around the same time. I can't understand everything he's saying, but I think I hear him utter a name that makes me freeze. A name that sends chills up and down my body every time I hear it.

It's not an uncommon name, but it's one that has haunted me for years. It's a name that I hadn't expected to hear escape his lips, and even now I'm second guessing what I heard. Could it somehow be...? No, that's crazy. Insane to even think about. Like I said, it's a name you'd hear walking through the supermarket, or anywhere really. But I can't help the rise of panic that is bubbling up inside of me, ready to burst at any second. Funny how a single word that you *thought* you heard sends your body into a spiral.

Suddenly I can't breathe as panic settles in.

14

Then: November 21st

I'm not sure where my parents currently stand on the D-topic (divorce). Mom hasn't brought it up and Dad just seems to dodge us both altogether. Making sure he's gone before we wake up and working late at the office so he misses dinner. When there's a change or something that makes him uncomfortable, like whatever is going on between him and Mom, he's like a turtle who retreats into his shell.

I study Mom closely. Not because of what Dad had mentioned about her new medication, but because ever since she'd talked to me about her and Dad that day, she hasn't been the same. Not really.

It's hard to explain.

Before, she would have just as many happy days as gloomy days. On the bad days she stayed in bed for hours. Somehow sleep helped her cope with whatever was troubling her that day. But this is different.

Mom has grown quiet. Even her steps seem lighter, as though she's in a constant state of tip-toeing through the house. Afraid if she says the wrong thing or makes the wrong move, we will all break into a thousand tiny pieces. Truthfully, we just might.

She hardly feels like eating whenever Dad or I are eating, she just walks into another room in the house and comes back when we are finished. She doesn't ask me about my day at school or bother to ask if I'd like to have any friends over.

When she does speak, it's like she's speaking through a muted volume. Her tone is soft and her words are slow. And she always says as little as possible, as though she isn't allowed to say too much.

It's a strange side of her I've never seen before. But I haven't been brave enough to ask Dad about it yet. While he's busy hiding in his shell, and Mom in her own sort of shell, I'm just trying to be the glue that holds us all together. And it's exhausting.

It's Friday afternoon and I just got home from school. I don't expect Quiet Mom to greet me at the door, but I'm surprised when I don't see her in the kitchen when I walk in. Backpack still on, I peer into the living room. The curtains are drawn, and the only sound is the soft hum of the furnace.

"Mom?" I call out, hoping she will respond in some way. *Where is she?*

I feel my heartbeat start to pick up speed as I fling open my parents' bedroom door. I suck in a breath, as though I'm entering something sacred. Of course, I've been in here before, but it's not like my parents have an open invitation to their room. This has always been their private space, and I've always respected it. It's like some kind of unwritten rule, I don't come in here, and they don't come in mine. The only times I've come in here recently are to check on Mom.

The first thing I notice about the room is how spotless everything in it is. The closer I glance around the room, the quicker I realize that the reason it's spotless is because there's hardly anything left in here.

All the shelves are empty. They are normally full of Mom's books. I haven't seen her pick up a book to read in a while, but she loves her collection with all her favorite authors, and it's odd that they aren't in her bookcases.

I step further into the room, my backpack starting to sag down on my shoulders from the textbooks weighing it down. I open Dad's closet first. He's always been the organized one. He mostly wears polos or button-downs and they are all displayed neatly, by color. His shoes are the same way, not a single one out of line. I let loose a breath. I had the panicky thought that maybe Dad already moved out, and they separated after all. Have they signed the papers without telling me? *They wouldn't, would they?*

Surely they wouldn't do that without talking to me about it first, right? Sadly, I don't know what to expect from either of them anymore. Panic creeps back in as I shut his door and move to Mom's.

Closing my eyes briefly, I ease her door open on the exhale. Opening her door wider, I step inside and gasp. Nothing is in here. Every little piece of her is *gone*. Her closet was never as neat as Dad's. Oftentimes she'd just thrown clothes, saying she didn't have time to fold them and would get to it later. But there is absolutely nothing here.

My worst fears have come alive. It's not Dad I have to worry about moving out.

It's Mom.

Now: November 21st

I didn't realize I'd been leaning on the door until it swung open under my weight and I stumble a bit. There is a brief moment where everyone's eyes are on me, but mine are drawn to his... *Denver's*. His greenish blue eyes catch mine from across the room, and everything in me tells me to *run!* Panic seizes my entire being, and like Cinderella dashing from the ball, I bolt out of there at lightning speed.

How could I have been so stupid?

I knew it was a mistake coming here.

Another mistake, again in public. I'm done.

I push through the front doors I'd come in almost an hour ago to be welcomed by a blast of icy air. It takes a moment for my eyes to adjust to the blackened sky. It's a beautiful, still night. Stars are dotted across the black sky, illuminating the faint outline of the towering, giant mountains in the distance.

When my eyes adjust I scan the parking lot for Wendy's car.

She's exactly where she promised she'd be. Of course, she is. I start quickly, making my way across the lot toward her when something brushes against my arm. What the?

I whip around and find myself face-to-face with a giant of my own. Denver. I still don't know what he's doing here, but it'd be better if I'd never decided to come in the first place. Every time I'm in his presence I only make a fool of myself, and tonight was no different.

The temperature has dropped by at least ten degrees, and I hadn't noticed how chilly it'd been before. Goosebumps pepper my arms like freckles underneath my lightweight sweater. I should have worn a heavier coat, but I'd left it at home.

"Wait," he rasps. He must have been running too.

He pauses a moment, his eyes flicking up to meet mine. His touch had been soft, yet strong. I've never noticed his muscles before, but I do now as we stand no more than a couple of feet apart. He remembered his coat at least, but it's leather and tight enough to show off his strength.

Growing impatient, I start to turn. Wendy will be disappointed, but she'll understand. She always has.

"Listen," he says quickly to stop my retreat. "I don't know why you came here tonight, but I'm glad you did."

I'm surprised at the softness in his voice. It's masculine, but gentle at the same time. I'm sure he means well, but he's wrong.

"Coming here tonight was a mistake, and I'm leaving." I start walking again.

This time he comes around to stand in front of me. Is he seriously cornering me in a public parking lot?

He must instantly read my expression because his eyes flare with an apology. He steps off to the side, putting his hands into his pockets. "Well, I don't think it was a mistake."

He goes silent for a moment, and I let him collect his thoughts. I don't feel a sense of danger from him, and I know Wendy is close by and is probably watching our conversation from her vehicle.

He tries again. "Look, I've been coming here off and on for the last six or seven years. They are a great group, and they genuinely care about the people that attend. Of course, there are a few regulars that have never left and probably don't miss a single meeting. They're just lonely and know that this is a safe place to talk about what they've gone through. But that's the beauty of it. We've all gone through *something*. And we've all lost people in our lives. I just think we don't have to do this on our own, you know? Life is hard, but being alone is harder."

A sigh of relief escapes my lungs. I must have misheard the name he said earlier. His loss is more recent, whereas mine was over a decade ago. I'm quick to brush it off, because it doesn't matter anymore. This will be the last time I see him. Despite this being a small town, I've lived here all my life and have never ran into him until recently. At least it won't be happening here again, because I won't be coming back.

When he finishes, I feel a tear trail down my cheek. I hardly ever cry anymore. For years that's all I did. I've cried so much I've finally run all my tears dry, at least I thought so. Until tonight. Why now?

He has no idea what I've lost. What I've done.

I swipe the tear away and silently pray it'll be the last.

When I don't say anything he continues. "And you're not the first person to walk out."

My chin trembles, and I dare to meet his eyes again. Up close his eyes are a sea green that reminds me of sea glass or a beautiful gemstone. "I– I'm not?" My voice quivers.

He shakes his head and smiles sympathetically. "No, not at all. It happened the last time I attended. And I'm sure it will happen again. They all understand. They've been there. Grief is hard. It's painful. Having the courage to share is even harder. Some never share anything about their lives, they just show up. That's all you can do sometimes."

You just show up. I hadn't heard anyone else say that before. Not since—

I guess that's what I did tonight. I wasn't what you'd call a willing participant, but I came. I had shown up. I am here.

I find my courage and dare to ask him something else. "Did you say you come here every year around the same time?" I know it's not fair of me to be nosy, but he seems to be a lot more open than I am. After all, he's well-known and liked here. He belongs here. I'm a stranger looking in, and I've lived here my whole life.

His eyes break away from mine and he looks back behind me towards the black, tall building we ran out of. "Yes, you heard that part right. I come here every year from November through February. Paying a sort of tribute I suppose."

February. I shiver at the thought, or maybe it's just from the cold. It *is* freezing out here and I can feel my bottom lip start to tremble. I hope he doesn't notice.

A tribute to someone. Someone he's lost. My throat tightens at this, and my eyes start to well up again. I bite my lip, refusing to let any tears escape this time. I won't cry. Not in front of him.

There are a hundred other things I could say right now, but instead, I blurt out, "I need to go. My ride is waiting for me." Plus, I'm sure my lips are turning a shade of blue by now.

If Wendy has paid attention to the time I'm sure she's at least spotted me standing here talking to Denver in the parking lot. I know she'll bombard me with questions as soon as I get in her car, but being interrogated is one of the last things I want to do right now. This is something that will just have to wait. I'm sure she'll understand. I'm suddenly exhausted, and my lack of sleep is catching up with me.

His eyes spark with something for a brief moment and then fade away. I get the feeling he would keep talking to me if I hadn't made another excuse to get away. Running seems to be the theme of the evening.

He nods, understanding. "Yeah, me too. I've got to get home

to Marvel. She's fully capable of putting herself to bed, but I like to be there, you know?"

I nod because I don't know what else to do or say. I don't have kids of my own so I don't know what he's referring to, though I can imagine. I tuck my head down and start to move, hoping he will let me pass this time. He does. He hollers one last thing as I make my way closer to my final escape.

"I hope you'll come back next month! Sometimes showing up is all you can do, Nicki."

That's the first time I've ever heard him say my name. And for some odd reason, I like the way it rolls off his tongue.

But I quickly push the thought aside. Because I don't think I'll be coming back. Coffee bribes or not.

16

Then: Thanksgiving Day

I am pulled out of bed by the wonderful smell of bread. Freshly baked hot rolls to be exact. Along with turkey roasting in the oven and bacon frying in the pan. My mouth waters before I even crack open my eyes. Ah, yes, my favorite holiday—Thanksgiving.

Mom was gone for three days. She was gone all day Friday, Saturday, Sunday, and was here again when I came home from school Monday. She had baked a pan of caramel brownies. She was back to smiling and asked me about my day as though no time had passed. As though she hadn't been gone for days, and this was our normal.

When I tried asking her about where she'd been the last several days, she just shrugged and said, "I'm back now, so what's it matter?" and carried on with whatever we'd been previously talking about. I let her talk because, for once, I had nothing to say to her. I wasn't sure which "Mom" she was that day—I was too terrified to break the spell and have her leave again. I couldn't let that happen. I wouldn't let it.

Now, three days later, Mom is in the kitchen dancing her way through one recipe after another. She's always enjoyed cooking, especially on big holidays like this one. I keep asking her if these are old family recipes, but she always dodges the question and replies with something along the lines of: *For goodness sake, can't a woman just enjoy cooking without it having to mean anything?* Which is true. Especially for my mom. She doesn't need a reason for doing the things she does, she just does them.

Like she is right now. Music is blasting from an old speaker in the kitchen. She's wearing her favorite checkered apron as she whisks mashed potatoes in a large bowl, swinging her hips along to the beat. She's a sight to see, that's for sure. Her long, curly hair is tied up loosely on top of her head. There are traces of flour everywhere. It's all over the countertops, the sink, and there's a light dusting all over the floor. Yet here is my mother, not phased by any of it one bit. Because she knows all too well that Dad will swoop in by the end to clean up all of her mess. I don't even have to ask where he is right now, because I know.

He's sitting on the couch reading the paper or watching the news. It's always the news. I'll ask Mom if she needs my help, and she won't answer. She'll simply shoo me away. She's in her zone and can't be bothered. It used to hurt my feelings that she didn't want my help, but over the years it's something I've learned to let go of.

So, naturally, I mosey into the living room to join Dad. I plop down in Mom's chair and ask if the annual Macy's Thanksgiving Parade is on. He nods and hands me the remote. Sometimes he watches it with me, but usually he continues reading his paper. We are rarely all gathered in this room together. While it's known as our "living room," not much living happens here.

I'm just grateful for his company today. Only this year, there's a wedge between him and I that wasn't there before.

Mom hasn't said the D-word again, and Dad never has. Its weight is hanging heavily over the entire house, yet we all keep pretending it doesn't exist. For all I know, maybe it never really did.

I become a zombie in front of the TV while I wait for Mom to call us both into the kitchen to eat after all her hard work.

ANOTHER DIFFERENCE this year is that we don't eat by two o'clock. We don't even eat by four. Thankfully, I ate breakfast and snacked with Dad earlier, sharing a large bowl of kettle corn. But now my tummy is rumbling with hunger again. She's later than ever this year, and I have no idea what is taking so long.

"Guys! The food is ready! Come eat while it's hot!" Mom finally calls us from the kitchen.

Dad heads off in the direction of the bathroom while I fold the blanket I'd been wrapped up in and drape it over the side of her chair. When I come into the kitchen I don't expect to see Mom grabbing her purse and keys. Wait, where is she going? She just announced that dinner is finally ready. Besides, it's Thanksgiving. *Our holiday.*

"Mom, where are you going? You said it was ready." I try to mask the rising frustration in my voice.

Her cheeks are flushed and more of her brown spirally hair has fallen loose around her face. She's digging in her purse for something. I can't figure out what she's looking for when we should all be sitting down to eat. I doubt any stores are open, and if she forgot something I'm sure we can do without it.

"What, P? What is it?" she asks me without looking up.

If I'm not mistaken she sounds almost like she's annoyed with *me.* But how can that be? She didn't want my help when I'd come in to offer several times. After the fourth time of being shooed away, I quit asking.

"We're hungry and you made this delicious meal... but you seem like you're upset. Let me help you, please," I softly beg her. I don't usually ask anything of her, but I want her to let me help this time. Just this once. I want her to *need* me.

This time her penny eyes meet mine. For a moment we just stare at one another, nobody moving a muscle. I think I'm the first to blink, but I'm not sure.

"I can't find my phone, P," she says matter-of-factly. She's digging through her purse for her phone. She doesn't even own a phone. What is she talking about?

"Mom," I say gently, "You don't have a phone."

Her eyes suddenly look glassy, and she glares at me like I'm stupid. Maybe I am. Maybe she's had a phone all along and never bothered to tell anyone. It honestly won't surprise me if she has one.

"Of course, I have a phone, P. How do you think I get around anywhere?" she fires back.

In all my life, I've never once seen her use a phone of any kind. She doesn't have any friends or family. I know she doesn't sit at home all day, but where she goes I've never figured out.

I'm too stunned to speak, and my stomach is still protesting underneath the confusion.

"I didn't know," I say quietly. I'll have to ask Dad if he knows she has a phone. I still can't believe she has one and never bothered to give me her number. Her own daughter.

"Of course not," she retorts, "I don't need to report every detail of my life to you. You're a freaking teenager, who knows what you do all day when you come home. I know you sneak my keys when I'm not looking. You've probably got a boyfriend you go and visit. Sneaking out at night so you two can do things. Are you having sex, P? Because if you are, I swear..."

Tears prick my eyes as I chew my lip. She is taking this too far.

How dare she make this all about me. It's Thanksgiving Day. She spent literally all day in the kitchen, refusing anyone's help, and is now making me out to be someone that I'm not. I thought my mother knew me better than that, but apparently, I was wrong. She doesn't know me at all. And maybe I don't know her either.

She did get one thing right though…

I am so mad I am fuming. I think I see actual flames through my eyelids. "You're right about one thing," I snap back at her, "I do sometimes sneak your keys. But don't you dare say those things about me when you know they aren't true. Heck, I don't even know what's true anymore because all that seems to be coming out of your mouth these days is nothing but a bunch of lies and broken promises—"

A hand slaps across my face, cutting off my tirade. And I know who that hand belongs to. My mother just slapped me. She *slapped* me. She's never laid a hand on me. Even when I was younger and acting out she never spanked me. That was always Dad's job.

Have you noticed anything different about her lately? She hasn't been herself.

I should have been paying more attention when Dad asked me about Mom that day. Maybe he noticed something off about her before I had. Maybe this is exactly what he was talking about. Dad saw this coming from a mile away, and when I look at my parents, *they* seem like the ones who are miles away from me.

But right now, I see what Dad may have been seeing from the start. He may have been witnessing an entirely different side to Mom that I've been too blind to notice. He asked me to pay attention to her, and I failed.

I stumble backward and yank her purse and her keys out of her hands. I don't tell either parent where I'm going but decide to go for a long drive. I need to clear my head.

Dad doesn't ask me where I'm going when I run into him in the hallway, and Mom doesn't try to stop me. Sometimes I wish they would. I wish Dad would chase me out the door and yell at the top of his lungs for me to come back home, but he never does. And I wish Mom, in all her anger and confusion, would yell at me that she is sorry for hurting me and beg me to come back. But she doesn't do that either. Neither of them says anything.

I pull back into the garage by seven. All the food is set out on the kitchen table, and it's warm. At least someone cares enough to warm dinner up for me, even if they don't care enough to stay and enjoy the meal with me. Instead, I spend the last little bit of the holiday stuffing my face. Alone.

Oh, and I did search Mom's purse for her phone. And in her car. Turns out she's now a liar. She doesn't own a phone. Probably never has and never will. Go figure. Why'd she have to go and make a scene today, of all days? Seriously, Mom.

I don't generally think of myself as a bitter person, but today it's all I can feel. Today, instead of being reminded of the things I should be grateful for, I'm left with a hollowness inside and a slow-burning hate for the two people I used to love.

Now: Thanksgiving Day

Wendy and her family arrive at our place shortly after two o'clock. Wendy and Rick are close to celebrating their twentieth year of marriage. Twenty! She'd mentioned to me once before that they'd married young, right out of high school. I thought high school sweethearts only existed in the movies. I didn't think that was real life, yet I don't exactly have a great picture of what forever love looks like when it comes to marriage.

They have two energetic daughters that keep them busy: Georgia and Hazel. I love their names and promised Wendy one day I'd use them in one of my novels. She blushed and said that wasn't necessary, but I know she'd love it.

Georgia is the younger of the two sisters, she just turned eight, and Hazel is now thirteen. Georgia has her arms full with some type of casserole dish, and Hazel is carrying a crockpot with home-made chicken and noodles. Wendy also made hot rolls, mashed potatoes, and roasted vegetables. Rick loves smoking meat and brought an assortment of brisket, pulled pork, and smoked ham. I can't believe they brought all of this to share with just me and Dad, but they've been joining us for Thanksgiving for the last five years, and I wouldn't have it any other way.

The Heckarts spread out their food along the counter. Since our kitchen is on the smaller side, Dad and I have moved our table into the living room and arranged the furniture so that there's plenty of room to comfortably eat and for the men to watch football.

After we get everything set up, we send the girls through the line first. Wendy tugs me back a little so we can have a moment to talk privately. I grab the pitcher of sweet tea I'd made out of the fridge and begin to pour us both glasses.

I hand Wendy hers and she motions with her head towards my bedroom. She wants somewhere we can talk alone. I don't often get nervous around Wendy, but she's also unpredictable at times when it comes to things that fly out of her mouth. I should be used to that by now, but it still catches me off guard at times.

We take our drinks into my bedroom. Suddenly I feel a little embarrassed for bringing her in here. She's been in my house plenty but the realization that this isn't my own home isn't lost on me. I'm less than ten years away from the big 4-0, and yet I'm still living at home with my Dad. I can't even use his health as an excuse to stay here. He's actually in great health.

Thankfully, I've never once felt judged by Wendy or her family. If they've ever had any opinions about me, they are careful to keep them to themselves.

"So..." Wendy starts.

She's wearing a sweater the color of a pumpkin and her nails are a bright orange to match. I stifle a laugh because her attire reminds me of Velma from Scooby Doo. She just turned forty a few months ago, but doesn't look a day over twenty-five. I haven't found a single wrinkle on her flawless skin, and she certainly doesn't look like she popped out two kids. She looks great.

She's standing against the door frame, eyes roaming around my room. My eyes follow her line of sight. What does she see? Does she look at me and see a woman who never grew up?

I shake my head to clear any doubt creeping in.

"So…" I retort back, unsure of why we came in here in the first place. I don't want to rush her, so instead, I take a swig of my iced tea.

"You said you were gonna tell me more about what you and Denver talked about the other night. You never elaborated," she says, looking directly at me and smirking. "Don't think I missed those heart eyes you were making at each other in the parking lot. You weren't hiding at all, I had a very clear view of the show. If I didn't know any better, I'd say you've got a crush on the tall mountain man," she added, her features bright with excitement.

Okay, so she wants to get into this now. This is the reason she brought me in here, to talk about Denver. Right. Last week I'd gotten into her car after the meeting and barely spoke a word to her the entire ten-minute drive to my house. I told her I was tired (which was true) and would relay our conversation to her later (which was also true). I just hadn't anticipated that the later time would mean *now*. She wasted no time pumping me for details.

She finishes off her drink and sets her glass down on one of my coasters on my desk, folding her arms across her chest. She's waiting for me to begin.

I take another sip from my tea and set it down on a coaster as well. I watch as one of the ice cubes melt and a trickle of condensation runs along the glass, collecting in a tiny puddle along the coaster.

I clear my throat and ask, "What would you like to know?"

A small laugh escapes her. "Everything," she replies.

"Well, he recognized me from the book signing and came up to me in the parking lot," I say, stating the obvious. She already knows this but she nods her head to tell me to keep going.

"And then what? What did he say?" she asks, leaning in towards me the slightest amount.

"He said he's been coming to G&G for six or seven years now and it's always this time of year," I say, hoping that's enough and we can talk about something else. It's only a matter of time before one of her girls finds us in here talking about a man. A handsome one at that. My cheeks burn at the thought.

"Oh, yeah? Huh. Did he say why he started coming in the first place?" she asks.

I shake my head. That was information he didn't offer up and something I was too afraid to ask further details about. The timing didn't feel right. Maybe it never would. *Who are you grieving for? What happened?* Because he could easily ask the same thing of me.

"He didn't say. He just said he comes this time of year between now and February." I try not to draw out the word February. I don't want to bring more attention to it. Wendy already knows what that month means to me. That's not something we need to discuss.

She nods again, as if accepting this. "I wonder what's happened in his life?" she says out loud, more to herself than to me.

Something he said that night has stuck with me. *Life is hard, but being alone is harder.* I know he is raising Marvel by himself. How long has he been doing that? Is that the loneliness he was referring to? Or is it something else? Maybe he lost his wife and really is alone. Maybe something bad happened. Something he isn't ready to tell me. Now he won't get the chance, because I won't be seeing him again.

Before I can say anything else Wendy speaks up, "So, when do you think you'll see him again? Did you get his number?" She smirks again at this.

I look away, avoiding her gaze. I know she means well, but I'm done talking about this. My nonexistent love life. It's Thanksgiving, and we should be out there enjoying the holiday with everyone else, not in here talking about a crush that won't go anywhere.

"No, I didn't ask him, and he didn't ask me for it either. It's okay though, really."

I suddenly feel her presence growing closer to me, her warm scent of jasmine wraps me up in a warm embrace. With a gentle touch her hand pulls my face back to hers. I look at her, really look at her. Her dark brown eyes hold mine for a moment before she says anything. I exhale and feel some of the tightness in my chest loosen.

"Do you like him?" she whispers.

Of course I do. I mean, what's not to like? But I don't really know him. Not like that. Not in the way she's asking.

I shake my head gently. "I don't know. I'm not sure."

She nods in return. "Okay, that's fair. But do you want to?"

I want to look away from her. But her eyes lock me in place. Ground me.

"Yes, but I—" I start but don't finish.

"Do you want to?" she asks me again.

"Yes," I say so softly I'm not sure she hears me at first, but she does.

She takes both of my hands in hers and I stare down at our hands. While mine are cold and clammy, hers are soft and warm like I expected they would be.

"Then don't stop yourself from at least trying to let that happen. You talk yourself out of a lot of things, Nicki. Don't let this be one of those times."

I hear Denver's words echoing in my head. *Sometimes showing up is all you can do.* Maybe he's right, perhaps they both are. Maybe this is exactly where our story should begin, rather than end. But I don't know... I don't know if either of us is ready for that. I don't know how he feels about me. Maybe he says those types of words to every new girl he meets, and I just happened to be *that* girl. I'm getting in my head again, I know I am, but I can't help it. I always do this. Talk myself out of something that might be good before I've really given it a fair chance.

It's fear talking, but will I listen to it this time?

"Nicki," she says to me softly, reining me back in, away from the negative thoughts that are pulling me under once again.

"Sorry, I'll, uh, think about it," I promise.

There's sadness in her eyes that wasn't there before. But she nods, understanding. Letting it go for now.

"Don't think too hard about it, or you'll just talk yourself out of it. If you like him, go back next month. Give it another shot. Give *him* another shot," she says.

"He did try to convince me to come back to another meeting," I say, shyly.

Wendy squeals. "Well, why didn't you lead with that? You have to go back! You have to give him a chance."

"Am I going to these meetings for me or for you? Hmm?" I challenge her.

She shrugs her shoulders and picks up her empty glass. "Maybe both? Okay, I'll drop it for now. Just promise you'll think about going back again."

"I promise I'll think about it."

"Good. I'm here for you, Nicki, and I'll always listen. I care about you. Let's get back out there before the food gets cold."

And with that, we enjoy our Thanksgiving feast. Without another word of a man with eyes grass green and teeth as pure as snow. We don't dwell in the past and we don't obsess over our future. We simply cherish the time we have together in each other's company.

Then: December 1st

Today's Sunday, which normally means going to the early service at our church, but Mom slept in again. I guess all those hours she'd spent in the kitchen on Thanksgiving was too much for her. Since then, every morning she stays in bed until at least ten, sometimes later. It's almost eleven, and she still hasn't gotten out of bed. We missed both church services today. I thought her new meds were working. I thought she was sleeping better. And that's when a new thought hits me: *what if she isn't taking her meds at all?*

I'm passing the time reading in the living room while keeping an eye on my mom's door, waiting for her to emerge. Eventually Dad folds up the newspaper he is reading in the chair and clears his throat before asking if I want to go for a drive.

Dad tries to take me out to practice driving every weekend. It's something I've started looking forward to because it's one of the only things we do together, just the two of us. He hasn't mentioned it, but I think he feels the same way.

Unlike Mom, Dad prefers to drive with the radio either completely off or at the lowest volume possible. It's been snowing since we started, but we are breaking soon for a late lunch. Dad and I make small talk as usual. He's in the passenger seat with his eyes on the road straight ahead. Snow covers the ground as I pause at a red light in town.

"Hey, Dad?" I start. He glances over at me for a split second then goes back to staring straight ahead.

His head slightly bobs in response, "Yes, Sweet P?"

"Um, how are you and Mom doing?" This is a topic I never bring up. Things seem fine-ish, other than Mom sleeping a lot again. I don't want to stir the waters, but it's always there on the tip of my tongue. Mom is always around when I'm with Dad, unless we're doing driving practice, and I'm never brave enough to ask in front of her. I feel like she'd give an entirely different answer than Dad would, and I want to hear the truth from him.

Dad is always straight and honest with me. Not that Mom isn't honest, but she's, well, *her*. And unfortunately, I don't always trust her judgment.

He fidgets for a moment with his beard. Typically in the winter he grows it out. I'm not sure if he just likes the look of it or it provides extra warmth, but either way he won't be shaving it any time soon.

"Oh, um, we are actually doing okay."

Short and to the point. The light turns green, and I ease onto the gas as I turn left onto a side street. We are headed to our favorite deli in town called Sam's Sammies (clever, I know). They have the best bread for their sandwiches and their soup is always delicious. Every time I try a different soup it's suddenly my new favorite.

When Dad doesn't elaborate I press on. "So... does that mean you two aren't getting a divorce?" Mom had seemed so distraught that day, but neither of them have brought it up since, and as their daughter, I feel like I have a right to know. If things are fine between them, great—but if not, if Dad were to take the house... where would Mom go? Surely, he wouldn't do that to her. To us.

He clears his throat, clearly not expecting the conversation to continue. "No, we are not separating. Um... I'm trying to get your mom to agree to come to counseling, but haven't had much luck."

Counseling? As in a shrink? What for? I know that Mom has been trying new medications, but talking about going to someone for therapy is entirely new and foreign to me.

"You're seeing a shrink?" I ask, confusion in my tone.

"Yes..." There's a slight hesitation in his voice I can't quite pinpoint. He clears his throat and continues, "And she's not a shrink, she's a therapist. She's actually really great, I think you'd like her."

This is the first I'm hearing about any of this. I guess it isn't exactly my business, but he's the one that brought it up.

"Why?" For some reason I can't fathom my dad talking to another stranger about his personal life. He doesn't even talk to me or Mom about anything remotely private, why in the world would he be meeting with a stranger? It doesn't make sense.

Unless... no. No, no. Absolutely not.

He said she. *She.* And whoever *she* is, Dad thinks *she's great.*

I slam the brakes so hard he gasps, and a car from somewhere behind us honks at me, loudly. I don't care. My head is spinning. My vision starts to blur. Dad is yelling something at me, but I can't hear him. I can't hear anything.

Someone is screaming. Is it me? Is it Dad? Is it someone else? I need to get out of here, but there's nowhere to escape. I am trapped. Cars are still honking and someone is still screaming at me, maybe it is Dad. I turn to him and yell back.

"Are you sleeping with your therapist?" I yell.

His eyes go wide in shock. They transform in a matter of

seconds. Shock. Anger. Hurt. Fear. But nothing to show that what I said isn't true.

He opens his mouth slowly to say something, but he doesn't have to. His eyes already told me everything. I can't believe it. I'm going to be sick to my stomach.

Horns are blaring, my brain is screaming, and my dad sits there and says nothing as usual, too stunned to move or do anything to remedy this horrific situation. I yank off my seatbelt and throw open my door right into traffic, right into the chaos of everything.

I am numb. I force my body to move, but it can't. I stand in the middle of the street, freezing cold and in a panic. I'm hyperventilating but don't know how to stop it. My head is pounding louder than my heart. Tears freeze along my cheeks, and I silently beg God to let my lungs freeze up too.

Because if I weren't breathing I wouldn't be feeling this way. I wouldn't have just found out that my dad, my *dad,* is having an affair with his *therapist.* Someone that is supposed to help you with your problems, not destroy an entire family. And Mom has no idea. *Mom...*

Suddenly something dry and warm wraps around me and pulls me out of the street. It feels like a blanket, but I'm still numb. I'm being lifted into the air and placed down into a seat. It's still warm from where someone was sitting. I hear a buckle click and doors slam from all directions. The car begins to move again, but I do not.

I am incapable of feeling or thinking anything right now. I close my eyes, and I succumb to the black.

19

Now: December 1st

It's been over a week since I'd walked out of Grieve and Grow. I've done my fair share of grieving, but am I continuing to grow? Because I think I've missed the growth part, despite being five feet, six inches. *Spider-Girl.* If I were a flower I'd have shriveled up a while ago. Everyone knows that flowers can't thrive in the darkness, and as much as I don't want to admit it, I haven't been living much differently.

Maybe I'm more of a mountain flower. I can still exist in the least likely of places and thrive in the harshest conditions.

If someone were to ask me if I was happy, and if I was answering them honestly, I'd probably say that I'm content. Which I realize isn't the same as being happy, but I'm okay with how things currently are. Dad stays busy with his work, and I stay plenty busy with mine.

The only luxury I don't have is a car because I don't drive. Dad doesn't usually seem to mind, and Wendy knows better than to bug me about it. She's brought it up occasionally before, but the conversation always falls flat because I'm not interested. But sometimes it's those instances where I'm reminded that someone out there still cares about me.

Cares enough to ask the hard things. The hard things I cannot ask myself. I stopped asking things a long time ago. Maybe one day I can start again.

WENDY HAS COMPLETED edits for my most recent novel. The past couple of weeks I've been pouring time into fixing certain character flaws and plot holes. She's good at what she does, and she's quick. I'm not her only client, but she's always on time with her edits. The editing process can often be grueling, and she gets that, so she never pressures me too hard once my drafts are back into my hands.

I'm hoping to have this final piece in the series ready to launch by spring. I've taken over the study for now. I concentrate better when I'm working in here. Not much light gets in, but it gives off the illusion that you're not really in the house at all. Like you're in a separate space altogether and nothing from the outside world can disturb you.

Which is ridiculous because Dad is just outside the room, but I like to imagine I'm the only one here and nobody can touch me when I'm inside. It's a safe haven. The perfect escape.

I've been working on edits for the last four hours straight, and my hands are starting to cramp. I've got a good momentum going, and I don't want to stop. Only a few more pages to go and then I'll take a break and eat something. My stomach is starting to protest.

My eyes are glued to the glowing screen when my phone pings

with an incoming text. Wendy. It's fine, she can wait a few more minutes. Another ping. Wendy, seriously?

When I finally look it's not Wendy. It's an unknown number. Which shouldn't surprise me too much. It's rare, but I do get spam messages from time to time. I pick up my phone to swipe and delete it when I notice the message:

UNKNOWN

> Hi, it's Denver from G&G. Wendy gave me your number, I hope that's okay.

Wendy did *what?* She asked me on Thanksgiving if I'd gotten his number and I said no. I didn't mean that as an invitation for her to get it for me! How did she even go about doing that? You know what, it doesn't matter. I can't believe she did that. And yet I can. It's exactly the thing Wendy would do. She knows me better than I know myself sometimes, and if it had been left up to me nothing would have happened. Hence, here we are and now he has my phone number. *He* has *my* phone number. I wasn't quite sure what to think about that.

I pause, unsure of how to respond, and decide to keep it brief. I'm not a big texter. I've always preferred conversations to be face-to-face.

ME

> Sure. That's fine.

DENVER

> She reached out to me. She got my number somehow and asked if I'd be able to take you to the next group meeting since she won't be able to.

The next meeting is three weeks away. Plenty of time to back out. Too much time allows me to overthink, which I'm already doing now. I'm not ready, and I'm not sure I ever will be. Besides, I'm not going. One and done. Check mark. Wait, why won't she be able to take me? Surely she said something to me about this, yet it's not ringing any bells.

A part of me wishes that she would have asked me first. Or at least allowed me the chance to see him again at the next meeting. But I haven't exactly committed to going. I'm still on the fence about it. About everything. I know she means well so it's hard to be mad at her, but I don't know the guy, not really. And now he has my number. Maybe it doesn't mean anything. This is simple, I'm turning it into something far more complicated than it needs to be.

I know I should give him a chance, but I'm scared. Putting yourself out there, exposed and real, is terrifying. I'm not ready. I'm not cut out for this. This isn't me.

I close my eyes and exhale before responding. I won't respond in frustration. Mom always reminded me of that when I was younger. All the times I was upset with her. Especially during those times.

The other part of me can't help but feel a little disappointed. Not that I'm interested in him or anything. I didn't notice him wearing a wedding band, but in today's day and age, that could mean any number of things. I can't assume he's single, and I can't assume that I'd be someone he'd want to date.

He doesn't want me. Of course not.

ME

Thank you, but that won't be necessary. I don't think I'll be going. Thanks anyway.

DENVER

It's no problem. You don't live far from me.

She also gave him my address. Now she's gone too far. But I suppose if she expects him to pick me up, he has to know where I live. This is getting out of hand quickly. Instead of responding, I do something even crazier. I call him.

He answers on the first ring. "Hello?"

I'm taken back by how rich and deep his voice is. Rich like the sticky, sweet syrup on Mom's homemade pancakes.

I can't recall a single time I've called a man other than my dad on the phone. How pathetic.

"Sorry, I don't like to text. Talking is easier for me," I say, a little embarrassed about calling him without asking first. He might be at work for all I know, I have no idea what he does. My cheeks flush, and I'm tempted to end the call. Overthinking as usual.

I can almost feel him smiling on his end. His voice is cheerful and light. "Hey, no problem at all. Me too actually. I realize it's still a little ways off, but she just wanted to make sure you had a way to get there."

I nod even though he can't see me. "Yeah, she tends to do that kind of thing. She's a good friend. I'll let you know if I plan to go or not."

"Not that it matters or anything, but I don't attend the full year. Just through February," he reminds me once again.

February. Why that month? Out of all the months in a year, why *that* one? If only he knew... but he has no reason to. Because his story isn't the same as mine. Sure, I'm curious to know more about him, but at the same time, I know better than to push someone before they are ready to share something. If he wants to elaborate, he will.

"That's right. I remember," I say, flatly. Not that I don't care, because I do. I'm not sure how to read him yet. I don't know if he wants me to ask the hard things like Wendy does, or if he'd rather I ask him something else, or nothing at all. I called *him* after all.

"Can I ask you something?" he suddenly blurts out.

That depends. Does he want to know my full name or does he assume that it's Nicki? Does he want to know why I blacked out at my own book signing? Why I bolted out of my first night of group? Why I'd come in the first place?

"Maybe," I offer instead.

"Why don't you drive? If you don't mind me asking. You don't have to tell me, I was just curious."

Oh, that.

"I... I'm just not comfortable with it." There's more that I could say, there always is, hanging on the tip of my tongue ready to gush out like a waterfall. But I don't let it. Not this time. Possibly not ever. He wouldn't understand. Nobody would.

He must sense the awkward pause on my end because he quickly moves on. "That's okay. It can be tricky navigating some of these roads around here. I'm a full-time EMT, and this time of year can be especially dangerous."

Yes, it certainly can be. So, he's an EMT. He saves lives for a living, I just write about lives being changed for the better. He's handsome, fit, and from what I can tell, he seems like a great dad to his teenage daughter. Yep, way out of my league. Maybe I should ask him more about her instead. I'm sure she's way more interesting than my lack of experience driving a vehicle.

"Wow, yeah I can only imagine. Uh, that's a tough job. Is that ever tough on your daughter, Marvel?" I ask, remembering her unique name.

"It is tough, but so rewarding. If you let me take you to our next group meeting I can tell you more about why I decided to become one. And yeah, sometimes it can be hard on her, but she gets it. She understands its importance and the sacrifice that comes with the job."

Is he bribing me with his life story so he can take me to the meeting? It's only a ten-minute drive. He may not have asked for my number, but is this a strange way of him asking me out? I'm probably reading way too much into this. I don't have experience in this area. I should probably get back to writing or find something to eat.

"Well, Denver, it's been nice talking to you, but I've got to go. I'll, uh, let you know what I decide." Even though I'd already made up my mind a while ago.

He laughs softly into the phone. Please, stop. I'm not going to let his charm sway me into saying yes. Will I? Maybe. No. Definitely not. Only Wendy has that kind of hold over me, and I'm trying to break that spell.

"Sounds perfect, Nicki. Is it okay to call you again sometime?" he asks.

My cheeks flush at his question. He said my name again. Is he flirting with me?

"Oh, yes. Of course."

"Great," he says.

"Good," I say.

"Have a good day."

"You, too."

Am I supposed to hang up first or is he?

"See you," he says.

"I haven't said yes yet," I say, making a light joke.

"Oh, right," he says.

"Well, then," I say.

"You can hang up, you know," he jokes back.

"Yes, right, of course. I was about to do that."

"Right." He laughs.

"Right." I laugh back.

I finally hang up the phone. What in the world just happened? Did I really spend the last half hour talking to a *man* over the *phone?* Yes, I think I did. Wendy is going to flip that her plan may have worked. What am I getting myself into?

20

Then: December 19th

I haven't gone back out with Dad for any more driving lessons. Even though he's the parent, and I generally respect authority, right now he's lost all respect from me. I simply don't have any left to give after learning about his affair.

So far, I haven't revealed his secret. But I have been studying Mom closely for any signs that she might know that something is going on. As angry as I am at Dad, I don't feel that it's my place to say anything to Mom. But for her sake, I hope he does. Or, I should say, for her sake I hope he quits going to therapy. Not that it's okay to brush this kind of thing under the rug, but I know exactly what it would do to her if she found out. It'd be much easier if he simply puts out the fire now and loves his wife again.

Sadly, looking back at their relationship, I don't know that I can truthfully say that either one truly loves the other. They aren't affectionate with each other. They never hug, kiss, or hold hands.

They are cordial with one another, but nothing more. It's depressing, to say the least.

The day I found out the horrible truth about my dad, I vowed I would never do that to someone else. I would never be unfaithful to my partner or spouse. I would never exist in their presence without love or warmth. I will never become my parents.

Now: December 19th

"Dad, I'm going out tonight," I tell him from across the table at lunch. Most of our meals fall out of sync with one another, but now is an exception. Today we are both sitting around the table, Dad in his chair and me in mine—eating salads together.

I used to love cooking. When I was seven or eight I dreamed of becoming a chef one day. Mom was always whipping up something amazing in the kitchen. The day I realized she wasn't coming back was the day I stopped cooking and baking. I couldn't come in here without seeing the memory of her in her checkered apron whisking, whipping, and chopping. I couldn't block out the loud music blaring from invisible speakers that no longer exist. For the longest time, I couldn't come in here without glancing at the fridge, expecting to see another one of her notes that read:

I'll be out for a while, Spider-Girl. There's some leftovers for you and Dad in the fridge to enjoy.

Love, Mom.

Now, I cook out of pure necessity, but nothing like I used to. The recipes are forever etched into my brain, but I can't will myself to make any of them again. So most mornings it's oatmeal, toast, or eggs. Lunch is a protein shake, salad, or soup. Dinner is always takeout or something from the freezer I can easily pop into the microwave. But from time to time I long to taste one of Mom's home-cooked meals.

Over the last few weeks, not only have I completed final edits on the last book in *The Honey Sisters* series, but they've been sent off to Wendy and are resting in her magical hands. It feels good to tie a bow on the series, but it's also left me with a bit of a hollow feeling inside. Since Wendy is my *only* female friend, over these last few years I've grown to know and love the fictional sisters and their unique stories as if they've been a part of mine all along.

Wendy hasn't dared to ask me if I'd be open to trying another signing when this story is released in a few months. To be honest, I haven't given it much thought, and every time I do, it reminds me of *him*. Speaking of... I glance back over at Dad who is using his right hand to shovel food slowly into his mouth and the other to hold open the newspaper he's reading. We never had a lot to say growing up, and that hasn't changed much. At least some things are a constant, even if they are a bit uncomfortable at times.

He doesn't acknowledge my comment until I clear my throat gently in an attempt to gain his attention. *Just look at me, Daddy, I'm right here.*

His gray eyes finally meet mine as he sets down his paper. He, too, clears his throat before speaking.

"Is that so, Sweet P? That's funny that you mention that because I have plans tonight too," he replies.

Wait, what did he just say? Dad has plans? Where in the world would he need to go? He rarely ever leaves the house and never has anywhere to be past six.

My stomach begins to tighten with anxiety, I push my salad away and look at him. *Really* look at him. My Dad leaves the house less than I do. Worried lines crease my brows.

"You have plans," I say carefully. "Tonight," I add.

He nods his head shyly, a slow smile curling through his lips. "Believe it or not, your old man has a date tonight."

I don't have any food left in my mouth, but if I did, I'd probably spit it out. What? My Dad has a... did he say *date?* But he doesn't date. He's never gone on a date, not even when he and Mom were still together... Unless he counts *her* as... No, we are past all of that. That was sixteen years ago. He's in his sixties now. Is this someone he just met or has this been happening for a while now and he finally dares to speak up?

When I found out about Dad's affair in high school, our relationship was damaged. Between Dad threatening Mom with divorce and cheating on her with his therapist, it took a long time before I was ready to forgive him. A *long* time. But when he became all I had left, things started to heal between us. Slowly but surely.

He calms my swirling thoughts with the simple touch of his hand, now resting on top of mine. He gives it a gentle squeeze like I used to give Mom on the days she'd had enough. The days she'd been too much, even for Dad, they'd retreat into separate rooms of the house. The days when shattered glass lay broken on the floor, and I was left to clean up their mess. When we'd all become strangers in a shared space. I remember it all a little too well.

Tears begin to well up in my eyes, and I find myself blinking rapidly to fight them away. He must notice, because he moves his hand away from mine and catches the tear before it has the chance to fall. He doesn't show it often, but at this moment I'm reminded that he does care for me. Possibly even love me. It causes my eyes to blur even more. What's happening to me?

"That's great, Dad," I manage to choke out.

I can't see if he has tears in his eyes as well, but he nods again and continues to wipe the moisture off my cheeks.

"Thanks, darling. What about you? You said you were going out too. Is it with your friend Wendy? I really like her, I think she's been good for you," he says, his eyes crinkling at the corners.

I gently shake my head and reach for a napkin to dab my eyes. I guess I shouldn't be quick to judge him for wanting to go out with someone. I'm glad he's finally found somebody he has an interest in spending time with, other than his grown daughter.

I have never gone on a date. I have never held hands, kissed, or done anything with a boy before. All hope of that was ripped from me when I experienced the worst thing possible at the worst time possible. I never recovered from it. I'm still trying to gather up all the shattered pieces from my mess.

Now, at thirty-two, I finally have my first date. Okay, it's not "technically" a date. I decided not to go with Denver to his G&G meeting this month, but I did agree to let him pick me up for a late coffee after it was over. With every minute that ticks by, I have to fight the urge to pick up my phone and cancel. Backing out is so much easier than saying yes. Making up excuse after excuse is less complicated than expressing myself to another human being, other than the pretend ones I write in my novels.

But I'm doing this. Wendy is preparing for her flight across the country with her family to somewhere warm and beachy. She won't be there this time to rescue me if I make another mistake. For all I know, this could be my biggest one yet. But I'll never know if I don't at least give it a chance. Give *him* a chance. The least we could do is become friends. Because God knows I could use another friend.

"Yes, she is good for me, but it's not Wendy this time, Dad. It's a man I met at the book signing I did a month ago." I don't feel like now is the right time to mention that I also ran into him at a grief group.

He doesn't know about that yet. I don't feel the need to share every piece of my life with him. Apparently, he hasn't told me everything going on in his either.

Instead, I add, "His name is Denver, and he has a daughter who enjoys my books. He'll be here around 8 p.m. to get me."

This time I notice his eyes. They suddenly look less dull and gray than they usually do, and they shimmer like a sparkly nickel. "That is wonderful, P. I hope it goes well for you tonight."

I reach across the table and gently squeeze his hand in mine this time. "You too, Dad."

I'm so proud of him for being brave and getting out there too. It's a really big deal that he's doing this. And not for me this time, but for him.

22

Then: December 19th

There are a few times a year that our house is exceptionally loud. When Mom is in her cooking element, you can bet she is in the kitchen not only wearing her favorite apron but also swaying her hips and singing off-key to all of our favorite 90s bands. And yes, I mean *our.*

I mean, I am a 90s kid, and I was raised in the 90s and early 2000s, so I grew up listening and jamming out to music Mom was always playing from that era. I wouldn't say Dad particularly cares for it, but he tolerates it when it's our turn to pick the music. He never fights for his music. At best, he will kindly ask us to turn the volume down a couple of notches. I think if he had his choice of music he would pick something Classical, instrumental, or silence. Anytime we are in the car together the radio is always turned off. Always.

Today is one of the loud days. I wake up to not only the smell of bacon grease, fried eggs, and homemade apple crumble muffins, but the music is on at a high volume at nine in the morning. Mom and I only wake up early when we have to, like on school mornings, and we heavily rely on digital alarms to pull us out of our deep sleep. Today is not only Saturday, but it's only six days until Christmas, and Mom and I have some shopping to do.

She's wearing her famous apron of course, but she's also a full-on Christmas elf this morning. She's wearing a bright green sweater wrapped in itchy tinsel everywhere and something on her body makes a jingling bell sound any time she moves.

Dad is sitting quietly at the table with a mug of coffee and his newspaper while Mom and I quickly scarf down our breakfast so we can hit the stores this morning. Dad mumbles something about going to meet a coworker for lunch later. When I hear that I make eye contact with him and glare. My expression says *you better not be having lunch with your therapist. You better not be seeing her at all.* His steel gray eyes hold onto mine, and his gaze softens, as if trying to reassure me that it has all been put into the past and he's moved on. I *wish* that I could do the same if that is true. For his sake and Mom's, I hope it is. He returns to his cold coffee and paper and I toss Mom her keys as we head out.

THIS TIME of year is seriously my favorite. There is snow piled up everywhere. The streets can get a little scary at times, but I've gotten more and more confident with my driving lately, and today I'm being extra cautious. It's the busiest time of year, and literally, everyone is out today for last-minute Christmas shopping. Only, we've never considered this to be last minute. It's how we've always done things. Dad buys a few small gifts early, he plans ahead that way and that's fine. But not Mom and I. She makes one of her lists before we head out, and then she checks them off one by one as we find them.

The list is never long though, I think it just helps her feel a sense of accomplishment to mark every item off the list. After we've hit six or seven stores and blisters are starting to form on our feet, we get hot chocolate from the vendor in the mall and rest our feet for a bit.

She always picks out three gifts for me to open on Christmas Day. One first thing in the morning, the second right after a late lunch, and the third I can open right before bed. She's done it that way for as long as I can remember.

To avoid spoiling the surprises while shopping, she will hand me a separate list of items. It'll list a few things she would like and a few suggestions of what to buy for Dad. She will then wander off into a different part of the store and have all her purchases gift-wrapped at the counter so no peeking is allowed. I've started doing the same for similar reasons. It's a fun little game we play. Over the past couple of years, it's even morphed into a bit of a competition to see who can, not only cross off items the fastest, but have them bought and wrapped first. She won last year, but I plan to win this one.

"Ready, set, go!" she yells and takes off to the right side of the store, and I dart towards the left. There are six total items on my list. Three each for Mom and Dad. I've never personally seen her lists, but she says hers has the same number of items as mine. I know she has to buy for Dad and me so I take her word for it. Let the games begin!

I don't even know how she manages to pick out the perfect gifts every single year, but she's an amazing gift giver. Always has been. Last year she got me a special edition box set of the entire Harry Potter series, a typewriter, and one of those old fashioned pen and ink sets. Dad bought me a new sweater and some perfume. Which were still great gifts, but they didn't exactly scream *me*.

I find the items on my list for Mom rather quickly. That leaves me with the three items left for Dad. I saved those for last. I still love him of course, but sometimes it's hard to show it. Bitterness creeps up like a spider, and sometimes I forget to shoo it away.

For Dad she wrote a leather wallet, a fountain pen, and a tie for work. In theory, those all should be easy to find. I'm trying hard not to run inside the store, but I have no idea how close Mom is to completing her list so I know I need to hurry. I'm in the men's department now, but I have no clue where they keep their wallets or ties... Think, think, think.

I'm concentrating so hard, zigzagging through each aisle while also trying not to miss anything, that I don't see the person right in front of me. OOF! I slam into a man's chest, and I nearly fall backward from the sudden impact.

I don't have time to run into strangers, I haven't even made it to the checkout line yet. I glance up and notice the man standing no less than two feet in front of me. Wow that's close. He smells so nice... fresh like pine needles. It reminds me of Christmas trees and the list! Shoot! I can't keep standing here.

"So sorry! Excuse me, I gotta go," I say quickly and try to awkwardly dodge the guy. Up close he doesn't look too much older than me. He looks like he's in his early 20s. Not that I care though, I don't have time to stand and chat.

"Hey, uh... do I know you from somewhere?

You sort of look familiar."

At his words, I take a moment to see him, really see him. His hair is light brown and messy, like he forgot to brush it this morning or he simply doesn't care. He's wearing one of those ugly argyle sweaters that old men wear and what looks to be expensive jeans of some kind. His eyes are a deep sea green, almost teal, and for a moment I find myself lingering in their depths. Earth to P, earth to P! I snap out of my fantasies about the guy in front of me.

I seriously do not have time for this!

What does he mean I look familiar? He's nice to look at, and there might be a very vague sense of having seen him before, but I know we don't know each other. There's no way I would've forgotten him if we would've met previously. If I wasn't in a rush maybe I would have said something nice in return, but what comes out of my mouth is anything but friendly.

"Nope, never met. Must be some other chick," I say, and I turn to leave again. My heels are now aching because we have been in and out of stores for the past three hours, buying random knick knacks, saving our Christmas gifts list for last.

Before I can get too far, I feel someone standing close behind me. I don't have to turn around to see who it is. I can smell the sweet pine scent. Why won't he just leave me alone and let me finish what I came here to do? I can't let Mom win again this year. This was supposed to be my year.

"What are you looking for? Maybe I can help," he offers.

I do think he means well, poor guy. I sigh dramatically and spin back around to face him. I take him in again. He's standing there with his hands in his pockets, looking boyishly handsome and a little shy.

"Why?" I ask, honestly curious about why the guy wants to help someone who ran into him and is being rude.

"I can tell you're in a hurry and that you don't know the store that well. I can help you find what you need if you don't mind."

There's no sense in fighting whatever is happening right now. I have to find these items before the game can officially be over, and let's face it, I don't know where to look. I'm obviously not getting anywhere on my own. So sure, he can try and help me. I give him a nod and a small smile.

I don't ask him his name and he doesn't ask me mine. He finds me a wallet and tie in no time, and I quickly thank him, give him a small wave, and take off for the front of the store, determined to win. I almost forget to look for a fountain pen, but luckily find one in the checkout aisle. It's not until much later, after we've been home for several hours, unloaded all our gifts, and placed them underneath our real Christmas tree, that I allow the butterflies to dance in my stomach.

All the lights are turned off, Christmas music is playing, and I'm reading by the lights of the Christmas tree. My nose is still filled with the smell of pine and the earthy scent of the mountains. My thoughts wander back to the stranger in the men's department and the butterflies take flight.

He'd asked me if he knew me. Although he looked a little familiar, I was certain I didn't know him. How could I forget eyes that were *that* teal and deep like the ocean? Maybe, just maybe, our paths had crossed somewhere around town. Afterall, it is a small town, and most people have mutual friends or some type of connection.

Everyone except for my family. We don't really know anyone outside of our private, little bubble, including the few families we know from church. If I'm being honest, I'm not sure I know how to make room for somebody else. But if fate really does exist, maybe our paths will align again. Who knows.

Mom takes up the biggest portion of my bubble. Most days I'm okay with that. If only I knew then how quickly I'd forget the kindness of a stranger. It's funny how some memories decide to fade away and others decide to stay. Little did I know that when I'd look back upon this day, all I'll remember was racing through store after store laughing and running until my feet were sore with my favorite person in the whole wide world. Because, at the time, I didn't have room for anyone else.

Now: December 19th

Denver's car smells like fresh pine. It's almost Christmas time, and his car smells exactly like the holiday. Growing up it had been my mom's favorite day of the year. She would go all out for it. She had boxes and boxes of decorations in our attic that we'd pull down every year. We had tinsel, nutcrackers, and flashing lights—the whole thing. But she was always particular about one thing. We were forbidden from buying a fake Christmas tree.

It had to be real, and it had to be cut from a real tree farm. It was probably one of my favorite things we ever did together, besides our crazy Shopping List Game that Mom always won. The year Mom left was also the last year we went out and bought a real tree. Dad and I never bought another. We couldn't bear to do it without Mom. Thinking about how little we decorate our house around the holiday now is depressing, and I push the thought away.

I'm pulled from my thoughts when I feel his eyes on me. *Denver's.* For a moment I almost forgot where I am.

I've only been sitting in here for about five minutes, but I'm already lost in thought. *Please don't screw this up already.*

"Where did you go just now?" he asks me softly.

I can feel his eyes on me, but I can't make myself look over in his direction. Not yet anyway. I'm so new to this. I'm sitting on my hands to keep them from trembling. I wonder if he notices how nervous I am. I still don't know if he's single... I should probably find that out real soon.

Here I am, drifting away again. "Sorry." I chew the corner of my lip, it's a nervous habit. "Your car smells like Christmas, is all." Not one-hundred percent the full truth, but it's a lot of it. Enough.

He must not have expected that to be my answer because he chuckles at my response, and when he does it's warm and smooth, like honey. Rich and full of flavor, and something I often lack in *life.* I barely know the guy, but he seems like someone full of life.

"That's a new one! I've been told it smells like many things before, but never Christmas. I like that."

So, I'm not the first person to mention the way his car smells. Good or bad. I can't help but wonder if perhaps it'd been another woman...

As though he can sense my thoughts, he adds, "I'm sure you remember my daughter, Marvel. Last week she told me it smelled like dirty socks. In my defense though, I had just gotten back from the gym. So it probably didn't smell the best in here."

Okay, so not another woman. It was his daughter. And, of course, he works out. What does this guy *not* do? This time I brave a small peek out of the corner of my eye, swiveling my head just the slightest bit.

His eyes are now focused on the road and not me, he's got one hand resting on the wheel and the other is resting on the middle console—dangerously close to where my leg rests. My face flushes, but in the dark of his car it goes unnoticed.

Unsure of what else to say, I decide to ask him more about his daughter. It seems like a safe topic.

"So, tell me more about your daughter. I love her name, I've never heard it before," I manage.

I'm not sure which coffee shop he's taking me to, or even what is still open this late, but he seems to be a safe driver, and something about him puts me at ease.

He switches lanes and glances over at me. I turn my eyes back to my window when he speaks.

"Yeah, it's not the greatest story ever, but believe it or not, I'm a secret nerd."

At this, I steal another glance in his direction. He doesn't strike me as a nerd in the least bit. He has broad shoulders and his muscles are lean. He's strong but not too bulky. Just right. Athletic, but not nerdy. Right now he's wearing a red, plaid flannel shirt and dark denim jeans. Nothing about him screams Nerd Alert!

If anything, he looks like he could be a male model for REI.

"Really," I say, unconvinced.

"Yes, really. I still am. I used to collect all the DC and Marvel comics as a kid, and then they started coming out with the movies for all the comics and I was toast. Please tell me you've at least watched the movie Marvel about the female superhero."

I can't tell how well he can see me in the dark, but I slowly shake my head no. I don't watch a lot of movies, and I haven't seen a single movie about a superhero. Lame, I know.

He seems taken back by this. "No? Iron Man? Spider-Man? Batman? Superman?" He pauses between each one, anticipating my answer.

I shake my head no to every single one. Even though one of Mom's favorite nicknames for me had been Spider-Girl, I can't recall watching Spider-Man with her. I've always assumed she came up with the name because of my long, skinny legs, but maybe I've had it wrong all this time.

I am not gaining any points here. But I can't lie to him. I have no reason to.

"Wow. Well, if we ever do this again sometime maybe you could try one with me," he offers quietly.

Wait. Is this him asking me on another date? If he's counting this as one. But where? If he thinks I'm ready to go over to his house...

I jump from the sudden warmth of his hand on my arm. How did it get there and why is he so *warm?* My heart begins to thunder in my chest, and my hand pushes down on the car's door handle without even realizing I'm doing it. Luckily, he has all the doors locked, and the door doesn't budge. I don't know if he noticed my freak-out, but his hand retreats, and I instantly feel the cold from its absence.

I look away. I've ruined whatever this is. He should probably take me home. Why was I thinking that I was ready to do this? Ready to meet somebody?

"Hey," he says gently.

I don't say anything back. I've already started the retreat inside my shell. It's what I do best.

"Nicki, can you please look at me?" he tries again.

But I can't. All I can do is look for a way out of here. I start digging inside my purse for my phone. But who would I call? Wendy isn't here, and Dad is out somewhere too. I didn't even bother to ask him who he was meeting. He probably thinks I don't care. But I do. So much.

We must have arrived at our destination because he pulls the car into a parking space. He puts it into park but doesn't turn off the car right away.

I can feel his eyes on me again. But I don't look to see if I'm right.

"Look, I don't know you very well, and you don't know me.

But I want to. I don't think us meeting was an accident. We met that day for a reason, Nicki. I... uh... I've been through some things, and I don't want to assume anything, but it seems like maybe you have too. I'm not trying to force anything upon you or rush into anything you aren't ready for or don't want. Let's just start with being friends, if you're okay with that, and go from there."

I nod my head gently. I'm afraid if I speak more tears will spill out, like they did earlier at the table with Dad. I don't deserve a guy like Denver. If only he *really* knew me. I came here tonight to try and give him a chance, and I think he deserves at least that.

"Okay, I think I can do that," I manage. I look out the window and almost laugh out loud when I realize where he's taken me. It's a bright blue and white neon sign I'd recognize anywhere. He's brought us to an IHOP. Most certainly not the place I imagined when he'd said he wanted to take me out for coffee and maybe even a bite to eat. But this works, this definitely works. I haven't eaten here in ages.

"Sorry, I know this isn't anywhere fancy, but I wasn't sure you'd want to come with me in the first place. So, I figured this might be a safe choice for a first da—" He pauses, glancing over in my direction.

Our eyes meet and I smile back this time, slowly peeking beneath my shell. "Do you want this to be a date?" I ask quietly.

His eyes crinkle in the corners when he smiles. Warm like honey. He bites his lip while nodding his head. "Do *you*?" He challenges me.

I can feel the pink rising back up my cheeks as I force myself to look away, staring into the neon lights my mother once loved, while admitting out loud in the smallest of voices, "Yes. I mean, I think so."

Heat radiates off my shoulder from his palm as he squeezes it ever so softly, a simple gesture, yet one that soothes me all over and melts me into a puddle of butter. Smooth and syrupy sweet, like my mother's pancakes that I miss so much.

"It's okay, Nicki, we can take it slow."

We smile and chat the evening away in a sticky corner booth in IHOP, drinking coffee and eating pancakes dripping with maple syrup.

Then: Christmas Day

Today is the day I've been waiting all year for—and no, not just because it's Christmas. It's because I know today is *the* day: the day my parents (mostly Dad) promised me a car! Okay, fine. Maybe they didn't *exactly* promise me a car for Christmas. But, I may have overheard them discussing a vehicle the other day, and I'm pretty sure it was for me. It's a *very* good sign that they're going to break the "you need to get your license before you get a car" rule. I'm so excited. Nobody or anything can screw today up. I'm simply not going to let it happen.

I wake up and it doesn't feel real, but there's no way I am still dreaming. Mom has taken off again, and I have no idea why. She's been missing for five days now. Dad doesn't have a clue where she might be, and without a phone, there is no way to track her down. He is concerned, but not enough to call the police. Her leaving is almost normal now, as sad as that is. But today is Christmas. Mom has never missed a Christmas before, surely she won't miss this one.

She won't.

I find out a few moments later that I am right. Despite Mom's absence over the last several days, she's home. Before I even step foot into the kitchen I can sense her presence in the air. She's *here*. I know it.

I can smell her famous butterscotch maple pancakes. Dad doesn't cook, ever. Frankly, I'm not even sure he knows how. Without Mom here we've been living off takeout and fast food. He's refused to let me cook because Mom will be home soon, and letting me cook is like giving up hope on Mom coming back. Something he wasn't prepared to do yet.

She didn't leave anyone a note this time, not even for me. I fight the burning sensation dwelling in my eyes. *Not today. She's here, she's here.* I believe it, I can sense it, but I need to know it's for real and not just a feeling. I need to see the proof of her existence.

Any doubt that had been previously lingering has vanished. Evaporated. As I make my way into our kitchen I see not one parent, but two standing by the table beaming at me over a steaming plate of freshly made hotcakes.

I notice something else. Dad's arm is draped across Mom's shoulders as though she'd never been gone, and everything is normal and fine. They aren't getting a divorce, and Dad didn't sleep with his therapist. It never happened—none of it.

Nothing has ever been normal or fine in our family. Especially not this. My parents don't even like each other anymore. But then I remember what day it is. Christmas. There has always been something extra magical about this day. Whether or not I believe in real magic, there's something about this holiday that can either bring out the best or worst in people. At this precise moment... it's bringing out the better parts of my parents.

I want to hold onto this. I want to wrap it up neatly and tie it with a pretty bow, because come tomorrow morning everything could change. It's as though we are under some sort of holiday spell and the moment it's over the spell will be broken and this day will have seemed like nothing more than a faraway dream.

We all sit down together at our table. Mom smiles at Dad and Dad smiles at Mom. And then they both smile at me. I smile back because it's contagious. I can't help it. I also don't want to add any more cracks to our fragile facade. Because I know that's all this is, but I'm not going to be the first to break it.

I stack my plate high with Mom's ooey gooey pancakes, my mouth watering at the sight and my tummy rumbling in response. The sticky sweetness from the syrup coats my mouth in a way that makes me feel like I'm drowning. Something about it tastes sweeter than normal. I'm not much of a milk drinker but I need something to help wash these down. I reach for my dad's mug of coffee and take a big gulp. I can feel both of my parents watching me in amusement, but I don't bother complaining. Maybe Dad helped her make these and that's why they taste a little different. I don't want to ruin this. Be polite. I thank them both for breakfast, and I'm completely taken by surprise by what happens next.

Mom ties a sheer, orange scarf around my eyes and guides me out the front door, out into the frigid December air.

I shiver as my slippers plummet into a pile of snow beneath me, but I'm too confused to let it bother me. Like a child about to whack a pinata, Dad spins me around three times. *One, two, three* they chant together. On the third spin, he places something cold and hard into my hands and peels off the scarf.

It takes me a moment for my eyes to adjust to the bright sun reflecting off every surface. That isn't the only thing that reflects in the light. I freeze in my tracks. *No way. No way!* Parked along the edge of our driveway is a brand-new Ford Explorer. She's shiny, new, and looks expensive. So expensive. We can't afford something like this.

I'm in a daze as my parents say words around me that I can't make out.

Today is Christmas. Magic is written in the very name. Today is special. Mom came home for *me.* Okay, maybe that part isn't entirely true. But she's here nonetheless. We are all here, as a family. They made me my favorite breakfast, and we are now standing out in the freezing cold staring at my brand-new *car!* I have a car!

Yet, none of this feels real to me. Despite the magic in the air, I can't help but sense that something feels very wrong. Nothing about this day has been normal. A more accurate depiction of our lives would be to take a snow globe and shake it all up, watching the snowman stand in place as everything around him erupts in chaos. That's us. We are standing still in the midst of a storm.

I should be jumping for joy. I should be hugging my parents and thanking them for this day that had been promised to me and come true. This is a promise that has not been broken. Yet I don't feel or do any of those things. I don't feel anything at all. I feel numb. Empty. Lifeless. Like I'm in shock.

I hear words and voices buzzing all around me but none of them stick. They melt and evaporate like the snow I'm standing in. My snow globe has been disturbed and my parents' voices surround me like tiny, little snowflakes, yet I hear nothing. They can't reach me.

I focus on the shiny black of my new car until it vanishes completely from my line of sight.

Their voices come across like static through an old radio. I can't tell who is saying what, they are both blending together. Swirling, mixing, chaotic.

"Say something, honey."

"You like it, don't you?"

"Of course she does. She's just in shock."

"Maybe we should all go for a drive."

"What do you say, Sweet P?"

I don't say anything at all. Because I can't. Because my entire world goes black as it all fades away. So much for this day and its Christmas magic. For the spell has finally been broken. *Again.*

Now: Christmas Day

*S*now *is pounding hard against the windshield. I can barely make anything out. I can't remember why I decided to drive in the middle of a snowstorm, but I needed to get away.*

My wipers are swishing at full capacity. I can't tell if it's the failed attempt from my wipers or how heavy the snow has gotten that is making it impossible to see, but I really should head back home. Or at the very least pull over and try to wait it out. But that could be hours, and I don't think I have an extra blanket in here. I would freeze if I stay inside the car.

I can't tell how fast I'm going but it feels too fast all of a sudden. It's as though something is making the car accelerate despite my foot attempting to brake. Something isn't right with the pedals. I need to get home. Which direction is home? Where am I? I can't see anything in this blizzard.

The car continues to rage forward while snow is now freezing onto my windshield. My wipers are no longer racing along with me;

they are frozen. This isn't looking good, not at all. I need to turn around and go back home, but I can't. There's a reason I left, and I can't go back. But I don't think I have much of a choice in this storm.

Dad is going to be furious that I took off with Mom's car keys once again. Mom's car keys. I'm driving her car. Mom—

That's when I hear the crash. Metal on metal and something else. Someone is screaming. Maybe it's me? I don't know. I can't see anything and I don't know where I am. Oh, no... What have I done? I have to get home, I have to... There's a loud ringing in my ears and someone shouting my name. They sound close. Someone has come to help me. They can bring me back home. Help is on the way...

I WAKE up in a cold sweat. I fly up in bed gasping for air. I can't breathe. What's happening? It takes a moment for my vision to clear and for me to bear my surroundings again. I can feel sweat dripping off my forehead and down my back. My hands are plastered to each of my sides, fisting the sheets beneath me. It takes me another moment to realize I'm not alone. There's someone else here in the room with me. It's Dad. But what's he doing *here*?

Dad calmly comes over to the side of my bed and starts to reach his hand out to me before changing his mind and dropping it down at his side. What's going on? My head is pounding, and I can't think straight.

Dad's eyes are his tired gray right now. I assume that I'm to blame this time. "Hey there, Sweet P," Dad says gently, daring to take the smallest of steps in my direction.

If I wanted to I could reach out and touch him, but I don't dare to move. I'm frozen in place, and my arms start to lightly shake.

"It was a bad dream, love, that's all. You've had them before,

I'm sure you remember... but it's been a while. You're okay now, you're safe." He tries to reassure me, but I don't feel safe at the moment. I feel sticky and panicky.

I do remember having other night terrors similar to this one. It's always snowing, I'm always driving, and I always wake up feeling like this.

I look up and notice that Dad is no longer in my room. The door is wide open and from somewhere off in the distance I can hear running water. Did he leave me to take a shower? Why did he leave me like this? I'm used to this, being alone. Figuring things out myself. But he'd come in here to check on me, and now he's... walking back into my room. He doesn't close the door all the way behind him. He leaves it open, just a crack, allowing a sliver of light to peek through from the hallway. His eyes crinkle in a soft smile as he moves towards me. There's something tucked into his hand and I look down. It's a wash cloth that is starting to drip onto my sheets. *Oh.*

I gladly take it from him and place the cool rag against my forehead. I instantly feel a little better. It's a small gesture, but it's something I can remember Mom doing years ago when I was little and had been sick with a fever or had woken up like this from a bad dream. How he still remembers is lost on me.

I can hear him awkwardly shuffle from one foot to another. He does that when he wants to say something but can't find the right words. I'm not sure if he's always been this way, but he has for as long as I've known him. My eyes hurt and are heavy, but I steal a glance in his direction.

He looks up at me, his eyes full of concern. I don't pull away this time, I hold his gaze in mine. "What is it, Daddy?" I ask like I'm six again.

"I just didn't know if it was something you'd like to talk about, that's all," he offers.

It's nice of him, really—but this is a nightmare that will haunt me forever. So, no, I don't want to talk about it. Thank you, but no thanks. But still, it's nice of him to offer. I don't remember the last time he'd wanted to just "talk."

"That's alright, Dad. But thank you," I say, closing my eyes as I press the damp rag into them.

"Okay, that's fine. Please know that I'm here for you, okay?"

Without opening my eyes I decide to ask him something. "Dad, what day is it?"

I'm not asking because I'm clueless, I'm asking so I can prove a point. I know what day it is.

"It's Christmas, honey," he says gently. He knows precisely what this day means to me. Or at least used to.

Christmas. I knew it. Of course, it is. I don't have some terrible memory of Christmas being awful, I'm not a Grinch (even though sometimes I can sure act like one), but this day, like all holidays, reminds me of the one person I wish that I could forget. Especially on days like today. Especially on *Christmas.*

My mom lived for the holidays, and without her here to celebrate them—well, they just aren't the same. We don't pick out a live tree from her favorite farm, we don't go see the town's annual lighting festival, and we don't stay up late pretending that Santa is real, even when I was long past the age for believing.

We don't do any of those things anymore. In fact, we don't do anything. Depressing, I know. Holidays are tough, but this one always hits the hardest. Every single year. And it's always the same terrifying nightmare that forces me awake in a panic this time of year.

"Merry Christmas, P. Why don't you get some more rest and then we can spend the day together, okay?" Dad offers into the silence that I've created.

I nod my head as I plop back down on my pillow, closing my eyes and pulling the blankets as high as they will go without covering my entire face. I drift back off to sleep in no time. I know Dad means it when he says he wants to spend time with me today, but the only thing I can hope for is to sleep the rest of the day away. And when I open my eyes again, Christmas will be over, and I won't have to face it again until next year.

No more bad dreams.
No more cold sweats.
No more panic attacks.
No more Christmas carols.
I can wait a full year, and do it all again.

26

Then: December 30th

So, apparently my entire Christmas morning hadn't been just a dream. Mom had really come home and Dad had really bought me a car. They won't tell me how much it cost but said I'd need to start looking for a job soon so that I could start paying for it. I knew there would be a catch. Nothing in life ever comes for free.

When I thought I'd drifted deeper into dreamland, instead I'd blacked out. There on the front lawn, luckily dodging the pavement. Panicked, my parents had driven me (together) to the hospital to have me checked out. I was kept overnight in case I had a concussion (thankfully, I didn't) and was released the next morning.

My parents were sent home with a stack of papers to go over with me whenever I was feeling better. I told them many times on the drive home that I felt fine, but they were in some kind of silent truce and said that we would "talk about it later."

Later could mean several things. Later could actually mean later, or later could mean never—as in it would be like everything else in our home that is swept under the rug. As it turns out, later means the very next day, as Mom drives me to my first therapy appointment. Apparently they don't trust me to drive my new car yet.

Therapy. The irony isn't lost on me.

Mom doesn't say much about where she'd gone for almost a week. And she doesn't return with much. Most of her things are gone. Whether she sold them all or gave them away I'm not sure, but she returned with two suitcases full and that was it. She'd moved back into her and Dad's bedroom and unpacked. I don't ask her if she'd hung her clothes back up in her closet or not. I want to ask her a million questions, but mostly I feel angry with her.

Angry that she'd left, *again*. Left without a note saying goodbye or telling me where she was going and how long she'd be gone for. Angry that when I'd asked her she just smiled and shrugged and said, "What's it matter, honey, I'm back now, okay? I'm not going anywhere this time. Promise."

Yeah, like how Mom and Dad promise a lot of things, yet they can't seem to keep many of them anymore. Mom doesn't know how to stay, and Dad doesn't know how to leave. It wasn't that long ago that he'd tried to escape through divorce papers and therapists... What was really keeping him here with us?

But that isn't the first time she's ever broken one of her promises. Once, when I was a freshman, she promised me if I got an A on this big school project that she would take me to go see this new movie I'd been begging her to see with me for weeks. I'd gotten an A, and she'd handed me a ten dollar bill. She hadn't said it was for the movies or that I could even still go. Either she'd completely forgotten, which was possible, or had changed her mind, also possible.

So, when she promises that she won't leave me again, I don't know whether to believe her or not this time. Will she forget promising me in the first place or will she change her mind? She's always been a bit of a free bird. I don't want to let her fly too far this time, but I also can't seem to pin down her wings either.

"I don't understand why I need therapy, Mom." I try to give her my best puppy eyes, hoping it will work on her. This appointment had apparently been in that big packet they'd sent home from the hospital. They were concerned about my health and recommended I at least get checked out by this health professional. Uh-huh, right.

I don't feel like talking to a stranger about myself, professional or not.

Her brown eyes bob and gleam as she glances over at me. For a second I hope Spontaneous Mom will burst out, and she will jerk the car around and take us somewhere new. Anywhere but the place we are heading. But she doesn't show any signs of changing directions.

"I know, Spider-Girl. Let's do what the doctors say, and we can be on our way, okay? We just have to show up. That's it."

Like *you*, I think to myself. You can disappear at the drop of a hat and simply show back up when it's convenient for you.

"What kinds of things are they going to ask me?" I can feel my body begin to tingle with nerves. I've always been a bit more on the introverted side, and the thought of having to speak to someone I've never met makes me anxious.

"Oh, I don't know. They'll probably ask you basic things and what happened when you passed out."

Maybe it won't be so bad. I'll show up and see what happens. Maybe I won't have to go back. They will sign their papers and send us on our way. Like Mom said. But what if she's wrong?

A question pops into my head, and I brave asking her. "Mom, has that ever happened to you? Passing out I mean."

She glances over at me again and laughs as though I've said something funny. Only it's not. I really would like to know. Now isn't the time for jokes. Not when we are only five minutes away.

A snort escapes her lips, causing her to laugh even harder. The harder she laughs, the angrier I get.

"Mom, stop," I say as calmly as I can muster.

Her laughter doesn't stop. Neither does my anger.

"Stop the car, Mom," I say louder, several degrees higher than the music that comes blasting out of the speakers.

That stops her in her tracks and she slams on the brakes, the volume of my voice reaching a level I'm not sure I've ever directed at her before. Until now. She stares at me. A car honks its horn from behind. I don't care. I want her to hear me. Actually, hear me this time.

"Let me out, now. I'm going to walk the rest of the way," I threaten, but I mean it. I have my hand on the handle, ready to bolt.

"No," she says, voice calm and collected.

"I'm walking, Mom, unlock the door." I try the handle, but it doesn't budge.

"No," she says again.

Are we really going to sit here and argue back and forth?

"I'm taking you to your damn therapy session, you're going to stay the full hour, and as soon as you're done, we are turning around and going straight home."

What I want to say is, "Dad is cheating on you, Mom, WITH a therapist! So, no—I'm not going!"

With hurt still lingering in my voice I manage, "I wasn't being funny, Mom. I was asking you a serious question."

She presses her foot on the gas, accelerating back up to speed, and ignores me. Her lips curl and she sneaks a small glance at me and then turns her attention back to the road.

"What was your question?" she eventually asks.

Okay, maybe she heard me after all. But only halfway.

"Never mind," I say and turn my back toward her. Away from her. I'm too frustrated to say anything more.

She turns the music up on the radio, and we don't say a word for the rest of the way to *therapy*.

27

Now: New Years Eve

Denver calls me at least twice a week. We haven't had a chance to go out again, but we've kept in touch. Wendy returned last weekend and has not stopped asking me about him. I can't say I blame her for being curious. It's not like I go on many dates, or any for that matter. This is big news. But not public news, we are still getting to know one another. As he said last time, *we can take it slow.*

He's on call a lot for his job, which makes his calls a bit sporadic at times, but truthfully, I don't mind. My heart leaps inside my chest every time my phone rings now, but I tell myself this is good for me. This is okay, and I'm allowed to have a friend outside of my writing team.

Dad, of course, says it's more than okay. He's basically become the female version of Wendy. Okay, maybe not as bad, but he does ask me about him often. Which is nice for a change, because usually there's not much to ask about. We know everything that goes on in each other's lives. But this is something new. Something we can talk about.

Speaking of new, Dad finally gave me more info about the lady he's started seeing. Her name is Deb, she also works in finance, and they met online about two months ago in one of their monthly meetings. They've been seeing each other for about a month now, and things seem to be going well. Her late husband passed away about four years ago, and she'd like to start dating again. I think he said she has three children.

Either way, I'm happy to see my dad happy. There's a soft glow about him that I'm not even sure he carried when Mom was still around. I've noticed the creases around his eyes are different even, as though it has very little to do with his age and more likely to do with him smiling and laughing more. I remember the light in his eyes dimming after Mom left, as though her absence had shut off something inside of him. But now?

I not only see an emotional change within, but a physical one. His gray eyes are shiny like a dime again, and the bags that had taken up residence underneath them are almost nonexistent. I haven't heard the TV on in the middle of the night in weeks—as though he's finally figured out how to sleep again after all this time. Whatever is happening for my dad, I can't help but want that too. It's contagious, and I can only hope a little bit of his glow will rub off onto me.

My novel currently rests in the hands of my formatter, and then it's off to my ARC team before it's ready to officially make its publishing debut. It's all coming together perfectly. I couldn't be happier with the direction things are headed. We are shooting for early March, as long as everything goes according to plan. And I know that things often go in the complete opposite direction.

I'm sipping on a late afternoon coffee when my phone rings. *Boom boom boom* goes my chest. I know in an instant exactly who it is. There's only one person that has that kind of effect on me right now.

I pick up on the second ring. "Hey," I say, trying not to sound too eager.

"What are you up to today? I'm sorry we keep missing each other. Do you have plans tonight for New Years Eve? I'd like to see you. I'll be off today by six and can get you at seven."

It's one thing having a conversation over the phone, but a completely different game seeing someone face-to-face. It terrifies me to do it again, yet I want to. I do want to see him again. I've never had anyone besides family I've wanted to be with when the clock strikes midnight.

"Oh, that's great. Yeah, I'm not doing anything. I'll be free this evening... but what about your daughter?" I hedge.

It's not that I don't want to see her again, but I'm not used to being around Denver yet. I'm not sure how she feels about me spending time with her dad. To her, I may be nothing more than a semi-famous author who signed her copy of my debut novel. Anyone that has their name stamped on anything in this town is automatically considered famous.

At times it's hard to wrap my head around the fact that he has a teenage daughter.

"I think she mentioned going over to one of her friend's houses tonight for dinner and to watch the ball drop on TV, but I could ask her if she'd want to join us. Or I won't ask if that makes you uncomfortable. I won't do anything you're not ready for, Nicki."

Ugh, so sweet. Sticky, syrupy, sweet.

"I hope you know that," he adds.

I do. This guy is seriously the sweetest. Is he real? I don't know what to say. I don't think I'd mind having her come along, but if she's already got other plans, I also don't want to make her feel like she has to say yes. Like I often did when it came to going some- where with my mom. No to her was a huge letdown, and I don't want to do that to Marvel. I don't know anything about her mother, and I'm not here to try and take her place.

"You can ask her if you'd like, I don't mind either way. I'll leave it up to you to decide." I hesitate before adding, "Um, can I ask you something?"

I hear a slight rustling sound coming from his line and wonder if he's shifting the phone to his other ear.

He answers quickly. "Sure, of course you can."

"Does she still get to see her mom? What happened with her mom, if you don't mind me asking?" I realize I'm treading into new territory, but so far he's been nothing but honest with me.

Denver blows out a whoosh of air from his end, and I worry I've asked too much. I wish that I could take it back, but it's too late.

"She does still keep in touch with her mom, yes. They do video calls once a week, and she spends the summers with her. Her mom doesn't live here so it's not the most convenient, but it works alright for them.

"As far as what happened with me and my ex... well, that's a story I'd rather share in person."

Of course, I shouldn't have expected him to offer me everything over the phone.

I nod my head even though I know he can't see me. "Yes, sorry. That wasn't fair of me to ask you that. I won't bring it up again."

"Nicki, please don't do that." He sighs.

"Do what?" I ask.

"Run away," he says.

"I'm not running away," I argue as my fingers find their way around a long strand of brown hair, tugging it gently.

"I want to tell you things, but not like this. I want to be with you when I share personal things, that's all," he says gently.

I don't say anything for a moment. But I know he's right. I don't mean to run every time I get scared. I panic and my natural reaction is to want to flee. It's all I've done for the last sixteen years.

I spent the first sixteen years of my life taking care of other people. Holding all the messy, broken pieces together. Until one day I suddenly couldn't hold onto anything anymore. Now, I can't even hold myself up. I simply don't know how to.

I've gone quiet again, and I'm sure it doesn't go unnoticed. I sigh and pull together all my bravery. "I like when you share things with me. I'm sorry that I have a hard time doing the same. It's just me and my dad here and we don't talk about anything... super deep. But I am trying to get better at it," I quickly add.

"Trying is all we can do sometimes," he offers.

"And also when we just 'show up,'" I remind him from when he'd told me that.

"Yeah, exactly like that. I see you were paying attention." He laughs softly in my ear and it's the most beautiful sound I've ever heard.

"I do from time to time," I joke. "Pay attention, that is. Um, so seven o'clock?"

"Yep, I'd love to see you. But only if you want the same. I won't come if you don't want me to."

I can't help but smile as I chew my lip. Of course I want to see him, if I can quit being a big coward when it comes to expressing how I truly feel. The way he makes me feel when I am with him.

"How are you always so confident?" I challenge him.

"I am when I know what I want," he remarks, and my cheeks are instantly on fire. It's a good thing he can't see me behind the screen right now because I'd be red all over.

"See you soon, Denver."

"You too, Nicki."

We both hang up at the same time. I hold the phone tightly to my chest as I flop down backward on my bed. I've never felt this way before, but I feel like I could fly. I can't wait to tell Wendy the next time I see her. She will be over the moon.

28

Then: January 3rd

As it turns out, I have not only an anxiety problem but also a problem with stress. Stress and anxiety are like oil and water—they don't mix well. According to my therapist (who's not half bad) and the doctors at the hospital, I suffer from a condition called psychogenic blackouts. I become so ridden with stress and anxiety I cause myself to pass out. Crazy, right?

My therapist, Dr. Gurkle, recommended I start taking medication for it, but surprisingly, my mother refused. She's on medication herself but doesn't want me to be on anything. At least not right now she says, she'd rather I continue coming to sessions once a month until my symptoms improve. Maybe it's for the best.

I don't argue, and Mom seems back to normal on the way home afterward. I don't try to escape the car, and there is no more talk of blackouts at all. Instead, we drive home with the windows down and 90s music playing loudly.

I want to ask her what would happen if I keep having these

kinds of episodes. Would I be allowed to drive? Would they still take me to get my license next week? What happens if I pass out in school?

Luckily, it doesn't happen again. At least not for a little while.

It's a new year already and I got my license with no trouble at all. Mom continues to drive her little red Coupe, and I drive my Black Beauty Explorer. I absolutely love it. Hands down—best Christmas gift ever!

Being with Mom this Christmas break has been great. She's been more Fun Mom, Present Mom, and Do-You-Have-Any-New-Crushes-Mom. She hasn't cleared out her closet again, and Dad hasn't threatened her with more talk of divorce. On the outside, their relationship hasn't changed much, but they are cordial with one another, which I take as a positive sign. No more broken glass in the house, and no more slammed doors. We still stay in our respective rooms and spaces, but we all come together at dinner just like we used to.

It's almost starting to feel like we are a family again. I can't help but think about the family that lives in the house full of laughter and light a few blocks away. The house with the young girl and the bright red mailbox. I wonder if they are truly a happy family or if it's all just a facade. Sometimes I feel like we are made of glass. We may look tough on the outside, but inside we're barely holding it all together. I wonder how strong our glue is right now.

It's been good seeing Mom smile and laugh again—not too much, but not too little either. She's also been cooking a lot more and even let me help a few times.

Dad seems to be in good spirits as well. He's polite with Mom and me and makes sure to ask us both about our day. I don't ask him if he's still seeing his therapist, because, truthfully, I don't want to know. We are all happy, at least I think we are... for now.

We are labeled fragile in bold letters, and I'm afraid that any tiny crack will cause us to shatter.

This year has been a little unsteady, but it's not too late to begin again. I just hope we can all hold on tight enough to each other. I hope it'll be enough this time.

29

Now: New Years Eve

Denver arrives promptly at seven. He'd texted me a little earlier telling me to wear something sparkly. I was in the middle of texting him back, asking where he was taking us this time and he replied with:

I got the hint. But seriously, where is the guy taking me? I'm assuming that this is a date (dangerous assumption, I know), and if that is the case, he's most likely not bringing his daughter with him. Although, I honestly wouldn't have minded if he did. I want to know more about her. I want to know what life is like for her at sixteen. *What his life is like raising a sixteen-year old.* I hope it's a lot different from how things were for me at that age. I try hard to shake loose the negative thoughts. Tonight isn't about my past. Tonight is all about us. It's time to move forward.

I can't believe he brought me to Bella Luna. The restaurant itself is built inside a cave. I've never actually eaten here before—we never had this kind of money growing up—and besides, I think it's only been open for less than two years. Wendy has come here on some of her date nights before. I didn't dare ask what it cost for them to eat here, but she says the food is to *die* for.

It's not damp and cold like you would think a normal cave would be. It is dark, but the entire place is lit with hundreds of candles everywhere, and it's incredible. A live band is playing in one part of the restaurant, and every waiter and waitress is dressed in black, formal attire. I end up deciding on an ombre sea-green dress that I wore the night I won a book award. Somehow it still fit just how I'd remembered. Denver hasn't quit staring at me since he first picked me up half an hour ago.

I've been perusing the menu for what feels like ages now, and I still haven't decided what to order. The menu itself is like a novella. The choices are endless, and don't even get me started on the dessert—which has a separate menu, of course.

I finally look up to see Denver staring at me. *He really needs to stop that.* I feel like he's undressing me with his eyes, and I don't know him well enough yet to read his thoughts. What is he thinking about? Do I dare ask him?

I clear my throat and take a small sip from my ice water. "So..." I gesture to the menu, "What's good here? And don't say everything."

He laughs. That beautiful, velvety smooth laugh. "No? But what if everything is good?" he teases.

I had a feeling he would say something like that. Little punk. "Well, in that case, I'll order the... uh..." I glance down quickly at the page I have opened and point to the first thing I find.

"Fried scallops with lemon risotto and balsamic roasted vegetables," I challenge again.

Is this what flirting feels like? I know nothing of the sort. I'm just going with it and doing my best not to second-guess the things that slip out of my mouth. Tonight, I've decided I'm not holding back.

He leans back in his chair, crossing his lean arms across his chest and smirking at me. "Ah, good choice."

Is he being serious or playing with me? Is this him flirting back?

"You say that like you're a regular here," I say, smirking a little.

"So what if I am?" he asks. His eyes find mine and he must read something in them because his eyes suddenly soften and his shoulders relax a little.

"I'm so sorry, Nicki, I didn't mean it like that... I... I've never been here before either. This is my first time." His whole demeanor has changed.

Because of me. Because of the doubt written all over my face. I did this, not him. Although, with the direction our conversation was heading, I couldn't be too sure I was the only girl he'd ever brought here.

I shake the thought away. I want to believe him. I'm pretty sure that I do. I don't have any real reason not to, other than the fact that trusting people isn't always the easiest thing for me. But I am trying.

"This is my first date," I admit quietly.

I glance back down at the menu so I have something else to focus on. I can do this. I won't run or try to escape when things get awkward. I'm going to stick this out. That's when I feel an extra presence looming over us. It's one of the wait staff ready to take our orders. I order the scallop meal I'd just recited to Denver before I'd gotten "weird eyes" and ruined the moment.

The moment the waitress walks away with our orders, Denver

leans in close. It's already a small table, and I can instantly smell his pine scent. I look up. My breath catches in my throat, but I force our eyes to stay locked. I don't allow my body to move away.

"Is it really?" he asks softly.

I nod my head quietly, "Yeah, my first date that's not at an IHOP," I tease, smiling at him.

He returns the smile, and a laugh escapes him. "Hey, what's wrong with IHOP?" He feigns indignation.

I shrug my shoulders, not saying anything. But he decides not to say anything either. I hope I haven't offended him, I was only teasing. Official date or not, it's a night I won't soon forget, because I'm with him. There's an awkward pause. Worry sneaks its way in through the cracks, and I find myself waiting.

Waiting for him to turn away or tell me this isn't going to work. I still don't even know how old he is. Or what his favorite color is or if he has any hobbies. What do I know about him? We agreed to take things slow, but am I the one rushing it?

Relax. Breathe. Stay calm.

Instead, I blurt out, "How old are you?"

He doesn't miss a beat. "I just turned forty this past June."

He's forty. Okay. That means we are at least eight years apart. That's not so bad. He's Wendy's age, and they both look amazing.

"What about you?" he asks in return.

"Thirty-two," I reply.

I rapid-fire another question, "Why do you go to G&G?"

Our eyes are still locked. We don't break eye contact. He takes a moment to respond this time, not backing away though. "I lost someone dear to me."

Tears form in my eyes because I know what that loss feels like all too well. Too well. *Don't ask. Please don't ask me. Only Wendy is allowed to ask me the hard stuff, and even then I don't give her much.*

I nod. I don't say anything. It'll cause me to break whatever spell is going on between us. I'll be tempted to run away, and I don't want to keep doing that to him.

"You?" he barely whispers.

No, I can't. I shake my head. He won't pressure me into saying it, I know he won't. I know it's not fair of me, but I simply can't. He wouldn't understand.

"Nicki... you don't have to tell me if you're not ready. But please, I won't judge you for whatever it is. I can tell it's something you've been carrying around for a long time. Sometimes it helps to tell someone... to unburden yourself. I'm here, and I'm not going anywhere."

He says that now. But he might. He absolutely might run in the opposite direction if he knew the truth. If only I really could tell somebody... would I finally be able to breathe? Would it release me from the pain and burden I've carried all these years? Or would it unleash new ones? It's too big of a risk.

"I appreciate that, but it's not something I can talk about. I know that's not exactly fair. I'm sorry, but I just can't."

Then he does something surprising, he leans across the table and grabs onto both of my hands. I am immediately lit up from the inside out, as though he struck a match and lit a flame within.

I can't believe this man. What is he doing? Why *me*? One of his hands leaves mine to wipe a tear that manages to escape down my cheek. Why does he care so much?

"Don't be sorry, Nicki. I want to be with you."

I believe him. I fully and wholeheartedly believe him. I don't want to let him go. If he lets go of me, maybe none of this will be real. I couldn't have made all of this up in my head, right? Even I'm not that creative. But this feels too good to be true. Can it be?

"You do?" I say softly back.

"Absolutely. We all have broken pieces, Nicki. And I won't promise that I can fix them. I don't have those kinds of powers. But I genuinely want to be here for you. I get the feeling that you haven't had anyone on your side for a long time... Is that right?"

I nod. That's all I can manage. I'm in a haze.

"I want to be with you if you want me to."

I do, I really do. I don't think I've ever wanted anything so badly in a long, long time. Fate be damned, I want this man.

30

Then: February 1st

Starting a new semester in school means new elective classes. I'm thankful to be out of gym class this semester, and finally in a class I enjoy: writing and literature. Okay, the literature part of it might be a little boring, but I am looking forward to the writing. It's a new teacher, Mr. Matthewson. I guess they just hired him this year, but so far he seems pretty cool.

By the end of the term we have to write our very own full-length novel, and I've been working on ideas for a mystery or a thriller, but I haven't quite nailed it down yet. It'll come to me at the right time, I'm sure of it.

He's told the class that he's already written three books of his own. I don't know anything about book publishing, but he looks young enough to have barely graduated with his degree and leapt right into teaching. I hope to have written at least one book by the time I graduate college. That is a big fat *if* I go.

I still haven't decided if I'm going to go anywhere. I mean, I still have time to decide... there's plenty of time to make up my mind about it, right? The thought of graduating from McKinley High and leaving Atlas Creek is just crazy to me.

I know my parents will probably protest if I decide to stick around (well, Dad would anyway, Mom would keep me forever if it were up to her), but I also can't just *leave* them. The very thought makes my stomach turn. So, I do my best not to think about it.

Because according to Dad, he thinks I should move to Denver and go to college there. I'm pretty sure that's where he met Mom. So, it makes sense. Mom always shrugs her shoulders at me when I bring up colleges and usually changes the subject.

The only exception to this happened a few days ago. Mom presented me with this new idea. A new kind of list she hadn't shown me before.

Mom is a big list maker, and she told me once how important it was to set goals for myself.

"It's a whole thing, P. You need to choose your goals carefully, set them, and then make a detailed outline. I'm serious about this, don't give me that look. Go get a piece of paper. I'll wait."

As per usual she was giving me her Stern Mom look, which meant she was absolutely serious and would not drop the subject until I did exactly as I was asked. I knew better than to argue when she was in Stern Mom mode.

I run back into the living room where she's sitting in her favorite chair in the corner by the big window, waiting for me to return with a pencil and paper. I sit across from her on the couch, ready to start writing out my goals.

"Okay, good. What is one of your biggest goals?" she asks me.

"Um, to graduate from high school?" I ask.

"Yes, that's a good one. Jot that down. Now make a bullet point list of what you need to do to obtain that goal." She taps her fingers along her knee as she waits for me to start writing them down.

It takes me less than five minutes. I glance back up at her and notice that she's studying me carefully in a way I've never seen her do before. It's always fun discovering these new little pieces of my mother, and this is one I haven't yet discovered. I tuck this little nugget of knowledge away to ponder later.

"So," she says, "What are they?"

"Oh, um," I start going down the list one by one. "Pass all of my classes with all A's or at least high B's. Put my best effort into all of my classes, especially the writing ones." I pause there, her copper eyes are shining.

"Why the writing ones, P?"

"I don't know. Those are just the ones I like the best. I don't know if I've told you before, but someday I'd like to become a writer." I blush as I admit this, recalling the time when I mentioned some ideas for stories and she'd rushed to the nearest store so that I could buy a journal for myself. She was both insightful and thoughtful. Pieces of me that sometimes I wish Dad saw more of.

My mom sits there still for a minute, not saying anything, and I can't help but worry our moment is lost. She's already moved on in her head to something else and doesn't want to play this fun little game of listing out my goals anymore.

But she does something else. My mom is always full of surprises. I never know what she's going to do or say next. Sometimes that can be exciting and other times it can be worrisome. She gets up suddenly and makes her way quickly across the room. She opens her bedroom door and disappears inside.

She's gone for at least five minutes.

When I'm starting to worry that I've lost her, she returns with a small, dark green notebook tucked beneath her arm. Without saying a word she walks back over to me and places it gently into my lap. She finds her way back into her chair and plops down with a heaviness that causes me to start to rise off the couch. That's when I remember the small weight inside my lap and glance down.

The journal is small and the green leather is worn and peeling. Written across the front in gold lettering is my mother's full name, Jolene Ann Larrs. I open the cover and leaf through the book. The inside is filled with her beautiful handwriting. It loops in and out of the lines on the pages. I've never seen anything like this before. It's beautiful.

Before I can explore the journal further, my mother clears her throat, and my attention is pulled away. I look back up at her, and she's wearing a new expression I can't read.

"Don't read that now. It's private. But I want you to have it. I've known you were a writer for a long time. You're always writing something these days and, believe me, I've noticed."

A random tear makes a run for it down the side of my cheek. I'm surprised by it and quickly swipe it away before she sees.

I hadn't realized anyone had noticed my love for writing. Especially her. Coming from her means something. Something more. My love for her swells and bursts in my chest. For the first time in a long time I feel *seen*. Seen by someone. Seen by Mom.

"This journal belonged to me, and now it belongs to you. It's mostly poems. I don't know if you even care for that sort of thing, but Dad has no use for it. I've been wanting to give it to you for a while now, just never found the right time."

Before I realize what I'm doing I'm up out of my seat and moving quickly across the carpet to her. She used to give me books and other things, but I never knew she'd written anything more than To-Do Lists and Grocery Lists. But this... this is special. This means *everything*.

I crawl into her lap and lay my head against her chest like I'm still her little girl. A child wanting to cuddle with their mommy, and I do just that. I'm so close to her now I can feel the rhythm of her heart against me beating, *thump, thump, thump*. I love this woman so much. I can only hope she loves me half as much. The other words that echo in my head as she holds me close, are *stay, stay, stay*.

She doesn't say a word but gently runs her fingers through my hair. Back and forth, back and forth. I don't know how long we stay like this. Dad isn't home from work yet, and I know she will have to start dinner soon. But for now, I soak every bit of her in. Vanilla and honey. Rich and warm. This journal may very well be the best gift I've ever received.

Now: February 1st

We'd hung around long past our reservation that night. We'd ordered dessert after our meal, and on our way home he surprised me with a midnight-boat tour. I'd been to this lake before, it was one of our favorite places to camp in the summer. We'd rent canoes or kayaks and fish for hours. Dad always fished, Mom and I would sit on the boat with our books and read until the sun was starting to set and it was time to cook dinner over our campfire. We called them "day-camps" because we never stayed overnight. We'd get there first thing in the morning, and then drive back home late, long after the sun had set. I'm not sure why we did it that way, but it was our family tradition.

Sally's in the Park had been one of Mom's favorite places. It's one of those hidden gems that, unless you ventured out to the state park, which we often did, you would never know it's there. There are newer restaurants in the park now of course, but this quaint little diner that overlooks the lake will always be a favorite place of mine. One of my favorite memories is of the three of us sitting outside facing the water and the mountains beyond, feeding french fries to the chipmunks. They would eat right out of your palm!

I remember almost everything about the place vividly, but I don't remember this boat ride. I wonder if it's something new. But then again we'd never stayed the night here. Maybe this had always existed, and I was only discovering it now. It was so long ago.

The boat ride was wonderful. There was live music, probably the type my dad would have enjoyed. It complimented the gentle rocking back and forth of the boat and calmed down my nerves. Because I was plenty nervous.

For it being a cold winter night in Colorado, the sky was clear and the boat was kept warm. We mostly stayed inside. There were a few other couples on the boat with us, and some seemed like newlyweds. Yet we seemed to fit right in among them. Denver held my hand and even danced with me during a slower song. He held me close enough that he couldn't see the dark pink color that had spread across my cheeks.

Several times we were asked if we wanted to order drinks, but I don't drink. I tried it once when I was in college and couldn't stand the taste, so I never touched it again. Now that I think about it, I don't think I'd ever seen Mom or Dad ever drink either.

I'm not sure if Denver would have normally declined alcohol on New Year's Eve, but he did. He politely declined each time they passed by, and I couldn't help but wonder if I had anything to do with it.

Promptly as the clock struck twelve, fireworks erupted from a distance. I'd never seen such a miraculous sight. Blossoms of yellows and bursts of oranges, reds, and neon purples illuminated the entire night sky right above the tallest mountain peaks. It was breathtaking. I couldn't believe I was seeing it for the first time. I hoped it wouldn't be the last.

Afterward, we headed back home, mostly in silence. I wasn't used to staying up this late anymore. I woke up early most mornings and worked all day, usually through dinner. By nine or ten at the latest, I was ready for bed. We didn't make it back to my house until after one a.m.

When he pulled up to my house, I didn't get out of his car right away. Even though I don't watch many movies, I'm not dumb. I *knew* what was supposed to happen when the guy dropped off the girl after their first official date. I've written about this scene in many of my novels. I know the part well, yet have never personally lived it.

I'm exhausted from the fun evening, but it's more than that. I'm afraid of what will happen next. Terrified actually. I hadn't thought this part through. Sure, we've talked on the phone and this isn't the first time we've gone out together... but it feels like the first time. Tonight was different. Tonight was special. I felt it, and I think he did too.

I want to be with you.

Yet, I can't leave his car. It's silly, I realize. I'm acting like a lovesick teenager, but maybe in a way, I am. I've never experienced anything like this before, so I have nothing to base it on. No pros or cons lists this time. Ground zero. The starting point.

"Nicki..." he eases gently.

I'm staring out my window at my house. I know Dad didn't wait up for me. I don't remember the last time we even watched the NYC ball drop on live TV. The porch light is on and so is the tiny light above our kitchen sink. *Mom's kitchen sink.*

I can't look at him though. It's been a great evening, and I should just get out and go. I'm making this super awkward, yet I don't seem to remember how to move. I need a push or a shove, an invisible force. Something. I'm frozen in place.

"Denver..." I whisper without looking over my shoulder. That is until I feel the heat from his palm resting on my shoulder, gently easing it towards him. He wants me to look at him. He wants to meet my eyes. *I won't run away this time, I will choose to stay. Stay, stay, stay, pleads my heart.*

I slowly turn in my seat and face him. His eyes look as tired as mine feel, yet he's smiling at me. Slow and steady.

"What are you worried about?" he asks.

He's like Wendy, cutting to the chase. No small talk, just straight to it. Okay. We're doing this.

"Everything," I admit. And it's the truth.

"Okay..." he starts. Pauses. Turning over my one-word response. But he doesn't run, he stays.

"Like what? Tell me one thing," he tries again.

"Um..." I pause briefly, I hate being put on the spot. I like to have time to think something through. But then that typically leads to second-guessing, which I'm trying not to do right now.

"Okay," I begin again. I take a deep breath in. "Well, I guess it's the fact that I'm so new to this. And I mean, it honestly has nothing to do with you or anything. Seriously... you're great." I laugh, but his expression doesn't match mine. He's studying me. Figuring out where exactly I'm heading with this.

I continue, "Well... I'm not great at relationships. I mean in general. I suck at them, actually. Wendy is my best friend, but she's also my editor and agent. Besides her and my dad, that's pretty much it.

"Like that book signing event. I never do anything like that, and being around people makes me so anxious I want to throw up or pass out—and sometimes I do both. But it just wasn't me. You see, I shouldn't have even been there that day, Denver. It was Wendy's idea—not her fault—but it hadn't been mine. And then I met you and your wonderful daughter... but you deserve someone *better* than me. Someone that doesn't suck at relationships with people. Someone that doesn't faint in public, run out of grief meetings, or try to escape the moment it gets hard."

I'm out of breath at this point. I can't stop myself. I'm on a roll now, and I can't slow down. I'm a train at full speed. Denver doesn't move, he doesn't speak, he listens. Listens as I steamroll any chance of us ever working this out. I'm doing what I do best.

"I know you asked me to name one thing. But that's impossible. Because with me there are a million and one things. And you..." my voice breaks, "don't even know the half of it."

Before he can say a word or try to stop me, I throw off my seatbelt and bolt out of his car. My feet have somehow become unglued and are in full escape mode now. I can't be sure if he's yelling my name, trying to get me to turn back around. I can't hear anything over the beating of my heart and my frantic breaths. I hate what I'm doing to him. He doesn't deserve this, but he also deserves better than someone like me. I know that for a fact.

I don't look back. I know if I do I'll be filled with regret instead of this adrenaline fire that's blazing hot within me. One look and he will extinguish every single flame. One by one. But I can't let him. I won't.

Goodbye, Denver.

AN ENTIRE MONTH GOES BY. It's February first now. The one month out of the entire year that I wish could be skipped or forgotten. Unfortunately, I can do neither of those things. Denver does try to call me several times, but each time I let it go to voicemail. I know I'm being cold, I've allowed my heart to turn back into stone. I did the very thing I said I would not do. But it's been done, and I can't change it now.

Eventually, all attempts at communication halt. He doesn't text, call, or even show up at my door. He's simply *gone*. As though he were never here to begin with. And it's only then, in those empty days without him, that I start to wonder if I was the one making a huge mistake.

32

Then: February 1st

Today is a typical Saturday. Mom and I ran a few errands during the day, and then I'd spent most of the afternoon writing in my journal and reading. We ate dinner, I finished my homework, then I showered and got ready for bed. But now it's barely after nine, and I'm lying in my bed wide awake.

I cannot stop thinking about the journal that Mom gave me. I can hear the soft humming coming from the TV in the living room, Dad most likely is still up watching the nightly news. I don't know if Mom's already headed off to bed, but I climb out of mine and walk over to the closet.

I flip on the light, and my eyes find what I'm looking for instantly. The shoebox I'd placed her gift in. I don't remember the last time I bought new shoes, but the box is in mint condition.

Crouching down on the carpet, I carefully open the lid. On top lies Mom's gorgeous green leather journal. I run my fingers over the gold lettering of her name across the front. Underneath her journal is mine, the tie-dyed one I pull out anytime a new idea strikes me. There are no full stories in there, just a bunch of ideas in the form of lists. I guess I'm like her in that way.

Maybe someday they can become something more than a collection of bullet points.

Underneath that are old receipts and recipes of hers I've jotted down on paper. I know all of her secret ingredients by heart. She didn't give me those herself, I've spent enough time in the kitchen with her that I've memorized them. How she tosses in not only one pinch of salt into her meatloaf but two. How she never buys salted butter because she always ends up adding it in herself anyway.

She also never wastes anything she uses. If she has extra of something, that just means she has to whip something else up, and she always does. I know her movements and recipes like the back of my hand. I know most pieces of my mother, except for this little treasure. I have never seen her write anything other than lists before, much less poetry—I'm intrigued, curious even.

The journal is soft to the touch and worn. The edges are curled already and several of the pages are dog-eared, something I never do in my books, but it's very her. I close the lid on the box and shove it gently to the back wall. Out of sight, out of mind.

I carry her journal tightly against my chest, as though I'm trying to keep it safe from the outside world, not that anybody else is looking but me. But still, I want to protect this precious piece of her. Something sacred and personal she had wanted to share with me.

Once back in bed and under the covers, I reach over to my nightstand and switch on my lamp. I turn to the first page and start reading. Sure enough, it's a poem—just like she said. Lots of them. There is no date to indicate how long ago she wrote this, but it has a title: *Fighting with Myself.*

"Fighting with Myself"
I had a fight with myself
It started while lying in bed
My heart couldn't agree with my head
I thought things I've never said.

The words tangled up in my hair
The toddler inside wrestled and cried
Because something in me has died
Can I at least say that I tried?

I had a fight with myself
I threw all the punches
Into my pillow, and in the air
Nightmares I can't tame anymore.

I had a fight with myself
I think I've let the devil win
How he likes to win
Where did I go again?

MY HANDS BEGIN to shake after I finish the poem. I... I don't know how I feel about it, about any of it. I have questions, so many questions. When did she write this? Was this a long time ago or something she wrote down recently? I quickly flip through the journal, scanning the pages. Every single one of them is filled. Cover to cover there are words on every page showcasing my mother's heart.

I don't know what to make of this one. It's many things, but it's also terribly sad and depressing. How much of this poem was real? Was any of this real? I read another.

"Words Unsaid"

I won't let it go to my head
These thoughts that try to escape
They won't ever leave this bed
You'll never hear the words unsaid.

Sleep feels like a fairy tale
My mind is a gear that doesn't end
No such thing as an OFF switch
On this machine in my head.

Close the doors, draw the curtains
End scene, let's begin again
A new leaf, a new season
Leaving the words inside my head.

I DON'T STOP READING until it's well past midnight. I read her entire journal cover to cover. It's *that* good. In some parts, I cried, and in others, I had to stifle a giggle so nobody would hear me and wonder what was up. I'm honored my mother trusted me with something of hers so personal, yet also a little scared. I had no idea some of her thoughts got so dark, but then again I can't say mine haven't either from time to time.

When I finally finish and I can't hold my eyes open any longer,

I tuck the journal quietly back into the safety of my shoebox and climb back into bed. Mom's birthday is coming up, and now I know the perfect thing to give her.

Now: February 4th

My mom's birthday is in ten days. I'm well aware that in ten days I will not wake up to the smell of her butterscotch maple pancakes. I will not be greeted by loud, overplayed 90s bands. I will not enter the kitchen to warm aromas, dancing, and laughter. I know exactly what I will be greeted with instead. But, that's in ten days. Today I'm going out with Wendy. Today she's more than my editor, she's my best friend.

I still have not attempted to contact Denver, and he has stopped trying as well. I know it's all my fault, and it feels stupid, but a part of me wishes he hadn't given up so easily. I'm not entirely sure what I would have done had he kept calling or shown up at my door, demanding to know what the heck was wrong with me.

But, if he had done that, at least I'd have gotten to see him again. Now, I've blown all hope of that happening away. I look and feel like a sad, mopey Eeyore. I have my long, straight strands tied up into a high ponytail, and I'm wearing boring clothes today. I have on a large, gray hoodie and jeans. I'd originally tried to leave the house in sweatpants, but Wendy took one look at me and sent me back into the house to change. At least she didn't say anything else when I came back outside wearing the same boring sweatshirt. The smallest of efforts seemed to suffice.

I'm in this strange state because I'm not even sure we dated long enough for this to be considered a break-up. We've only gone on two dates and called each other a handful of times. Does that count? Wendy had asked questions of course, but she was careful never to push me for more than I was ready to give. I gave her the bullet points, the highlight reel. She'd simply nodded and all she had to say was, "Yeah, men suck."

Which I suppose can be true, but that isn't the case with Denver. He didn't suck—I'm sure he still doesn't. I am the dummy who sucked everything up. Wendy is just too nice to tell me that to my face. And now, well, here we are.

We pull into the lot of a local craft store and park. I'm not here for anything in particular, Wendy asked me to tag along, promising me coffee afterward. I think she was surprised how quickly I agreed this time. I'm not a total snoot, and I reminded her that she's got to quit bribing me with drinks and want to have a coffee with me because we're friends. She blushed and agreed.

We walk inside and I'm surprised to find it full of people. I mean, it's a Monday, and people do go places every day of the week, but it's also a *Monday*. Wendy's grabbing supplies to decorate Valentine's Day boxes for her girls to take to school and she's got a list. Of course, always a list.

"I can't believe your book comes out next month," she chimes in beside me, her arms already full of supplies.

Honestly, I can't either. I think this last piece in the series means more to me than anything else I've written thus far. Something about it is just so *personal*. I haven't discussed that bit with

Wendy yet, but I think somehow she knows. She knows me better than anyone, maybe even myself at times. It's a little scary.

"Me neither, but I think I'm ready," I say, picking up a card off the shelf in front of me. It's a Valentine's Day card. I flip it open, scan the words, and place it back where it belongs.

"Yeah?" she asks. Her arms are getting full. I could offer to help her carry some of her things, but it might be best to grab a shopping cart instead.

"Yeah. Hey, let me go get you a cart, you're about to have a landslide there." I laugh and she glances over at me, her eyes creasing with a grin. She nods her head and mouths a thank you.

I make my way back to the front of the store where they have all their carts lined up in a neat row. I grab the first one I come to and pull it out. Great, this one has a squeaky wheel. Before I have a chance to trade it for a new one, a group of teenage girls saunter in through the front entrance.

There's at least five or six of them all together. I'm terrible at guessing ages, but they look like they could easily be high school students. I look away and pull out a different cart, this time without a squeaky wheel.

I'm heading back toward Wendy when I feel someone tap gently on my shoulder. It's a different touch this time, it's not coming from a strong man's hands (*his*), but someone else's.

I start to turn my head but they walk around the side of the cart, facing me. At first, I'm annoyed. It's one of the teenage girls that just walked in. What does she want? Does she recognize who I am? Every now and then when I'm out in public someone will recognize me and ask me for my autograph. I always say yes, and thus find myself reaching in my purse for a pen out of habit. My hand is already halfway buried inside my bag.

Before I can ask if she needs me to sign something she speaks, and the words that come out have nothing to do with me being an author, but everything to do with me being *me*.

"Nicki? Is that you?"

Now that I'm facing her head-on I see it. I know exactly who she is. I've only met her one time, months ago now, but she has one of those faces that isn't easily forgotten. I remember her blue eyes and soft, long blonde hair.

"Yep, it's me. What are you doing here, Marvel?" Denver's daughter is here. *Here* in the craft store with me and Wendy. Of all the places, out of all seven days in a week, what are the odds she'd run into me here, today?

Okay, I'm overreacting. It's a craft store for crying out loud. She probably got out of school and is stopping by with some of her friends. No big deal. She's allowed to shop here as much as anyone else. I'm instantly reminded of the man I'm trying hard to forget. But it isn't working. It isn't working at all.

She laughs softly. She's got a beautiful laugh, just like her father. I'm standing here like a fool with a girl I barely know when I should be helping my friend out instead. Yet there is something, something so painfully familiar about her that I can't place. *What is it?*

She must notice me staring. She laces her fingers together in front of her and offers me a gentle smile. "Um, how are you doing? Dad's uh, mentioned you... Like a lot." She laughs again. Pure gold.

"He does? I mean did?" I sound too eager, too hopeful. She probably means in the past tense. He used to talk about me, but not anymore. Now there isn't anything to talk about.

"Yeah, of course. He's still crazy about you, ya know?" she says.

No, I don't know. I don't have a clue.

I shift a little on my feet, left to right and back, like my dad does when he's nervous.

"I'm sorry that I haven't called... I just, I have some things I've got going on," I tell her. It isn't exactly a lie, I definitely have some stuff going on—but it isn't true either.

She nods her head in agreement. "Yeah, that's alright. We all do at times. He's pretty understanding when it comes to that stuff. Anyway, it's good running into you."

She starts walking back towards her group of friends.

"Marvel?" I call out to her, before I can stop myself.

"Yes?" she returns.

"Do you think he'd answer if I tried calling him again sometime? When I'm ready, that is?" I'm terrified to know the truth, but not knowing is so much worse. It's all I can think about. He said he'd wanted me, but does he still? Has that changed?

"I do. I really do." She doesn't hesitate. "In fact, you should come over for dinner sometime. It's always the two of us, and I mean, he's cool and all, but he's my dad, ya know?" she adds.

Yes, I do know. Believe me.

"Oh... I don't know... I'm not sure that's a good ide—" I start to say, but she stops me. Something in her eyes tells me she's serious. She's a confident kid, I'll give her that.

"Look, I'll have him call or text you. Whichever you want. That way it's coming from him and not me, okay? Let's say Friday night at six. Does that work for you?"

I suddenly love this girl. I don't know her yet, but I want to. Her smile is contagious. Bright like summer sunshine.

I blink a few times, processing this conversation. Is this really happening? Will he even say yes? What if this all turns out wrong and...? Stop. Don't go there. It's going to be fine. Breathe.

"Are you sure he's going to go for this?" I ask, hesitating. I trust her, but I still have my doubts this is going to work. She wants me there, but does he?

She nods her head as she digs inside her purse, pulling out a folded-up receipt and a pen. She scribbles something quickly on the paper and hands it to me. I look down, it's her address.

"Friday, at six?" She cocks an eyebrow, waiting for me to confirm.

Okay. Let's give it another shot. "Okay, I'll be there. But only if he invites me as well."

"Deal." And she sticks out her hand for me to shake. I gladly shake her hand, and we seal the deal.

AFTER MARVEL and I part ways I finally meet back up with Wendy. She said she'd wondered if I'd forgotten or wandered off somewhere. When she went to check on me she saw who I was talking with. She'd ended up grabbing her own cart and finished her shopping without me. I feel a little guilty but not too guilty. I'm floating. The very thought of seeing him again is just... everything. It would be everything. I hope it all works out, because I'm not sure how well I'd take disappointment right now.

Wendy and I spend the next hour cozied up in a coffee shop along the same shopping strip. We talk about her family and what she's got planned this year, and we talk about the prospect of my upcoming date. It feels good to have her in my corner. I don't even want to think about what I'd do if she wasn't.

Then: February 4th

I get to work right away on Mom's gift. It's a Tuesday, and her birthday is the following Friday. I don't have a lot of time to pull this off, honestly, but I'm using every spare moment I can to make it happen. I'm not sure I have the same gifting gene that she has. Dad is okay at giving gifts, but I think he only gives because it's expected of him.

Last year for Mom's birthday, since it also happens to be on Valentine's Day, we took her out to her favorite place to eat, Sally's in the Park—it's this cute little diner that sits inside a state park. Afterward, we spent the rest of the evening driving through the park, sightseeing all the wildlife that tends to come out at dusk.

Other than the gift I'm preparing, I don't have a whole lot else planned for her yet. There's an art show next weekend that I'm pretty sure she mentioned once, but now that I'm trying to remember, I might have the wrong date. I could try asking Dad, but I haven't yet.

Dad doesn't know what I'm working on. He thinks I've been busy studying for exams in my room. I do have a test coming up, but I'm not studying tonight. I jump at any little noise I hear throughout the house. Dad is most likely working in his study right now. He's gone all day at work, and sometimes after dinner, I find him in his office answering emails.

I nearly fall out of my desk chair when someone knocks on my door. I quickly find something on my desk to cover up the evidence of what I'm doing. It's my math textbook, and I jerk it open to a random page, grabbing a pencil from the holder so it looks like I'm in the middle of studying for something important. I am quite obviously not. I can only hope it's not obvious to whoever it is on the other side of the door.

The knock comes again, and I realize I'm supposed to invite them in. A sigh escapes me and I say as pleasantly as I can manage, "Come in!"

It's Dad. His hair is disheveled, and he looks older somehow. I don't remember him having creases by his eyes and along his cheekbones. He's older than Mom, but he's aged this past year. Even though I've given him the official invitation, he doesn't make any further movement into my room. The door is barely cracked, and he peeks in at me as though he's afraid of what he might see in here. I may have forgotten to put my dirty clothes into the laundry hamper, but my bed is made like it usually is. Nothing else should be out of place, except for the textbook I'm not using.

"Hey, Sweet P, I'm sorry for intruding like this, I just..." he trails off and so does his gaze.

The glow of the hallway light behind him illuminates his face, and for a moment I don't think I recognize this man standing before me. I blink, and it's just my dad standing there. Hmm.

"Dad, you aren't intruding. You're allowed in here, you know," I say. And I mean it. I don't know when we set these hard, do-not-cross lines, but I'm sick of them. I wish they never existed in the first place.

He shuffles from one foot to the other, still not making any move closer to me. I close my textbook. It's a risk, but one I'm willing to take. I invite him in this time.

"Dad, I want you to come in. Please," I say. I can't recall the last time I said those exact words to him. Maybe I never have. After all, Dads are supposed to tuck in their daughters each night and kiss them on their foreheads. It's not something I miss, because I don't remember it happening in the first place. But right now I want him in here.

He hesitates for a moment, but then slowly makes his way in. He's wearing an old, checkered robe. If I remember correctly, I think it was a Christmas gift from Mom a few years ago during one of our crazy shopping escapades.

He leaves the door open a tiny sliver, like he's trying to create an easy escape. Standing in my room, he looks awkward and uncomfortable, so I motion for him to sit. The only obvious place is my bed so he takes it.

"I was just coming here to ask if you had any ideas for Mom this year," he says quietly. He's always spoken to me at a hushed volume. Mom's volume often changes frequency, but Dad's rarely does. Like the highs and lows of a valley, Dad's voice flows like a stream.

I swivel my chair so I'm facing him. I lean back slightly, folding my legs up in my chair. I take a moment to think before I blurt out the first thing that comes to mind. I'm contemplating how much I want to give him. I'm still a bit angry with him for wanting to divorce Mom last year and having an affair. The two biggest elephants in the room we've never once talked about.

As though he can sense a shift in me, his grayish-blue eyes lock with mine. His smile fades and concern is written in the lines on his face. Worry, fear. I've seen that look before. The day I found out that he—.

"What is it, P?" he asks.

Don't run, don't run, don't run. Stay, stay, stay.

"Why did you want to leave Mom?" I force out. An ache spreads throughout my stomach as I feel it start to twist in knots. I shouldn't be bringing this up. He came in here to talk about fun things like planning Mom's thirty-fifth birthday. I forget how old Dad is, but I think they are close to ten years apart in age. They'd met in college her first year, fell in love, got pregnant with me, and the rest is history.

He folds his hands into his lap and stares down at them. For a moment I don't think he's going to answer me at all, after all the door is still open, pleading with him to walk back through it. It's not too late to retreat.

It's a feeling I know all too well. *Run.* All we've ever done is run. I want to be done running. It's exhausting. I'd never really noticed it before, but I see it now etched in the tired lines on my dad's face. What has he been running from? Maybe we aren't that different after all.

"Your Mom and I got married young. I don't know if you know the entire story, but believe it or not, I used to be a professor," he starts.

My eyes go wide at this. I have not heard this version of the story. I've only heard it from Mom, and hers is quite different.

"Really?" I ask, "What kind of professor?"

"Guess." He glances up at me, but he isn't smiling.

"Finance?" I suggest.

He nods and looks back into his lap. "Yep. I was a professor at the college Mom attended. I won't bore you with everything, but we fell in love her freshman year, and because she was a student at the time and showed up pregnant in my class..." he trails off.

The sick feeling in my stomach doesn't go away, it gets worse. I'm not sure why he's telling me all of this. Why does it matter now? *Mom slept with her professor? No, she definitely left that part out.*

"I had no choice but to resign." He sighs sadly.

"But you did have a choice to marry her or leave her," I quickly add, "right?"

He nods again. "Yes, that is true. We both wanted to get married. Although, it was a mutual agreement," he says, acting as though it was some sort of contract and not my parents' marriage.

"I'm not sure either of us planned for it to happen that way," he says, hesitating.

I'm not sure how I feel about this, any of this. I'm trying hard not to judge something that happened so long ago, but I'm having a hard time with it. Mom slept with her college professor, and he was forced to resign. Whether or not they'd meant for that to happen, it did. Dad had been forced out of a profession he loved because of Mom. Yet, they still got married and stayed together all these years.

Did they only stay together because of *me?*

He continues before I can choke out all the questions that are starting to bubble up to the surface.

"We did things a bit out of order. Looking back, we both should have done it differently. I should have waited until she was no longer my student to pursue a relationship with her. We should have dated for a while and then talked about marriage. We sped up the timeline, our timeline. When we should have taken everything much slower than we did.

"Sweet P... I know this is all strange to hear coming from me. I know. I'm not sure if this is something I should be discussing with my daughter, but it isn't right for either of us to keep anything hidden from you. And for that, I'm truly sorry."

A tear escapes my eye and lands in my lap. I quickly swipe it away as another falls. I swipe that one away too. As hard as it is hearing this truth coming from my Dad, I'm glad it's coming from him. We mostly dance around each other with small talk and side hugs. I never get much more from him, but all of this? I'd take this side of him any day. The ugly, the messy, the broken pieces he keeps locked away like the secrets in my mom's journal.

I want *this* Dad.

"I want you to know that I love your mom. I truly do, so much. She's not always an easy person to love, but I have never stopped loving your mother. Yes, I have made some mistakes. Terrible ones, as you already know. I was at a really low point, and I didn't see how to fix our marriage at the time. It was wrong of me to do that kind of thing to her. I know that. I really do. And I have not gone back to that lady again..." His voice is starting to tremble.

That's when more tears start to fall down my face like rain in a storm. I let them.

"Promise?" I squeak out.

"Wh-what is that?" he asks, glancing up at me with a look in his eyes like he's forgotten who he's been talking to—lost in his own world, like Mom often is. His stone eyes meet my copper ones. We hold onto each other's gazes. Neither of us wanting to let go of the other.

"Do you promise that it's over with that other woman?" I whisper, forcing out the word 'other' as though I've said a dirty word. I don't know if Mom can hear us, and I hope she's not listening somewhere in the house.

He catches on and lowers his voice too. "Oh, yes. One thousand percent. I'm never doing that again."

I've heard of men cheating on their wives before, that's nothing new to me. I'm also aware that they will often do it repeatedly. But somehow, someway, I'm choosing to believe my dad. If he says he's done, then he's done. I believe him.

At least... I want to.

"Does Mom know?" I ask softly.

"No. She doesn't. That's not why I wanted the divorce, though." he says.

"Oh." is all I say.

"I'm not sure that I'm right for her."

What does that mean? They've been married for almost seventeen years, how can he say that?

He clears his throat. Mine suddenly feels parched too.

"But you said that you love her," I say confused.

"Yes, and I do. Always will. But you know how she is, Sweet P. She's a free bird, she beats her own drum, and doesn't have a care in the world. That's great—I love that about her. But sometimes I feel like she's trapped, like I'm the one caging her in. People like her don't want to be tied down to someone. And to be honest, I'm not sure her medication is working anymore," he says sadly.

I jump at this. "What do you mean? What's wrong with Mom?" I say, forgetting to keep my voice to a whisper.

"Nothing. I don't know. Something's off." He doesn't say more, doesn't elaborate. But I want answers. No, I *need* them. What is he talking about?

"But she's seemed fine these past couple of months. She hasn't left in a while, and she's laughing again. That's a good sign, right?" My voice breaks again. I think back to some of the poems I'd read in her journal, and I quickly shove them back down.

"Yeah, that's the thing. You never really know what version of her she's going to be. I'm a little worried is all. She's been unwell for a while, and I've tried everything I can think of. I just don't know anymore.

"I didn't come in here to burden you with all of this..." He waves a hand in the air, as if all of Mom's problems are merely floating in the air and we can reach out and catch them. I wish that I could.

"I want to make this birthday extra special for her. Don't worry, I'm not leaving. I'm not going anywhere, okay? I realize that's not going to fix anything. I know how much you love and care about your Mom, that's why I want you to help me plan this day. I want to do this together. With you, for her." His voice breaks, and tears leak out of his wrinkly eyes. At this, the dam in me bursts open and rivers of tears flow down, down, down.

Just like I'd done with Mom a few nights ago, I make my way over to Dad and curl up in his lap like a little girl. He doesn't back away or tell me I'm too big to be held. He wraps both arms snugly around me and holds me. I feel his warm tears soak the top of my head, and I don't care. I haven't shown this man enough love over the past couple of years, or maybe ever. But I want to start. I want more moments like this. Because even though it hurts in places, it's something real. And real things I can hold onto.

"Okay," I manage through a blur of tears. "I'm in." And I mean it—one thousand percent.

Now: February 7th

His text comes in later that evening. I'd had a great afternoon with Wendy, and she'd dropped me off back home in time for dinner. I had purchased a chicken salad sandwich from the coffee shop and stuck it in my purse for later. Gross, I know, but I knew my options would be limited at home.

Dad's been going out more with Deb, and he's gone most evenings. I've only met her in passing twice. I don't know if he's embarrassed to be dating at his age, or if he doesn't feel ready to bring her around me yet. Either way, as soon as he's off work for the day he goes out. Where—I don't have a clue, but I am happy for him.

Denver's text is short but sweet:

DENVER

I see we've been set up for a date by my sixteen-year-old. Hope that's okay with you.

Of course, it is... honestly, I didn't think I'd get a chance at another one. I'm thankful for Marvel's interference. She's much braver than I was at her age.

I quickly send a reply:

ME

It'll be good to see you again. I'm looking forward to it. 

I add in a happy face emoji at the end to let him know I mean it. If he knows me even a little, I hardly ever use emojis.

He doesn't reply but instead 'hearts' my message. That's good enough for me. Now, for the hard part. What in the world am I going to wear?

*   *   *

I settled on wearing a royal blue, silk dress shirt with a V-neck and pearl buttons. I hardly ever wear skirts because of my Spider-Girl legs, but I did remember to shave at least—thus, I make an exception and pull out the black leather skirt. Afterwards both the top and skirt will go back into Wendy's closet, where they belong. We are not the same size, but she's also the type that has a hard time getting rid of things, especially when it comes to clothing. She's certain her daughters will wear her clothes someday.

Wendy drops me off at exactly six. I gawk at his house as I make my way to the door. His house is gorgeous. It's not a large house, but it's modern and up-to-date, unlike our home, which was built in the early 70s. We've had to fix a lot of things over the years, but I don't think it could ever look anything like this. I know it's bad to compare, and I shouldn't—but I can't help it.

I must still have my mouth hanging open, because Marvel giggles as she opens the door, motioning for me to come in. Part of me is shocked to see her here holding the door open for me, yet another part isn't. It seems exactly like something she would do. She's the kind of person who never feels like a stranger, rather she feels like someone you've known for a very long time. I feel comfortable around her, and that's saying a lot.

I take my shoes off and leave them by the front door, along with my purse. I don't know if that rule applies here or not, but it seems like the polite thing to do. Wendy's family makes a small attempt at the shoes-at-the-door thing, but mostly they get thrown around in places that were aimed somewhat near the door.

We pass an enclosed office to the right with giant glass doors, and on the left is a small reading den. She leads me down a small hallway that opens up into the kitchen/living room. This place is incredible. I feel like I'm dining in a five-star hotel rather than someone's house. The kitchen is no comparison to our tiny, square kitchen that barely fits our table and chairs.

Denver is standing over the stove with his back turned to us. He's flipping something in a large pan that smells amazing. There's a line of vegetables laid out, already chopped into neat pieces along a cutting board, on the large island table behind him. The island has full bar seating and, along the far wall, is a window that faces out front with a large, farmhouse table in front of it. I am so amazed that I think I've forgotten my manners. Oops.

He must realize he's not alone in here and turns around to greet me. His hair isn't as long as it was a month ago. It still falls in gentle waves along his face, but shorter, and the stubble on his face has grown out. I like this new look on him. He's always been handsome, but tonight he's even more so. Maybe it's that we haven't seen each other or spoken since New Year's. I didn't think I'd ever miss someone of the opposite sex, but I did. I really missed him.

"Hey," I breathe out. I'm still shocked that I am standing here, in his house, with him. I don't want to jump to any conclusions, but he wouldn't have gone along with Marvel's invite if he didn't want me here. Right? *I want to be with you.* I could only hope that was still true.

"Hey Nicki... uh, wow, you look great. It's good to see you again," he says.

I smile and nod toward the food he's preparing. I don't want to be too much of a distraction.

"I don't want you to burn anything on my account." I joke, waving in the direction of the food on the stove.

He shakes his head and laughs. I missed that laugh. "Are you questioning my cooking skills?"

"I would never." I cross my heart, teasing him. This is fun. This is okay so far. It feels good being here with him. I hope he feels the same way.

Marvel is standing in the doorway, smiling and laughing with us. Denver waves his daughter in and she joins us. I help her set the table while Denver finishes up. I offer to help but he waves me off, says that I'm the guest and he wants to serve me tonight. Some other time maybe I can cook for him. Yeah, maybe. I haven't cooked for anyone in ages, including myself... but for him, I might. I won't say no yet. It's time I start working on saying yes more often. Starting now.

Denver cooks rib-eye steaks, Caesar salad, and roasted vegetables. I'm not a vegetarian, but I don't eat a ton of meat. I would choose a McDonald's cheeseburger off the dollar menu before I'd go out and buy myself a nice steak. But Denver has cooked them to perfection. He has come up with his own spice rub that is amazing. Everything is delicious. And to top it all off, he made the cheesecake for dessert. Who does that? I used to love baking, but I haven't even attempted cheesecake. I have never met anyone else who has owned up to that, it's impressive.

I ate way too much tonight, but I was too polite to turn anything down, and to be honest, I couldn't get enough. If I didn't think it'd be rude, I'd ask if he could make me a to-go plate after I leave tonight. There are plenty of leftovers, but I don't ask either of them that.

I thought dinner might have felt awkward. Our last conversation hadn't exactly been great, and I'd probably said some things I shouldn't have said. But tonight has felt anything but awkward. Both Denver and Marvel have made me feel like I belong here. As though I come here every Friday night, rather than being here for the first time.

We are in the middle of discussing plans for Valentine's Day when his phone rings. He apologizes and excuses himself from the kitchen. He returns a moment later with a look in his eyes that says *Stay.*

He's on call tonight, like he is often for his job as an EMT, and he has to go. It's urgent, but that's all he can say. I get it and wave him off. I'm sad to see him go already, but he says he thinks he should be back in an hour or so if I don't mind waiting for him to return. He leaves it up to me and doesn't pressure me either way. He's never pressured me about anything, and I love that about him. I know this sounds crazy, but I think I might actually *love* him.

I DECIDE to hang out with Marvel for a bit. She's seriously the sweetest kid, or rather teenager, I've ever met. I haven't met many, but still. She's great. She offers me a tour of the rest of the house. She briefly opens the door to Denver's room, and I'm positive that I blush as I peek inside. It smells exactly like him.

There's a guest bathroom in between her room and her dad's, with the guest room right across the hall. Next, she shows me her room. Her room is decorated in pink. Her walls are a faded pink, and her bedsheets are a brighter shade. She has a large, white desk in the corner with one of those big, fuzzy swivel chairs. The largest wall has a giant built-in-sized bookshelf that looks custom-made. I'd bet anything Denver made this for her. It's amazing. He's amazing. I wish he were here.

We opt for watching a movie in their living room to pass the time. I keep checking my phone to see if he's texted me, but the only new messages I have are from Wendy, checking in on me. I send her a quick smiley emoji (my second one of the day, what's gotten into me?) and a thumbs up. Things have been great so far. I'm glad I came tonight.

Since I was deprived of my share of superhero movies, Marvel decided to pick the movie she was named after, *Marvel*.

When the credits roll I am left in awe. I cannot believe I've never watched superhero movies. It was amazing and all these years I've missed out. I can't wait to watch another one sometime. Maybe next time can be with him.

It's a little later than I'd originally told Wendy, so I shoot her a text asking if she can come pick me up. She replies instantly that she will be here in twenty minutes. I feel bad for not waiting longer for Denver, but it's already after ten and I'm fading. He can call or text me tomorrow.

I'm not much of a hugger, but I hug Marvel and thank her for the wonderful evening. It truly was a night to remember, and I hope it can happen again real soon. She smiles and thanks me for coming. I put my shoes back on and bend down to grab my purse. As I'm bringing it up to my shoulder it knocks something off the long table by the front entrance. I look down and see that it's a picture. A picture that is now lying at my feet, cracked. Oh, no.

I quickly bend down to grab it, careful not to cut my hand along the glass. I apologize to Marvel but she's quick to reassure me that it's not a big deal, it's just a frame and can be replaced. I'm carefully placing it back on the table when I notice something strangely familiar about it.

I look more closely at the image. There's a man in the picture that I can only assume to be a younger version of Denver, and he has his arms around a girl. She's got pink rosy cheeks and her hair is almost the color of snow. It's so white. So blonde and beautiful, just like Marvel's. I've always thought there was something familiar about Marvel, but I could never put my finger on it, until now.

I hesitate, and my voice comes out shaky when I ask her, "W-wh-who is that? In the picture?"

Marvel comes around me to get a closer look. I don't turn around to see her expression, but I get this awful sinking feeling in my gut. Dread.

"Oh, that was Denver's little sister. She died when he was younger... It was an accident... a bad snowstorm... they didn't even see her—"

I don't hear anything else. I had no idea she was somebody's sister. I had no idea it was *his* sister. Oh, my god. I sink to the floor, numb.

I can't hear anything she is saying to me. All I see is white snow falling all around me. It doesn't stop falling. My entire body goes rigid, and I'm frozen to this spot in the middle of her foyer. I thought I could run forever from this terrible thing... but it's found me once again. And this time I cannot run.

36

Then: February 7th

It's a week until Mom's big birthday surprise, but I think Dad and I have it all figured out. If she overheard any of our conversation from that night, she doesn't show it. So far, I think we are in the clear. It's Friday, and today she is driving me to another therapy appointment.

I have my license now and can drive myself, but she says that she wants to go with me. Probably to make sure I go, but rather than asking her why, I let it be. If she wants to sit in the lobby for a solid hour while I mostly nod at the therapist, fine. My therapist is okay, but it all seems a little pointless to me, if I'm being honest.

Dr. Gurkle is the type that you never catch smiling. She is all professional and all business. She does not laugh when I try to crack jokes to ease the mood, nor does she smile if I offer her a compliment. I haven't given up hope though. I know one of these days she's going to crack, just the tiniest sliver, and it'll be gold. It's all I want from these sessions anymore, and it's quickly become a bit of a game.

After the evaluation with Dr. Gurkle, I was scheduled to see her once a week. Always on a Friday afternoon immediately following school.

I have an idea.

"So, how are you doing today, Phoenix?" she asks me in her monotone voice. She sits behind a dark mahogany desk that looks extremely important and expensive, while I sit in a cheap, worn, leather chair that has probably seated a thousand butts before mine. I try not to think about it too much.

"Fine," I retort, bored. I don't know why I still have to come here. I haven't had any more blackouts, and I'm doing fine. I'm okay, really. Can't she see that?

She sits there with a large laptop, taking notes every time I speak. I don't have a clue what she is writing about me, but I'm not sure I want to know either.

"How have your stress levels been lately?" she asks me for the hundredth time.

My answer is always the same. I hope she's getting paid a decent amount, because I can't imagine sitting here like this every day with people like me if she wasn't.

"What are you doing for Valentine's Day this year?" I ask her, and she glances up at me from the computer. She doesn't crack a smile. Darn. I'm not done yet.

She raises an eyebrow and leans back into her comfy, leather chair. "Why do you want to know?"

"I just wondered if they gave you the day off. They should since it's a holiday and all," I suggest.

She doesn't appear phased or impressed, but she's paused clacking away at her keys for the moment. I have her full attention.

"Is that so? And what do you plan to do on this holiday?" she asks me. Back into therapist mode. The woman is a machine. I'm not phased, not one bit.

"Oh, loads. It's also my mom's birthday," I say.

She quirks her eyebrow again and nods. For a second, I think she's going to slip, but she doesn't. It's as though she really wants to but knows that smiling would be unprofessional.

"Really? Well, that's quite the celebration then. A birthday and a holiday."

"Yep," I say, smirking.

"And do you get the day off?" she asks me.

Her question has thrown me off guard. What is she playing at? Has she figured out my little game? She is good, I will give her that, but how good are we talking here?

"Well, no... I have school that day," I say flatly, my voice full of disappointment. There was a time or two when Mom pulled me out of school for the day, calling it a "family day," but nobody's brought that up this year. As far as I know, it's a regular day. Except for the surprise Dad and I have planned after school and work. It can still be special.

"Ahh, I see. Well, like you then, I too have to work that day. Somebody's gotta pay the bills, right?" She winks at me.

It's not exactly a smile, but it's close. Does that count? Wait, what is she talking about?

"Do you make more money than your husband, Dr. Gurkle?" I ask, onto something.

She's never once mentioned her husband, but she's wearing a ring. If I can get her talking about herself, the focus will be off of me. Brilliant.

She types something quickly into her computer and then closes the lid. She places both of her palms down gently over the device, looking directly at me.

"I think that will be all for today, Phoenix."

I can't tell if I've upset her or if she's back to playing *her* game with *me*. I think she's caught on to my little tricks. Oh well, it was fun while it lasted.

"Oh, alright," I say, defeated. "Guess I'll see you next week then." I scoot back in the chair, getting ready to stand.

Then she says something surprising. "That won't be necessary. We are done here. Good luck out there."

For a second I feel confused. I don't understand. I came here thinking there would be no end. I'd be seventy-five and retired, and she would still be asking to see me every Friday to talk about the same things we always talk about. Now that it's over, I'm not too sure how I feel about it. What if I'm not okay? What if it does happen again? Maybe I was wrong about her, maybe I should have been listening more to the things she was saying, rather than tuning her out.

"I don't think I'm ready," I admit, my voice small. I'm done playing our game for now. I'm serious.

"I think you're ready for more than you give yourself credit for. I know that you're a bright girl with big ideas. You're passionate about the people you love and you love deeply. You're going to do amazing things someday. I believe it."

Wow. I take back anything negative I've ever thought about the lady. I'd even written a short story about her that didn't paint her in the best light. I'm a little embarrassed about it now. I'll trash that piece as soon as I get home.

"You got all that from sitting here with me while I make jokes and say mean things about you in my head?" I say, in disbelief.

At that, she breaks. A smile forms in slow motion across her face, and I memorize it. Especially if this is the only time I'll ever witness it. But I'm here now, and I take a mental snapshot.

"Well, I didn't know about the mean jokes part..." she says, and I blush at that.

She continues, "But, yes. I see great potential in you. Don't sell yourself short, kid. Now go on, get out of here. And hey," She pauses as I push in my chair and fully stand up this time.

I meet her dark, beady eyes that no longer look like an evil witch's but someone that truly cares about the people she meets. "Yeah?" I ask.

"I hope your mom has the best damn birthday." And guess what she does? She smiles a second time.

Maybe I was wrong about therapists. Maybe not all of them are bad people. Maybe some *do* want to help people with their problems. Maybe that's exactly who she is. And maybe not all of them sleep with your Dad.

If someone like her can believe in someone like me, maybe there is hope for everyone. I bounce out of there with joy in every step as I walk out to find my mom.

Now: February 7th

The next thing I know, I wake up in a hospital bed. I'm surrounded by whirring machines and constant beeps. I don't sense anyone in here with me. I have no idea how I got here or why I'm here. *Why am I here?*

The room is dark save for the soft glow of glistening snow outside. I'm mesmerized by the steady fall of the snowflakes coating the cars in the parking lot. I watch them fall to the earth one by one.

I let my mind wander for a bit. The last thing I remember is having dinner with Denver and Marvel at their house, and oh... it suddenly hits me. The picture frame. I broke it. A frame can be easily replaced, the mistake I've made—the damage I've done—cannot.

I feel a warm hand reach out and touch me. At first, I jerk away as though I've been burned. I hadn't known anyone was here with me. As soon as I realize who's touched me, I reach back out for her with tears running down the sides of my face.

Wendy wraps her arms around me and holds me in place. If only we could stay like this, because I don't think much else is holding me together. The one piece of my past I've kept locked up inside for sixteen years. I'm terrified of what that will look like now that it has come to light.

"Oh, honey... it's going to be okay." My best friend assures me.

If only she knew the truth, and pretty soon she might. Nothing has ever seemed okay, and quite possibly, never will be.

I shake underneath her, sobbing into her shirt. I'm a snotty, teary mess, but she doesn't seem to mind. Maybe being a mom helps you get used to that, although I'm sure it's a little different coming from a grown woman. I don't feel like a grown-up at all, I feel like a very small child right now.

I hear someone else come into the room, but my eyes are too blurry to make much of anything out. Wendy softly pulls away and smooths out her clothes. They are now disgusting because of me, but I guess that's what best friends are for.

I wipe my eyes on my hospital gown and finally see who it is. It's a female doctor. She's got darker skin and kind eyes. Her hair is pulled up into a high ponytail, and she's holding a clipboard against her chest. She offers me a sympathetic smile as she introduces herself as Dr. Erica Cline.

"Hi there, Phoenix," she says, using my real name.

Remembering where we are, I chance a glance over at Wendy, watching for her expression to change at the mention of it. We've known each other a long time and my name isn't a secret to her, but it's also not something I've gone into great detail with her about. I'd said something along the lines of it being an old family name, but I prefer to go by Nicki. She accepted it, no questions asked, because why wouldn't she?

I nod. I have no words for her. I'm tired, and I still don't understand why I'm here. Did Wendy bring me here? Where is

Marvel? I look at her again, but she's not looking in my direction. Her eyes are glossy from tears, but the doctor has her full attention. Good, at least one of us is of sound mind here.

The doctor is saying something to me, but I am not listening. My head is swimming, and I can't remember how to swim. Wendy reaches over and squeezes my hand to reassure me. I squeeze hers back.

"Is it okay if you come back in a little bit? I'd like to have a few minutes with her if that's okay with you," Wendy says to Dr. Cline.

The doctor smiles a tiny smile, kind of like the one my therapist gave me on our last day together.

"I just need to check on a few things for her, and then I'll be out of your hair. You're welcome to wait in here while I finish up," she tells Wendy as though I'm not right here in the same room as them.

She quickly checks my vitals and writes a few notes on her chart before she exits the room with a smile and a nod. She closes the door behind her, giving the room back to Wendy and me.

Before I can ask her a million questions, she stands up and looks like she's about to walk out as well. What? No. I plead with my eyes. *Don't leave me here. Stay, stay, stay.*

She must sense my despair because she reassures me. "I'll be right back, Nicki. But there's someone else here who wants to see you." She gathers up her purse and book she must have been reading and walks out.

I should have begged her to stay. Now I'm in here alone. I want to go home, I don't want to be here. Somebody please tell me what's going on.

The tears are starting to rain again when the door opens back up. This time, a tall man walks in. A man I would recognize anywhere... Denver Marks.

HE COMES in and sits down on the edge of my bed. At first he stuffs his hands into the pockets of his uniform. But then he quickly removes them as though he changed his mind and folds them in his lap. His familiar gaze meets mine, and I can almost sense a change in the air when it happens. I hold my breath, waiting for whatever comes next. Maybe he has some answers for me since I haven't gotten them from anyone else.

"Denver."

"Nicki."

We both utter in the same breath.

"You first," I say. I press two fingers to my temples as I feel a headache coming on, and I rarely get headaches.

He lets out a long sigh. His cheeks are a bit flushed like he rushed here, and he's still wearing his EMT uniform. Has he been home yet?

"Marvel called me immediately. She said you'd blacked out in the middle of the foyer. What happened, Nicki? Are you okay?"

No, I am not okay. I'm not sure I ever will be.

I shake my head no, and more tears fall.

"Nicki, talk to me. Tell me what's going on," he pleads with me.

I should just come out and say it, the real truth I've been running from. I've been running for so long, and I don't think I can do it anymore. I can't outrun myself.

"Tell me about your sister," I say, quietly—my voice crackly and on the edge of breaking.

He stares at me, confused. Sadness laces his expression. "My sister?" he asks, not understanding.

Why would he?

"Yes. The picture on the table by the front door. I broke one of the picture frames and Marvel said it was of you and your little sister," I say. I know who she is, but I want to hear it from him. I can't say what I need to say yet, because I don't know what it will do to him. *Or what it will do to me.*

"Right. Oh. She did mention something about that happening right before you blacked out," he pauses, a second too long.

My bravery is cracking, threatening to flee. No, not this time. I take a deep breath. I will not run.

"I had a younger sister... We were twelve years apart, but we were also really close. She was all I had, and she meant everything to me. She died one winter in a terrible storm..." His voice cracks and I bite my lip, not sure how much more I want to hear. But I force my attention on him. I don't look away.

"How did she die?" I ask.

He breaks eye contact first, and I find myself grabbing for his hand. As if this is the most natural thing in the world, sitting here in a hospital room, holding hands, talking about his dead sister.

"How did she die?" I repeat softly after a few moments of silence.

"It was an accident... The storm was getting bad and someone just... they were driving too fast down our street, and she'd been sledding down our hill in the front yard. We had this really big hill that was great for sledding in the winter. Her sled was going too fast and she slid right into the street. The driver didn't see her... she was killed instantly."

Bile rises in my throat, and I grip his hand tightly. I can feel myself starting to shake. A ripple waves through my body as I fight the start of a panic attack. Denver's tear-filled eyes find mine. He's found me. Does he know? Has he figured out the truth?

"What is it, Nicki? Why are you suddenly asking me all of this?"

"Is she the reason you started going to Grieve and Grow?" I ask, genuinely wanting to know. I know it's not fair to leave him in the dark like this, but he will find out soon enough. Once I explain there is no turning back. I remember the night I'd run out of the group and overheard him talking about his sister. I can't believe I hadn't put two and two together. Until now.

I assumed when he'd said he had been going to G&G for the last six or seven years that he meant that's when grief struck him. It couldn't have possibly happened a long time ago, sixteen years to be exact. But I was wrong. I was wrong about a lot of things.

I still remember seeing the news article titled *Police Still Searching for Hit and Run Driver of 12-Year-Old Girl.* There'd been a picture of her, and I recognized her right away. The girl I'd seen standing at the bright red mailbox. And there had been someone waiting for her at the door when she'd gone inside, I remember him now. But somehow I'd cast him from my memory at the time, and his name had been left out of the article. I'd had no idea they were siblings before then, only what had come out in the paper later.

"What does that have to do with anything? Nicki, tell me what's going on. What does my sister have to do with anything?" He raises his voice an octave. He doesn't sound angry, just confused and frustrated.

"She has to do with *everything*," my voice breaks, coming out in pieces like shards of glass. I can't manage to get more words out than that. I know I'm not making sense but I'm trying to. I really am.

"What? What do you mean?" he asks, confused.

"Your sister. She's part of the reason I went to G&G that night."

"You knew my sister?" he asks.

No, not really... I want to say.

I shake my head. "No," I say softly.

He releases our hands and grabs me by the shoulders. His touch is firm, but not rough. He isn't trying to hurt me, but he's frustrated and wants me to tell him what I know. What I've always known.

My voice fractures as I choke out a sob. "I was there that day. The day that your sister died. It was me that had been driving down your street... and I—I'd been trying to get away from something else terrible that had happened. I didn't see her. I could barely see out my window and suddenly... I am so, so sorry, Denver. I never meant to. I–I'm sorry." I am sobbing now. A blubbery mess, as I should be.

He doesn't move to wipe my tears, and I let them fall.

Denver stares at me, frozen. His eyes scan me as if trying to decipher what I'm saying but it's not registering. It's not clicking, and I can't say that I blame him.

I give him more. "Your sister *died* because of me, Denver. I'd only made the connection a few hours ago, or was it only a moment ago? I've lost track of time. When I recognized the girl from the picture at your house, I had no idea she was someone's sister... *your* sister. I never meant to hurt you this way."

I know there's nothing I can say to make any of this remotely okay, but I want him to at least believe that it was an accident. Please, believe me. I would never hurt anyone on purpose—I am not my mother.

For the longest time, I thought I'd blacked out that day. I wish that I could blame my diagnosis for that careless, tragic mistake. But it had nothing to do with that. All it'd taken was poor visibility and my phone ringing in the passenger seat for my focus to shift and ruin everything in a matter of seconds. I'd tried calling my dad many times earlier that day, and when he'd finally decided to call me back—I never should have tried to answer his call. If I hadn't, maybe his sister would still be alive.

"No." He shakes his head and quickly stands to his feet. He shoves his hands through his hair and then down the stubble along his face. The expression on his face dances in front of me like a slideshow. Anger, hatred, hurt, to the most unbearable kind of pain that can only be caused by death itself.

"You're telling me that you hit my sister with your car and then just drove away? Are you kidding me? You figured this out just now? Then what? Were you even going to tell me, Nicki?" he practically screams at me. This time when he says my name it sounds like a dirty word that leaves a bad taste in his mouth.

I am telling him all of this now! What did he expect me to do? Say, "Hi, my name is Phoenix, and I did something terrible when I was sixteen—I think I killed someone."

I cower back in the bed, but I have nowhere to go. Nowhere I can hide. I have to face him. I have to face this. I will not run away. I will choose to stay. I am through running. I'm done.

"You don't understand... I..." I trail off. Where do I go from here? How can I pick up the pieces now? Just a couple of hours ago we'd sat around his dining table eating, laughing, and talking about Valentine's Day. In a single moment, everything has shattered and broken.

"What don't I understand, Nicki? Tell me," he demands.

I've never seen this side of him, and it's scaring me a little, but I know I can take it. I deserve this. Everything he has to fire my way, I deserve it and so much more. What I've done is *unforgivable*.

"I wasn't okay that day... I'd witnessed something horrible, and I was trying to run away when I hit your sister. I should never have left home, but I couldn't bear to be there any longer. The storm was getting bad, and I was trying to make it back. I got turned around, and it happened so fast. It was an accident..." My voice breaks on the word 'accident,' and I pause for a moment, closing my eyes, forcing myself to remember.

I begin again. "I didn't see her, I swear. I thought at the time I'd just hit the mailbox. It wasn't until weeks later that I saw the article in the paper and put two and two together. By then it was too late... Denver, you have no idea how sorry I am. Really... please."

I'm begging. I don't know what I expect him to say, but something. Tell me it's going to be okay, like Wendy had only moments ago. Tell me he somehow forgives me and this can all be put to rest.

Tell me I'm not some horrible monster. Tell me that he still cares about me, enough to try and figure our way out of this hell together.

His eyes turn to stone, a color I'd never seen come from him before, and I know I'm not going to like what he says next.

"I'm sorry, too," he starts, "I'm sorry that I ever met you."

And with that, he leaves me here the way that he found me, alone. Exactly as I imagined he would once the truth came out. I saw this coming. I expected this. But it doesn't make it hurt any less. The people I love the most always find a way to leave me, my mother had just been the first.

"I think I'm in love with you," I tell the now empty room as a tear trickles down my cheek. The snow continues its steady rhythm, like the thrum of my own heart breaking inside my chest.

38

Then: Valentine's Day

I've been waiting all year for this day. Today is not only Valentine's Day, but it's my mother's birthday. Although I still have school today, I set my alarm a full hour early. The first part of the birthday plan is to make Mom's favorite breakfast—just as she's done for me all these years. It's about time I return the favor.

In no time the kitchen is filled with the wonderful aroma of maple syrup and butterscotch, with a side of brown sugar bacon. Forget the calories today, today is something worth celebrating.

Savage Garden's *I Knew You Before I Loved You* is playing in the background, and I start singing the lyrics.

Another familiar voice joins in as she sings the line leading into the chorus... *Mom.*

❋ ❋ ❋

THE SOLID HOUR that we have together goes by in a blur but in the best way. I finish up breakfast while she sets the table and continues to sing 90s songs. My mom's got a beautiful voice, and I love it whenever she sings. Dad had to go in early for work today but promised he'd be home in time for the birthday festivities tonight.

I was able to finish up Mom's biggest birthday surprise with help from Dad. It all came together quickly because of him. I'm glad we decided to team up and do things together this year. I hope it will mean as much to her as it means to me.

Mom drives me to school, she insisted. How could I say no? She said there would be no buses today to or from school. Supposedly, there's a blizzard forecasted to hit later this evening, and they didn't want their buses caught out in it. School hasn't been canceled yet, it rarely ever does around here, but the school email mentioned it could close at a moment's notice if the weather gets too bad.

Mom hasn't let on that she's aware Dad and I are up to something. But she has made it clear that no matter what today's weather has in store, she wants to spend as much time as possible with me today. After all, today is her big day.

I hug her and wave goodbye as I climb out of her car.

For it being a Friday, school seems to go exceptionally slow. I end up having tests in three of my classes that feel like they are never-ending. When the final bell rings, I leap out of my chair and dart out of the door. I can't escape fast enough. All throughout the day students kept checking outside to see if anything had changed in the weather, and to everyone's dismay it hadn't. It'd been an ordinary Friday, filled with the same exams as always, along with the same teenage drama.

No crazy winds, and not even a single flurry had fallen from the sky yet. The skies had remained clear all day, in fact. There was no sign of a storm coming. It wasn't completely out of the ordinary for the weather forecast to predict wrong... but so far they were way off. If I knew better, I'd say the storm probably isn't happening at this point.

Mom said she'd park in the student parking lot and wait for me. I scan the lot for her unforgettable bright red Coupe but don't see it anywhere. She must have gotten stuck in traffic or didn't check the time and is running late. It certainly wouldn't be the first time.

I check my phone for the time. School let out at three-o'clock, and it's now a half hour later. My stomach clenches, but I shouldn't start worrying just yet. Maybe she stopped to get herself a treat somewhere. If only I could call or text her and find out what's keeping her. But no, she still doesn't have a phone. It's times like this I wish she did.

Three-forty-five, four o'clock. An hour late. I have waited outside for my mom for an entire hour. The only cars left here are the teachers and school staff that haven't retreated yet for their weekend. Where is she? Is she okay? Did she forget? It'd been a long time since she'd broken one of her promises, but I stopped believing in those a long time ago. I trusted her this time—now, I'm starting to doubt all over again. And I'm getting worried. What's keeping her?

I sigh and do the thing I hate doing, but I do it anyway because she's left me with no choice. I call Dad. It goes straight to his voice-mail. Great. I hang up and try again. Once again it goes to voice-mail. I leave a brief message this time and hang up. Fine, I'll start walking home, and maybe he'll call me back and come get me. It's only about a ten-minute drive from our house to the school, but getting there on foot takes a lot longer, even with some shortcuts I can take.

I've also been watching the sky steadily turn bleak and gray over the past hour. There are clouds everywhere, and they are a dull gray, as though they hold something darker within them. The air feels colder now and a frigid wind has started blowing. At least I wore my hat and gloves today. I snuggle into my jacket as much as I can to avoid the bitter wind that has kicked up a notch and start making the long trek home.

IT TAKES me a solid twenty minutes to make it back home. By the time I get there, my cheeks are lobster red, I can't feel my fingers or my toes, and my legs and feet ache from the long walk. A few cars honked at me, and one even sprayed me with a snowdrift pile when I'd turned a corner near our neighborhood.

All the lights are off in the house, and there is no sign that Mom is here. I go straight into my room to jump into a quick, warm shower. As soon as the water pelts my skin I instantly feel better. I give myself a few minutes to thaw out, and I'm out in less than ten minutes. As soon as I dry off, I check my phone for any missed calls from Dad but have none. He must be in a meeting or something with his phone on silent. He is supposed to get off work early tonight for Mom's birthday, but it's nearing 4:30 and he hasn't called back yet.

But where is Mom? There is still no sign of her. It's her birthday and she's missing. Fabulous and so typically her. I start flipping on lights as I walk through the house. Like a kid playing hide and seek, I wonder if I am supposed to start calling for her. I yell, "Mom?" Nothing.

The house remains silent. Hmm. Oh, I should probably check the garage. If her car is still here that means she's home. Probably in the shower or reading a book in the sunroom like she does from time to time.

For a moment, I'm hit with a sudden realization. My stomach tightens at the thought of walking into her room and seeing all of her bags packed. Or worse, her room empty again—only, she's left us for good this time. *Where does she go every time she disappears?*

I open the door to the garage and find her car parked in its usual place. I'm instantly flooded with relief. If her car is here that means she is in the house somewhere. If she was thinking of running away she hasn't—yet. I run my finger along the hood of the car. It's completely dry. If she'd been out recently it would still be wet from the snow.

I walk back into the house and continue the search. There is a chance she might be sleeping. That would explain why she'd had all the lights turned off and her door closed. She seemed to be sleeping better and hadn't slept in this morning. She'd joined me for her birthday breakfast and sang and danced with me. She didn't seem at all tired like she used to get. But maybe she'd done more during the day while I was at school. I hesitate going in for a moment, because if she is sleeping I don't want to disturb her. After all, it is her day, and a nap may have very well been on her list of things to do today. I'm positive she'd made a list. Just like I have.

Dad will be getting home soon, and we have dinner plans. We had originally planned to take her out to this cute little Italian restaurant that opened up last year. We've only been a handful of times, but each time I remember Mom gushing about how much she *loved* their lasagna.

We quickly had to change gears when we heard about the storm coming through, and Dad came home yesterday with all of the ingredients for me to put together our own version of the lasagna Mom loved. I've never attempted to make it before, but I have a recipe to follow, surely it won't be that hard. But if it was going to be ready at a decent time, I need to start it soon. Dad had offered to help, but I told him he could be in charge of picking out a cheesecake from the store on his way home from work today. He agreed.

I don't know how long she's been sleeping, and I need to get her up. Knowing her, she probably forgot to set an alarm and didn't remember that she was supposed to come get me from school. I better go in.

I carefully crack open her door. The moment it opens I'm overcome with her scent, honey and vanilla. It's become my two favorite scents. I dare to push it open a little further, and I peer inside.

Sure enough, there she is, sleeping soundly in her bed. I let loose a sigh of relief. The curtains are drawn, and she has a candle still burning on her nightstand. There's no telling how long that's been going so I make my way over there quickly and blow it out.

I turn and face my mother. She hasn't noticed my presence yet, she's in one of her deep sleeps. Her fluffy down comforter is wrapped tightly around her body, keeping her snug and warm. I'm tempted to say screw the list, I'll just lie here with her. I don't want to wake her, I've changed my mind. Dad can wake us both up when he gets home.

I start to climb into her bed when I notice something I hadn't noticed before. Her wedding ring is placed neatly on her night-stand, beside a bottle of pills. I slowly move the covers off of her, wanting to get a better look at her hand. Maybe she always takes it off when she sleeps, and it's just something I've never paid atten-tion to until now.

She still hasn't opened her eyes and asked me what I'm doing in here like this. I reach for her hand. My hand lightly brushes the hand that is missing her ring, and it's cold to the touch. Too cold. Something isn't right. She's wrapped up in thick blankets, why are her fingers so cold? How long has she been like this?

"Mom?" I say, nudging her again, less gently this time. Her body puts up no resistance to my gentle push, and I gasp. I have to keep trying. I don't understand what's going on, and I need her to say something to me. Anything.

I try again. "Mom? Mom?" I say a little louder, panic starting to rise in my chest. Why isn't she moving? Why is she not waking up? What is wrong with her? She was fine this morning. I was with her. I hugged her and she said, "I'll see you later my Sweet Phoenix."

"Mom! Wake up! This isn't funny. I'm not joking or playing any of your dumb games. Say something! Say something to me!" I am screaming. I am screaming at my mother just lying here, doing nothing. I feel angry. Why is she doing this to me? Come on Mom, this isn't funny...

"Mom, Mom." I don't give up. I rip the sheets completely off the bed. I turn on all the lights. I'm not playing around. She's given me enough whiplash over the years. I love this woman with my whole freaking heart, but whatever this is I've had enough of it. Come on...

"Mom, Mom." Nothing. Silence. The worst kind of silence.

"Mom, Mom." My pleas are growing weaker. Something is shifting inside me, I'm not sure what it is. I'm not sure what anything is right now, I just want my mom to wake up and tell me everything is fine. She's fine. Open your eyes now, Mom.

"Mom..." I collapse in tears on top of her chest, which doesn't feel warm and comforting like it usually does. As I lay there I realize something else. Her heart is not beating beneath me. Her chest is not rising and falling. And that's when it hits me. My mom isn't sleeping at all... my mom is... no, no, no!

"Mom..." I say one last time. This woman that I love. This crazy, insane woman drives me up the wall sometimes. This piece of work, this, this... no, no. There's no way that she... she wouldn't have. She couldn't... She wouldn't do this to me. To us.

Today is her birthday. Her *birthday*. I have plans for her... Dad and I have all these plans, and we don't get to do any of them. Her gift. I was supposed to give it to her after we finished dessert... She was going to open it and... Now, she never will. I'm lying here and she's just... no. Oh, god, no. *NO!*

Mom...

Mom...

Mom...

Now: Valentine's Day

The hospital discharged me the next morning. Wendy had offered to take me home with her for a few days, but I politely declined. She'd already done enough for me. *More* than enough. Instead, I let Dad take me home.

At first neither of us spoke. Dad would look over at me every couple of minutes, as though he wanted to say something, but then he'd retreat back into his shell. Eventually he mustered up his courage. "What happened, Sweet P? Do you want to talk about it? I'm here for you."

I mean, what was there to say? I just told the man I love that I killed his sister sixteen years ago?

The truth would crush my father, maybe more so than it had Denver. *Denver...* Denver is on my mind, and I can't stop replaying our last conversation in my head.

I'm sorry I ever met you.

His words had stung badly, they still do. The doctor had

returned shortly after he'd left, along with Wendy. Wendy could tell something had happened between us, but I wouldn't tell her what that was. Whoever said "the truth will set you free," is a liar. It didn't set me free. If anything, it did the opposite. I'm forever a slave to the truth I've held captive all this time. The truth robbed me of the one shot I was ready to take when it came to falling in love, and now I was suffering the consequences. Suffering bad.

But I saw this coming. What good had I possibly imagined coming from this? You don't easily get over this sort of thing. What if the roles had been reversed and Denver had told me about something terrible he'd done to someone I'd loved? What then? Would I have it in me to forgive him?

The truth? I don't know. But Denver had sixteen years to process the loss of his sister. If I said something to my dad now, I would be blindsiding him. Yet, he deserves to know the truth about that day. As much as I can muster up the courage to tell him. It's a secret I've been holding onto for half of my life, and it's time I let it go. I promised myself no more running. It's time he finally knows the truth about his daughter.

I waited until we got home and he parked the car before bursting into tears. The dam had broken open, and I couldn't stop myself. After I calmed down a little bit I started at the beginning, relaying the details of the past I'd kept hidden from him for over a decade. At first he just listened, his eyes wide with concern, nodding here and there. It wasn't until I started crying again at the mention of finding Mom in her room that day, and what had happened with Genny that he lost it and a few tears slipped down his cheeks.

He didn't reprimand me, he didn't scream at me like I'd pictured him doing a thousand times—he reached across the driver's seat and held me. Held me like he had that day in my room when we'd both fallen apart and needed one another. This moment had been no different... we needed each other. *Life is hard, but being alone is harder.*

We both had been trying to go through life carrying the weight of our own grief, alone, when we could have held onto each other this whole time. How did we not see that? Why didn't I tell him sooner? I'm glad he knows now. It's like a huge weight has been lifted off my chest.

When we finally pulled apart and dried our eyes on napkins stashed in the console, he looked at me with his big, shiny eyes and said, "I love you. I loved you then, and I love you now." And that was it.

That was all that he said to me, and somehow it was enough. It was something he used to say to Mom when she was having a hard day. There's a deep comfort that resonates in me hearing him say the same thing to me. Because I know what he's saying without having to say it. He will always love me, no matter what. No matter what kinds of terrible things I've done in my past, and what kinds of mistakes I'll make in the future. He loves me, and that will never change.

THIS TIME when one of the doctors wanted to prescribe me something to help with my blackouts, I said yes. I don't think it'll solve all my problems, not even close, but maybe it could help take away at least one of them. I can't keep doing this on my own, and I'm done trying to.

My book is still scheduled to release next month and I'm not sure if I'm ready for it now that it's almost here. Even though it's barely been a week, Wendy has been the sweetest. She comes by every morning, and she lives clear on the other side of town. It's not exactly a quick drive over for her, yet she makes being here for me seem so effortless. Because for her, it probably is. She wants to be here for me, and as much as I can muster, I let her.

She always brings me coffee and a treat for later. Today, knowing how hard this day is for me, she brings me a little more than usual. Today she shows up with a mocha raspberry latte, chocolate-covered strawberries that look divine, and a new romance book I haven't read yet. She's too good to me, and I don't deserve her kindness after what came to light a week ago.

She stays for about an hour and then says she's meeting with a client and can pop back in later if I'd like. I thank her for everything, and she heads out.

I pop a strawberry into my mouth and then put the rest in the fridge to snack on later. Dad has a day planned with Deb. He asked me at least a thousand times if I was sure it was okay with me that he go out today. I reassured him a thousand times that I was fine. I know he's trying to be extra sensitive to me today, especially after I broke down to him recently, and I appreciate it.

But it's been sixteen years, and he's finally dating someone again. I want him to be happy, and I don't think that will happen if he stays here all day with me. Besides, I've noticed a change in him. Physically and emotionally. There are less bags underneath his eyes and his eyes have transformed from a dull-gray back to a shiny nickel. Dating has brought him back to life, he isn't simply going through the motions, he's out there living again. He deserves every bit of this.

Especially since I'm already in a funk. Not only because of what happened with Denver but because of what this day means to me. A constant reminder of what's missing. *Who* I'm missing.

They say that memories can fade with time, and I do believe that to be true. There are things I don't remember. Like learning how to ride a bike, or the time I broke my arm hanging upside down in a swing. And then other memories that won't ever fade no matter how much time has passed. They become a permanent part of you. A core memory. Wherever you go, they go. That is how it is with the memory of my mother.

Most parts I don't want to erase. Like all the times we'd spent together laughing, dancing, and acting like fools in our kitchen. In this kitchen. All of our day-camping trips and all the other holidays. Before she'd forever ruined this one for Dad and me. Honestly, I don't know if it's still ruined for him. It's not something we bring up or talk about. Not anymore. For a while, it seemed like it was all we'd talk about. It was all-consuming. But then, one day—like Dad moving her chair in here, the very mention of her name was not a part of our conversations. Like my name had stopped being a part of mine.

Phoenix died when my mother died, and she won't be coming back.

Dad, unfortunately, didn't get this memo and still calls me the nickname they both used often, Sweet P. I hate it and I love it, but I'm at a point now where I've decided to leave it alone. I don't want to take anything else away from my dad. I lost my mom, but he lost the love of his life. Well, maybe they weren't soulmates, but he did love her. I do know that.

Since Dad isn't here today I curl up in his spot on our couch. I snuck one more strawberry because they are just too good, and decided to start reading the novel Wendy had brought me. The front cover is super cute. It has an animated-looking couple holding hands with flowers and a bakery in the background. I'm sure it's a romantic comedy, but it's probably what I need right now. She knows me so well.

I'm barely finished with the first chapter when there's a soft knock on the front door. What in the world? Is Wendy back already? I told her I'd be fine today, and if I wasn't I'd text her. I'm not great, but really, I've been worse.

The knock comes again, this time a little louder. Okay, okay! I'm coming.

"Coming!" I shout as I find something to mark my page. I close my book and climb off the couch, making my way to the front door.

A blast of chilly air greets me in my flannel sweatpants and 90s band tee shirt. I haven't showered today, and I probably look hungover. I am not, by the way, but to the outside eye, you'd never be able to tell the difference from first impressions.

The person standing before me is every bit the opposite of how I look and feel. She's wearing a bright red sweater dotted with pink hearts all over, and light pink leggings to match. She looks like she walked out of a greeting card.

It takes me a moment to realize that it's Marvel. Standing here on my porch. What is she doing here?

"Oh, Marvel. Hi. I'm sorry," I say, shocked and confused. Did Denver send her here to remind me to stay away for good? Did I invite her here while I was still in the hospital? Parts of it are still a blur from that night. She'd been there with me when I'd passed out.

She folds her arms across her chest and softens her gaze. "No, don't be. I am sorry for barging in on you like this. I didn't have your number, but I found your address on our fridge. I hope you don't mind. Can I come in?"

Oh right, where are my manners? Still shocked at the sight of her, I wordlessly wave her in, and she gladly obliges. She takes her white, fuzzy boots off at the door and I peer outside. Sure enough, she drove here in her little white Sedan.

I offer to make her some coffee and she politely accepts. After I make both of us drinks, I bring them into the living room and sit with her on the couch.

She brings the warm mug to her lips and smiles. "Mm, this is good. What kind is it?"

"Oh, thank you. It's just a vanilla latte with a drizzle of honey. Nothing much," I say, chewing my lip. It's a drink I've started enjoying in more recent years. I can no longer smell the scent that my mom used to wear, but somehow, whenever I make this drink, it comforts me.

"Oh." She takes another sip. "Well, it's tasty. I like it."

I smile back at her. I don't know why she's here, but I've

missed her. She's so easy to be around, and I thoroughly enjoy her presence. Even if she reminds me of her dad, who may be off-limits permanently.

"Sorry," She says again, setting her mug down in her lap. She stares at it for a moment and then looks up at me.

She's sorry? What for?

"I should be asking you how you're doing, not about this delicious coffee! Sorry about that. How are you, Nicki? I mean, really?" she asks me, her voice soothing and gentle.

My first reaction is to wave her off like my mom used to do with me, but I stop myself. Instead, I pause. I want to answer her honestly.

And, honestly, I am feeling a little better, despite everything. At least the truth is out now.

"I am doing okay, I think. I mean, right now I am. After you leave that might change, but for now? I'm okay," I tell her.

"My Dad told me what happened," she says, our eyes meeting.

He did? How did that go? Does she hate me now, too?

I don't say anything in return. I turn to my drink, I need something else to focus on. But I'm still listening.

"And I don't think it's entirely your fault," she continues.

I must not be hearing her correctly, because it's absolutely my fault. My life may have been wrecked that day, but my mistake could have been avoided if I hadn't been so reckless myself. If I had only stayed home and waited for Dad to get there. Or, if I'd never gone to school at all that day. Spent the whole day with her, maybe she wouldn't have ended her life. Maybe she would be here with me sipping vanilla honey lattes. Maybe...

"What do you mean?" I ask, still not making eye contact.

"He said you'd mentioned something about running away from something that day. Don't think he missed that, Nicki. He heard every word you said."

Every word? This time I look up at her. I'm frustrated, but not at her. She wasn't a part of this, and none of this is her fault. "But he still walked out. He left. He's done."

"Yeah, he did. He was," she admits.

She's brave for coming here, but I'm not sure what she wants from me. What does she hope to gain from any of this? The damage has already been done.

"It took him time to admit it, but he also realizes that something is missing from your story. Something you didn't say."

She's right of course, but she doesn't know that. That part of the story is in the past, it doesn't matter anymore. She's gone.

"Well, there's nothing to say. What's done is done," I say into my cup as I take another long sip. The hot beverage usually calms my nerves, but this is getting me amped up. My blood is pumping as if I'm on a sugar high. Maybe I am.

"I think that's where you're wrong. We all have a story to tell, whether it's good or bad. I believe there is more to your story than you shared. Just like I know he wouldn't have walked out if he had only decided to share his *full* story with you," she says, looking me directly in the eyes.

Her crystal blue eyes pierce my dull pennies. They do not shine today, but she has me intrigued. There's more to the story? About him or his sister? What did he not tell me?

I'm assuming that his daughter knows this story herself? Is that why she's come here? To tell me the truth that her father has kept buried? Like I'd buried mine?

She must read this in my eyes, because she gently shakes her head no, finishing off her drink and placing it on the table.

"No, I didn't come here to tell you his. That's not my story to tell. It should come from him. But I want to hear the rest of yours first. Why were you out that night, Nicki? What were you doing out in the middle of a blizzard?" she asks, point blank.

This girl sure knows how to throw punches. She has guts, more than I do.

No running.

I turn to face her completely and tell her the rest of my story. Every little detail. Starting with my mom's birthday, to my complete and utter devastation when I'd found her at home, after walking home from school in the snow.

I broke in that moment. That day I lost not only my best friend but the only friend I'd ever truly had. In a matter of seconds, my entire world had split wide open. And when things break, so do I. I have a bad habit of trying to run when something goes wrong. So, I ran. Like I have plenty of other times, not knowing that this one time would be the one that I'd regret the most.

By the time I finish, we are both in tears. She leans across the couch and hugs me. I don't give out hugs freely, but right now I long for her warmth—her embrace. I let her arms wrap around me, just like I used to do with my mother on her really bad days. If only I had seen through those bad days and known then what they'd meant. I hadn't paid enough attention to the signs of her depression to know how serious it was, until it was too late.

I was too late.

She's the first to pull away. She reaches for a tissue on the coffee table and hands it to me. I blow my nose, unashamed, and look back at her.

"Nicki, I don't know how many you have told that heart-breaking story to... but I need you to hear this. I don't think you're a terrible person. You made a bad mistake, but we all do. Seriously, who hasn't? Don't—let me finish." She holds up a hand, and I swallow my arguments and let her continue.

"I realize not everyone's mistakes cost somebody else's life, I get that. But listen to me. You were only sixteen, Nicki, my age. You had witnessed the worst thing imaginable and did what you thought was best at that moment. And yeah, it turned out it wasn't. But it was an *accident*, Nicki. They said the storm was really bad and there were all kinds of accidents that day. His sister was not the only one... I can't imagine losing a parent like that. And I won't try to. But I don't think you can blame yourself for her death. She made that choice, just like you made the choice to drive away. Nicki, I forgive you."

She what? Did she not hear anything I just said? How can she after what I've done? The pain I've caused him and his family. And I tried to run from it. Who does that kind of thing? Me, apparently.

Coward. That's what I am. My mother ran away from her own life, and I ran away because of what she'd done. I'm not that different from her.

"I forgive you," she says again and takes both of my hands in hers. My hands are trembling and the tears I'd previously wiped away have returned.

"How? How can you? After everything?"

"Because we are human. And I think you deserve a second chance. Half of your life you got to spend with your mother, and the second half of it you've spent beating yourself up for a mistake you never forgave yourself for."

How could I possibly begin to forgive myself for this? What I've done can't be erased. It's too much. I cost somebody their life... all because I'd lost someone in mine. However, she is right about it being an accident. A horrible one at that, yet it had never been intentional. If I hadn't been out in the first place, and if I hadn't been trying to answer my phone... I don't even know how to forgive myself. Where would I even begin?

"I think Denver needs to hear this. Give him a second chance, and I think he will let you back in. Slowly, but I think he will come around."

I'm not so sure that's a good idea. Just when I'd gotten my hopes up about mending things, everything came to a crashing halt. One I don't think is fixable. I don't think my heart can handle another person walking out of my life. He's already done it once. I walked away first when he tried to fight for me, but I didn't let him. I should have though. Doesn't he deserve the same from me?

"He's never going to let me speak to him again," I say. Hoping that isn't true, but I don't see how it couldn't be. I dashed all hope of that away with the truth.

"I think once he hears the rest of your story, he will be more open to sharing his. Look, I'll try talking to him, but the monthly G&G meeting is next Thursday night. It's the last one he will be going to this year. I'll even give you a ride if Wendy can't. Give him another chance, and I think he'll do the same."

"And what if he doesn't?" I ask.

"Then at least you know you tried."

She's got a point there. She hugs me again and thanks me for sharing my story with her. I end up giving her the rest of the chocolate-coated strawberries before she leaves. She gladly takes them and promises to share them with her dad. I'm not ready for her to leave, but at the same time, I'd like some time to myself.

I close the door and turn off all the lights. I light a candle for Mom, her favorite vanilla scent, and I curl up in a ball on the couch and cry myself to sleep.

Then: Valentine's Day

I don't know how long I stay here like this. I don't know much of anything right now. The only thing I know is that Mom isn't waking up. I've pounded and screamed and fought and even yelled at God. Nobody heard my cries. Nobody but me and my mother's lifeless body. I should do something. I can't stay here. I'll either keep crying, screaming, or start throwing up. Or all three.

I should call 9-1-1—that's what I should do. That's what I should have done ten, fifteen, twenty minutes ago. I have no clue how long I've been like this, but I can't stay. She's still my mom, of course, but not really. It's not the same. I can't... I can't look at her and think of the mother I saw earlier this morning. My brain doesn't know how to go back there.

I shut her door behind me. Did I remember to turn the lights back off? Does it even matter? I should call Dad. He can call the police or whatever he needs to do. Or maybe he's already on his way home. Do dads have the same type of intuition that they say moms have? Maybe he can sense that something is terribly, terribly wrong. He'll be here soon. I have to believe that.

Maybe she's just passed out and someone can come and revive her. Some type of emergency crew, right? Isn't that what they are for? But she is ice cold and her heart isn't beating.

I'm starting to panic because I don't know what to do. My body is urging me to *move, move, move*—yet, I can't. I am paralyzed.

Suddenly, I can't remember where I left my phone. Did I leave it in the bathroom when I came home to take a shower? I am so selfish! If I hadn't taken a shower first thing, maybe she would have woken up. Maybe she would have been okay. I can't believe I didn't check there first. *What kind of daughter am I?*

I look like an insane person. After five minutes of pointless searching, I start shouting out the only thing that makes sense, because I can't be rational right now, I need to find my phone.

"Hey, Siri!" I start yelling in every room of the house. Again and again and again.

It's not until the tenth or eleventh time shouting nonsense in an empty house that a knot forms in my stomach. Please, no. Tell me I didn't. Tell me I did not leave it in my mother's room. I don't want to have to go back in there to get it. I can't face it all again. I can't face *her* again right now, but I don't think I have a choice.

I crack open the door and quickly scan the room for my phone. I call out to Siri one last time, and she chimes back in a chipper voice at my feet.

Oh, thank God! I quickly grab my phone and slam the door shut again.

I tap the screen and glance down at it. The time reads: **4:41** in dark, bold letters. There are no missed calls from Dad but one message instead. It reads:

DAD

> Hey, Sweet P. Excited for our big night tonight. I got caught in another meeting at work, but we should be wrapping up soon. Sorry, I'll be a little late. You can start dinner without me.

A little late. He promised me he'd be home early tonight. He'd said those exact words to me last night before I'd gone to bed. Not just because of the storm that was heading our way, but because of what this day meant. All that we'd had planned, together. He isn't on his way home. I am here alone.

Sweet P. Short for Sweet Phoenix. The last two words I'd ever hear come out of my mother's mouth. A name I never want to hear again.

I am so mad at him right now that I want to throw my phone. What's the point of having one if the people you are trying to get a hold of don't answer? Well, *screw him*!

Without a second thought, I grab a coat and Mom's keys from the entry table and get in her car. I'm crazy enough to go for a drive right now. 4:45. It's going to be getting dark out soon. The sun starts setting in about half an hour. But that's all I need. Scratch that. I don't have a clue what I need right now. I just know it isn't this. I can't be here alone. *Alone.* I have to go. And nobody is here to stop me from doing it.

THERE IS MORE snow on the ground than when I first came home, and more is coming down. The glow from the sun is barely visible, clouds are obstructing the view. I know it's probably really stupid to be driving in this kind of weather, but I couldn't stay at the house either. Not with Mom... My thoughts trail off. Void. Empty. Numb.

Today was supposed to be for *her*.

Today was her *birthday* celebration.

Today was a day that came around every freaking year. What was she *thinking*?!

I didn't even check to see if there were any pills left in the bottle beside her bed. I don't know if she'd left them there on purpose for someone to find, so nobody would question how she died. Or if she'd taken a few pills too many and hadn't meant to overdose. What if this was all a mistake and she'd never meant for anything terrible to happen? I'll spend the rest of my life wondering and always be left with questions I'll never get answers to. And my mother, a woman of many words, of many notes scattered about our home, left us with nothing. Silence. And that is far worse.

I increase the windshield wiper speed since the snow is coming down heavier now. 4:55. I should turn back around, but then what? I know I'm not thinking straight, but how can I possibly? I'm sixteen, and things like this should never happen. Especially on days like this. On a day when most of the world will be filled with love, romance, and chocolate candy hearts. My heart is nothing but the crushed up pieces at the bottom of the box. This day is forever ruined.

Should I have sucked it up and called the police? Yes. Should I have tried to call Dad again? Also, yes. But I didn't do either of those things, and here I am driving my mom's car, which smells just like her, in the middle of a snowstorm. Smart. I didn't think about what I was doing when I grabbed her keys and pulled out of our driveway. But then again, neither did Mom when it came to a lot of the things she did. Maybe we are more alike than I thought.

No, I take that back, *I am nothing like her.*

5:00. Any minute Dad will call me, and I can ask him what we should do. I'm terrified. I feel sick to my stomach, when normally at this time we'd be home preparing dinner. Not now. Not tonight. Maybe never. I don't think I can eat anything ever again.

5:05. Dad still hasn't called. I can't erase the image of my mother lying there cold in her bed. It's forever etched into my brain like a permanent scar.

I don't have a destination or a plan, I'm just driving. Seeing where the roads or fate takes me. Whichever. Or Dad to tell me to pull myself together and come back home. But he doesn't. I'm left to my own devices, and to be honest, I'm not too sure that I trust myself. I don't have anyone left *to* trust. So, instead, I'm doing what Mom taught me best—to run away.

I turn another corner. Nobody is crazy enough to be driving out in this but me. The roads are starting to get very slick, and every time I come to another stop I have to pump on my breaks. The sun is completely hidden from view now and the sky itself is shifting from a grayish blue to a velvety purple. 5:10. A sure sign this is completely stupid, and I should give up and go home. I can't remember what I'm trying to accomplish, but whatever it is, isn't working.

I don't realize I'm crying until I suddenly can't see. I swipe quickly at my eyes with my sleeve but it's no use, more continue to spill out. I don't have wipers on my eyelids, and can't swipe the tears away at full speed like I can the windshield. But even the car is having trouble keeping up with the snowfall now. 5:15.

Okay, I really should turn back now. I pump my brakes again, but I can feel my tires starting to slide around. This isn't good. I've driven in snow before, but not like this. Not *this* much. As much as I hate the thought of going home right now, I don't have any other choice.

Just then, something starts to make a vibrating sound in the seat next to me. I glance over to the passenger side and see the screen on my phone light up. 5:18. Someone is calling me. It takes me a moment before it fully registers. *Dad!* Dad is finally calling me.

I don't have a clue what I'm going to tell him, but I need him right now. He's all that I have left...

I lean across the seat, still pumping my brakes, and grab my phone. I sit back up in my seat and glance down, ready to swipe to answer—*crunch.*

Suddenly my ears are ringing. I hear the worst sound imaginable. I hear metal grinding against metal and it's ten times worse than fingers grating on a chalkboard. It makes my bones rattle. I grind my teeth so hard I start to taste blood. My head slams against the window and everything stops. Even the snow.

Everything in my world slows down to nothing. I can't see a thing, like I'm caught inside a snow globe. The snow is falling in a thick blanket outside, and there's a relentless waterfall of tears streaming down my face... no, this is so much worse than I could have imagined. My whole world is being shaken in every direction. Everything fades to black. I pray this time I won't wake up from this nightmare.

Now: February 20th

It's been almost two weeks since I left the hospital, and I'm still trying to wrap my head around everything. My new medication seems to be working out okay, and so far no side effects that I've noticed. If anything starts to seem off I'm sure Wendy or Dad will be the first to notice. They are both watching me closely, making sure that I'm okay. It's nice having them care so much, but at times I need my own space. Maybe it's time to start revisiting that idea once again—the idea of me finally moving out and living life in the real world, without my dad a couple of rooms over from me.

I don't have a clue what it's like, but I honestly think I could handle it. I'd move somewhere close, obviously, so I could still see Dad as often as I wanted or whenever he needed me. But we both have been living separate lives for over a decade now, the only thing we share when it comes to this house is occasional meals at the table. Dad does just fine on his own, and if things continue to progress with Deb, like I hope they will, he might eventually want her to move in with him. I don't want to be in the way of that happening. I'll add that to my to-do list for this weekend. Start looking for a new place to live.

I've replayed my conversation with Marvel many times in my head. She hasn't shown back up at my doorstep, and it's still been radio silence from Denver's end—not that I expect anything else from him. Not really. I checked my phone a few too many times and had messages I typed out and ready to send before I'd chicken out and delete the text. I don't want to push him. If and when he'll ever be ready to speak to me again, it has to be on his terms. He'll have to come to me this time.

"Are you sure you want to do this?" Wendy asks as she pulls into the familiar parking lot of Grieve and Grow. It feels like it's been ages since I'd run out of here during that first meeting. I haven't braved coming back, and tonight is the first night in months. I'm also nervous about how Denver will react. Did Marvel tell him I would be here, or will my presence be a complete surprise? Well, I'll find out soon enough.

I wipe my sweaty palms on the sides of my legs and take a deep breath and exhale. "Yes. I need to do this."

I ended up telling Wendy everything after I'd melted down two weeks ago. She's my closest friend, she deserves to know the truth. She took it all rather well and held me in her arms after I was finished. She made us both steaming cups of hot tea with honey and we stayed up past midnight talking about it all. I don't deserve her friendship one bit, but she's stuck by my side the longest. She didn't run when I told her the truth.

"Okay, hun. I'll be right here when it's over, okay? And if you end up needing to leave sooner because it's too much, I don't mind taking you home earlier. Whatever you need, I'm here for you." Tears brim her eyes, and I lean across the seat to steal a hug from her. I'm getting a little better at the whole affectionate thing. It's warm and inviting and says everything that I can't get out right now.

I push open the car door and climb out. I'm going in, I can do this. I can do the hard things. No running.

THE ROOM IS ALREADY full by the time I grab a few refreshments and find a seat. Quickly scanning the room, I recognize most of the same people from before. I'm just missing the one familiar face I was hoping to see. Denver isn't here yet. There's a chance he isn't coming at all. I don't know how much he knows, but Marvel said that he needs to hear the rest of my story, and I think she's right. I only gave him the second half of it. But the first part matters, too. He's not the only person that lost someone that day, and he doesn't know that.

Sam, the leader, sits down in her chair at the front of the circle and opens us up with a prayer. Did she pray last time? I must have missed it somehow, been too much in my head. I pop a piece of a cookie in my mouth to help calm my nerves and keep my hands busy. It's a short prayer, yet somehow it helps my body relax. I let it. I let her words about hope, peace, and courage wash over me, and suddenly I don't feel as afraid as when I first walked through the doors.

As soon as she says amen she starts going around the room and asking if anyone has anything new in their lives to share, any updates, or anything at all they'd like to talk about. The room is mostly quiet, but a few speak up. Someone named Pam shares about her husband that passed away earlier this year and how, for the first time, she was able to visit his grave. Somebody else says they lost their last grandparent and how that's been hard, but they are planning to take a family trip to their grandma's favorite place when she was a kid.

I swallow down the last little bit of nerves that are fighting their way up to the surface. I force them down and clear my throat. I'd like to go next.

I start with my name, my real one this time. Phoenix Jo Larrs. I tell everyone that's the name my mother gave me. Hearing that name now is painful, it brings up so many memories that I've tried to erase. Yet, I can never seem to. As I'm saying it again out loud, I wonder if it's the name I should be using. I've run from my own roots for so long, and I'm sick of running. Tonight will be a new starting point.

Sam lets me continue, so I do. I tell the entire group about my mother. About her highs and lows, her good days, and her bad days. I tell them about how she had always been the love of my life. I loved her with my entire being, and one day she ripped that all away from me—without my permission. The day she took her own life, she took a large chunk of me with her. I have never been the same, everything has changed. Dad is all I have left, and we barely speak to each other.

I decide not to share what else happened that day after I found my mother. Maybe not all secrets are meant to be shared, especially in a room full of strangers. I don't know who else may have lost someone in that way. Besides, the one person I wanted to hear all of this isn't here. He already knows the rest of the story anyway. He ran away as soon as I confessed. I'd been hurt, but I also expected that very thing to happen.

Sam thanks me, and I see several other heads nod in agreement after I finish.

"That was very brave of you to share with us, Nicki. How are you doing with all of this today?" she asks me.

"I'd like to start going by Phoenix again if that's okay. I shouldn't have taken that away from her, even though she isn't here anymore."

I've blamed her for sixteen years for taking a huge piece of me. Maybe that part of me will always be with her. But I'm not faultless either.

"Absolutely. I think she'd love that."

"And to answer your question. Honestly? Most days I don't feel like I'm okay. Most days I feel like I'm drowning. I miss her so much... everyday. But I am also grateful to still have my father with me. He's been so supportive of my writing career, and he really has taken great care of me. We became each other's everything when we were left with nothing. When I believed I deserved nothing after what I'd done. But if my father could still love me despite my past mistakes, maybe someday I can too.

"He's happy again, and I'm working towards that myself. One day at a time, baby steps. It's been sixteen years, but not a day goes by that I don't think about her. I will never stop loving her, even after what she did." And for the first time, I realize that's the truth.

Sam nods and thanks me again and they move on towards closing the meeting. I fight the urge to get up and leave. This was my fifth time telling my story in a week, and I was beginning to feel its weight. It was a lot. But I push through until the end before standing back up.

I help the rest of the group stack their chairs, overcome with emotion, yet relieved for having opened up again. The more times I retell my story, the easier it's starting to get. Little by little. Maybe this won't be the last time either. I can't help but feel disappointed that Denver hadn't heard any of it. The one night he was supposed to be here, he hadn't shown up, and now my chances of talking to him are running out. *If* he is even willing to listen to me. His words replay in my head like a broken record, *I'm sorry I met you.*

I grab my things and walk out of the double doors. I don't see the person standing right outside the doors and slam into their chest. On instinct, my palms instantly fly up in front of me, and I quickly realize my hands are on this *man's* chest. My gaze flicks up to the person towering over me and when I realize who it is I gasp. It's Denver. He *came*?

"Hey," he offers.

I search his eyes for anger or hatred at running into me like this, but I don't find either. Instead, I find something else. It's always something else. If I'm not mistaken it looks a little more like he's glad it was me that had run into him. Is he? No, that couldn't be. He said he wished he never met me. I remove my hands from his chest and stare down at the ground.

His hand reaches out and cups my chin, lifting my face back towards his. He's not a lot taller than me, and I can feel his warm breath against my face. Warm and sweet, like honey and cinnamon, and it makes my whole body tingle.

"Denver... what are you doing?" I barely breathe out. Suddenly, I feel a little self-conscious. Here we are in a public place, and anyone could walk right out of those doors any minute. He doesn't seem phased one bit.

"Is it true? Is all of that about your mom true?" he asks me, gently.

How much did he hear? Had he been here the whole time? Why hadn't he come in?

"Yes. It is." I say, unsure of what's about to happen next.

His eyes search mine and his soften. A complete turnaround from our last encounter at the hospital. I'm not understanding.

"I am so sorry... Really, I am. I had no idea. Why didn't you tell me?"

I sigh and step slightly away from him, giving us both a little space.

"I'm honestly not sure... I think because I thought you needed to know the other part first. I had just made the connection to your sister earlier that evening, and it was eating away at me. I couldn't continue being with you knowing something that big about that night. I'm so sorry that I blindsided you with that, but you deserved to know... you deserve a lot more than what I can give you," I say.

"Can we go somewhere else to talk, Phoenix?" he asks, using my full name. He used my birth name, the one my mother had chosen for me. The gesture is simple, yet sweet, and it isn't lost on me what it means for him to say that. I nod my head yes.

"I just need to let Wendy know, she's waiting for me outside." I gesture in that direction and he understands.

"Okay, I'll wait in my car for you. I won't run this time," he says, and I believe him.

I run out to Wendy's car and fill her in on the latest. She smiles and tells me this is a good sign. I hope she's right.

I find my way back to Denver's car while 90s band Keane's song *Somewhere Only We Know* plays in my head. Mom is here with me tonight, and I feel it. I look up towards the heavens and whisper, *Love you, Mom.*

42

Then: February 20th

Mom's funeral was on Monday, three days ago. Dad planned the entire thing, which I am grateful for. It is enough just waking up in the mornings, much less planning the most dreaded part about the end of someone's life. They tell you that life is short, but really, they have no idea.

To be honest, I don't remember much of it. My brain has been in a constant blurry state. Dad offers to take me out of school for a couple of weeks, but I know as soon as it's over I'll still have to face everyone. Might as well rip the Band-Aid off now and go. Besides, it keeps me away from home, and thinking about *her* and what she did in *there*.

At first, Dad and I barely look at each other.

Despite my protests about staying home, he's decided to take some time off work himself. Good for him. He never bothered to take enough time off for family vacations, but because Mom is no longer around anymore, he's allowed a "vacation." I know I'm being a bit harsh, but I'm not myself. How could I possibly be? And Dad doesn't know the other half of it. He doesn't know about *my* accident.

I don't have a clue how I made it home that day. When I think about it, I seriously consider it as some strange miracle. As though a guardian angel (maybe it was my mother, who knows) guided me back home. I do remember parking her car in the garage and being greeted by my wailing father as soon as I came in. It only took a moment to register that he'd found Mom the same way that I had. I'd been too mad at him for not answering any of my calls, so instead of speaking to him about where I'd been, I came home and shut myself in my room that night.

I didn't even come out when the police had come to talk to Dad and take Mom away from us. It made it all feel too real, too final. The police wanted to ask me some questions, but my father waved them off. He said if anything came up about my mother, he would give them a call. I don't think he ever called, because what was there to say? Her death had been no mystery.

She downed all of her sleeping pills along with all of her depression/anxiety pills. There is nothing left to question. It's plain and obvious. I'm not sure if this was worse or not, but she didn't leave a note of any kind. Nothing. My mother, with all of her lists and poems, couldn't find it in her to write a final goodbye. For that, I can never forgive her.

The big surprise we had planned for her birthday was her *new* book of poems. I'd taken her old journal and typed up every single one and bound them into a new cover Dad and I had designed. The front cover had a Phoenix bird, one of her favorite mythical creatures. Underneath the bird was her name typed out in a fancy, handwritten font. And now she'd never get the chance to see it, feel it, hold it. I'd been too late.

Since he's been home a lot more, he's attempted to cook a few meals. They aren't great, but they aren't terrible either. At least he is trying, it's more than I can say for myself.

Tonight's dish is classic spaghetti and meatballs. I can't even remember the last time I had this meal, probably when I was in elementary school and I'd been a super picky eater. It's not something Mom made when she was still alive. If she could only see us now, what would she say?

"I'm thinking about moving my position to work from home so I can be here for you more. Uh, I'm... I'm sorry I haven't been around as much as I should've been, kiddo," he says, slicing a meatball on his plate and taking a large bite.

I poke around at the food on my plate. I'm not really hungry. Everything makes me think of Mom, and it doesn't feel right eating without her. It's pathetic, but I can't help it. If she were here we would not be eating boxed noodles with a canned jar of tomato sauce poured over the top. Mom would have made noodles from scratch along with her rosemary vodka sauce and homemade meatballs.

I'm not sure what he expects me to say to him, so I say nothing at all. The silence between us is common anyway, he probably won't even notice. He does.

"Sweet P. Look at me. Please," he tries. His gray eyes look even more tired than before. The lines underneath his stone gray eyes are even more pronounced, deeper, fuller. I don't think he's slept much since he found Mom. I'm not sure how it's possible to sleep again... she looked so peaceful. I thought she'd been sleeping. I would give anything if she had only been asleep when I found her.

"Don't call me that," I say instead, ignoring the hurt look in his eyes.

"Do you want to talk about it?" he asks, and at this I look up at him.

"Talk about what?" I say flatly.

A sound like a sigh escapes his lips before he brings a hand to his mouth and clears his throat. "Your Mom. That day. You've shut yourself away in your room, and I've wanted to give you some space."

Space. That's a funny thing to say. He gives me plenty of space. Like I need even more of it right now, but that's not exactly fair of me. This time I put the distance between us. I have to.

I close my eyes. I don't want to be angry with him. He should have answered his phone sooner. He should have been home with me. There were a lot of 'should-haves' that day that turned out to be empty promises instead.

I don't answer him, not right away.

As if he can read my thoughts he says, "I should have been there. I should have picked up the phone and came to get you from school. You never should have walked yourself home. I should have seen Mom first, not you. Nobody should have to see their mother that way, and I wasn't here to protect you from that. I wasn't here... I wasn't..."

Dad's voice breaks, and for the first time ever he sits there and sobs in front of me. Big fat tears are rolling down his unshaven face. I can only recall seeing my dad cry twice in my life: the day of the funeral and right now.

At the sight of him burying his head into his hands, my eyes moisten too, and a single tear escapes. It's at this moment I realize something—or maybe I'm just remembering something I'd forgotten... Dad is broken too. I'm not the only person that broke when Mom died. He did too. He is hurting right here with me. I am not as alone as I feel.

I scoot out of my chair and walk around the table to him. His body is like a rollercoaster, heaving up and down with every breath he cries. I've never seen him cry this hard, and it only makes me want to hold him tighter. It's not just daughters that need to be held by their fathers; sometimes, it's the other way around.

I lean across his back with my arms draped around him in a bear hug, the warmest embrace I can manage. We stay like this for a while, until finally he starts to lift up, the tidal wave subsiding. I wipe my eyes on my sleeve and sit back down in my chair, watching him. Hoping he's okay.

"Dad?" I say softly. Gently. I don't want him to retreat back inside the shell he often hides in.

"I failed you that day, P. And I'm *so* sorry. So unbelievably sorry," he says, and I know full well that he means it. He means it with his whole heart.

I shake my head. "No, Dad. You didn't fail. It's no one's fault, okay?" That is mostly true. If I am allowed to be angry at anyone, it should be Mom. We wouldn't be sitting here having this conversation if she were still around. If she had only stuck around... but I can't go there right now.

He's not to blame. And he still has no idea what else happened that night. The terrible mistake I've made. I am not guiltless. I am to blame for my own wrongdoings. A sin he may never know.

He hesitates, but he nods his head in return. "Okay, Sweet P."

"Dad..." I say, quirking my eyebrow up at him. It takes him a minute to figure out what I'm talking about and then a tiny smile crosses his features.

"I'm sorry, it's a habit. I've always called you that."

"I know," I say, quietly averting his gaze, adding, "but so did Mom."

I don't have to look at him to know he now understands the weight of it. What hearing that name does to me every time he says it. But a small part of me doesn't want it to go away.

"Okay, I'll try my best not to use it. I want to be here for you, okay? I need you as much as you need me. Are you okay?" he asks.

"I'm fine," I lie. Neither of us are fine. I don't think we know how to be "fine," but nobody ever means it when they say it anyway.

He sighs and eats another bite. I stare down at my plate, poking and prodding, not eating.

"I know it's going to take us both some time to get there. Probably a long time. Just... know that I'm here okay? I'm not going anywhere," he says.

At this I look up at him, my eyes intense and angry. Like a

switch has been flicked on, suddenly the anger I'd pushed down is now bubbling up to the surface.

"Don't say that. Don't you dare say that to me. Mom used to promise me things all the time, and she hardly kept any of them. So don't you dare promise me you won't leave me too. Nothing bad will ever happen to you, and I won't be left alone to fend for myself. Don't," I spit out, rising from the table.

His eyes flash something I've never seen before, but he just sits there, unmoving. Stunned by my outburst.

"I'm not promising anything..." he says carefully, cautiously, afraid of me.

I'm afraid of myself.

"But as long as I'm able to, Lord-willing, I will be here for you. That, I can promise."

I excuse myself and leave the room. I spend the rest of the night reading through Mom's journal. I fall asleep reading the last poem she ever wrote, one that she'd written for me. The one I've read so many times I know it by heart.

"Phoenix"
Eyes of fire, full of desire
My little girl this is for you
You're my spitfire, my ride or die
I'd do anything for you.

You take hold of the pen
Like nobody I've seen
And you dream
Higher than the moonbeams.

Light of my life

You light up my world
If only I could keep you
In it forever.

My little girl
Stay young, stay bold
With wings like a phoenix
And a heart made of gold.

Now: February 20th

His car smells exactly the way I remember it, pine and cinnamon—like Christmas. It doesn't take long to warm up. It's still fairly chilly out in late February, and I am fully enjoying the heated seats feature. If I ever muster up the courage to drive again, it'll be in a car with heated seats.

"So, how much of what I said tonight did you hear?" I ask, holding my hands out in front of the heater vents. We haven't left the parking lot yet, maybe he was just planning to sit here so we could talk and then drive me home later. I'm not sure, but even after all that's happened between us I feel safe with him. I always have.

"All of it," he says back.

I can feel his gaze on me and my cheeks heat.

"I was running late tonight, and then I saw you in there sharing with the group. I had no idea you'd even be here tonight, and I didn't want to walk in and interrupt you. But I heard everything."

I nod and fold my hands in my lap. So maybe Marvel hasn't said anything after all. Maybe she just wanted to hear things from my side. Denver and I are both adults and can make these kinds of decisions for ourselves and she understands that. For her age, she's really smart and mature. There's silence between us, but it doesn't feel uncomfortable. It's okay.

He continues, "I am sorry about what happened to her. I can't even imagine losing someone I love like that."

I glance over and our eyes meet. I don't look away. I don't want to.

"Yeah, me too. I loved her a lot, and I'm so sorry about what happened that day... I shouldn't have ever run from it. I didn't realize what had happened until weeks later when I saw the article about it in my dad's paper. I'd been completely out of sorts, and I was having a lot of blackouts. It was a very difficult, confusing time. Denver, I never meant to destroy your family that way. I cannot tell you how truly sorry I am... For everything," I barely manage to get out.

He surprises me by reaching across the seat and swiping a tear that has escaped down my cheek. It's a simple gesture, but his touch is tender and gentle, and I find myself craving more of it. His finger traces a soft line down my cheek and finds a loose piece of hair that he tucks behind my ear. Who is this guy, and how can he be sitting here with me right now? Knowing what I've done. The pain I have caused him and his entire family. They have no idea.

"It's in the past, Phoenix," he says my name again.

I love the way my name sounds coming from him. I want to hear him say it again. Why did he ask me to come here and talk to him? Is he ending things once and for all? I've handled far worse news. But I'm also not sure how well I can handle another goodbye right now if that's what this is.

He continues, "It happened a long time ago... I'm sorry I ran out on you. I just couldn't be in there with you. I needed a little bit of time to process everything. It hasn't been brought up in *years*. But, I am glad that you did, because there's something I haven't told you."

He removes his hand from my face and takes my hand in his. I've never held anyone else's hands but my mom's... but right now, holding onto Denver's like this, I don't ever want to let him go.

Please, don't let me go this time. Stay, stay, stay.

"My sister and I were twelve years apart. My mom had a nasty divorce when I was younger and they'd been separated most of my life. I have no ties whatsoever to my biological dad. She'd been dating a new guy for a while, and they were getting pretty serious. He'd talked about moving in with us. He was okay, I guess. Mom got pregnant before they got married. He ran as soon as Genny was born."

Genny... He'd said her name the same night I'd run out of the group. Her name had been the reason I'd run in the first place. I hadn't stayed to listen to the rest, I thought I knew enough. But I'd been too wrapped up in my pain to stay for his.

I wanted to be here for it now.

"That's terrible..." I say and he nods. I relate to it well. All I've ever done is run away. Not anymore. I am done trying to escape from the things I can't escape from.

"Mom raised us by herself most of our lives. It was all we knew, and she was a great mother. She passed five years ago from cancer. Anyway, I got married right out of high school. She was the only girl I ever fell for, and at the time, I thought she was my forever. Funny how forever can quickly shatter," he says.

Don't I know that truth all too well.

"On the day of that terrible snowstorm, my wife went into labor with Marvel. We barely made it to the hospital in time. Genny called after school, complaining that she was stuck at home by herself and begging me to let her come to the hospital. But I told her no. Marvel hadn't been born yet, Genny was just eager to meet her.

"The winds had picked up on our way, and the hospital was clear across town. I knew Mom would be getting off work at five, and I'd told Genny she could sled out in the front yard while she waited for her. I hated crushing her spirits about meeting her baby niece for the first time, but Mom and Genny would get to see the baby as soon as we made it back home. It was awful telling her no at the time, but I had no idea it'd be the last thing I ever said to my baby sister.

"Mom wasn't back from work yet when I told Genny she could play in the yard. And, well, you know the rest..."

I am so ridden with guilt that, without thinking, I try jerking my hand out of his grasp, but he holds me there. He doesn't let me run, I look up at him and his expression whispers *stay*.

"For years I blamed myself for what happened. If I had let her come to the hospital the day Marvel was born, maybe she'd still be here. I could have called her a cab or had a buddy from work pick her up, but I did none of those things. Instead, I'd told her to stay home and play in the yard. I'd told my sister no the day my baby girl was born, and gave her permission to do the thing that killed her. I carried that guilt with me for years. Sometimes, I still do. Yes, I was mad that someone would be careless enough to drive off. But I blamed myself *more*."

I can't help the tears that are falling now. Neither of us makes a move to wipe each other's tears, we simply let them fall. I had no idea about his daughter being born the same day his sister died, at *my* hands. And yet, here he is telling me that he blames himself for her accident more than he blames me. How can that even be possible?

"It's why I became an EMT. I wasn't able to save my sister, but I want to save others if I can. Every person that I help reminds me of her in some way. We may have been over a decade apart, but she was all I had, and she meant everything to me. Every day, I live for her. I don't hate you, Phoenix. I was hurt, yes. I might still be if I'm being fully honest. But I don't hate you. I don't think I could ever hate you.

"For the longest time, it was hard looking at my daughter, who was young, bright, and perfectly healthy, and not feeling this terrible guilt that maybe I didn't deserve her. She was too good for me, and I wasn't good enough. Here I was, twenty-four at the time, with a newborn to take care of, while grieving the loss of my sister. Those were the hardest years of my life. I started drinking, and for two years straight, I didn't stop. I was living in a nightmare. Before long, my ex threatened divorce. I pulled my act together for my daughter, but soon realized that I was no longer in love with my wife. Our marriage and relationship wasn't the same as it had been before. We both knew it, but she came to the realization sooner—I'm sure my drinking had been a big factor that tipped the scale.

"We did the back-and-forth thing for a while, but even that got to be too much. By the time Marvel was four and starting preschool, Evelyn left town and never came back. I hadn't touched alcohol for two years and will never touch it again. I haven't to this day. Marvel stayed with me full-time, but would visit her mother during the holidays. After a while, that changed and she only wanted our daughter during the summer. She's a teacher and has summers off. I've only been on a few dates since my separation, and nothing has been serious. Not everyone wants a single dad with a daughter, you know?" He laughs a little at that, and it's so good to see him smile again.

More. I want more.

I laugh a little too. I want us to be okay, but I have no idea where we stand right now. I'm letting him call the shots. I'm ready for anything, but I don't know if he is. For all I know, he's slowly prepping my heart for heartbreak. So much for ripping off the Band-Aid this time.

"I do," I say softly, unsure if he's heard me. Hoping maybe he didn't.

He did. He wipes his own eyes with the back of his hand before touching my cheek again.

"I haven't felt anything toward anyone for the longest time... until I met you," he says, gently stroking my cheek.

It feels so good, and I'm tempted to lean into his hand, but I don't. *I'm sorry I met you* keeps playing on repeat in my head.

Had he meant it? Does he mean everything he's saying now?

"I would like to try and make this work if you do. But you'd have to promise me something first," he says.

I slowly shake my head. I don't know what he has in mind, but I don't make promises. Promises are too easy to break. And I don't want to break whatever he's asking of me.

"I can't promise you anything, Denver. I can't promise you that I'll be perfect and won't screw something up. Because I'm sure that I will. I can't promise that I'll always show up when I'm supposed to or even be good girlfriend material, because trust me, I'm not—" He puts two fingers against my lips, shushing me.

I smile through them. What is he doing?

"I'm not asking you to promise any of those things. I'm only asking that you'll give me another chance," he offers. He takes his fingers away and cups my chin, tilting my head closer to his.

I can't help but look at his lips. Full and perfect, and I want to kiss them. More than anything, I would love a second chance with him.

"I should be asking you that question. You want to give *me* another chance? After everything I've done?" I choke out, fighting tears again.

He nods, without hesitation. "Yes, after everything. I'm not perfect either. I've got my share of sins too. I can share all of them with you sometime, but that would take up another evening. So, what do you say, Phoenix?" he asks me again.

I do something bold. Something I've never done before. Something completely out of character. I place my hands on either side of his face, feeling the soft prickle of his stubble between my fingertips, and I kiss this beautiful, wonderful man. *Mine.* He's mine. This isn't the end after all. Maybe this is the precise place where we can begin again.

Dad and I continue going through the motions. After three weeks of grinding my teeth through school, Dad decided to pull me out. At first, I refused. I did not want to take online classes. School still sucked, but at least I wasn't home. It had been a much-needed distraction, but my grades were starting to slip, and I had trouble focusing in class. Who could blame me though? The teachers wanted to do whatever they could to help me, but I had stopped caring altogether. Dad picked up on this quicker than they did and pulled me out, which surprised me. He'd never seemed to notice me before.

Our lives have been divided into Befores and Afters. Before Mom died... I loved reading and writing, but now I can't pick up a book or a pen. Before Mom died... I had what I thought was my best friend for life—now, I have no one.

After... our family fell apart. After... we became empty shells, barely living. After... We forgot who we once were because this new way of life overtook everything else. One day you wake up and can't remember what it was like before. Because that felt like a daydream, and this is reality.

I peel myself out of my thoughts and focus back on Dad. He's been more attentive than he's ever been. It's kind of nice, but it's also strange.

He offers me a deal. Not a promise, he says, but a deal. Okay, I'm listening. If I start bringing my grades up at home, he'll find me an online school where I can complete my courses and still graduate by next summer. It's an accelerated online program and I'll be able to graduate early. He'll also let me start doing my schoolwork at our local library. I think it's a great idea and eagerly shake with him on it.

I'm not quite there yet, but I'm hoping soon he'll see enough improvement that I can at least work on assignments somewhere else. I'd say yes to doing homework just about anywhere. Anywhere but here.

Dad surprises me when he comes home with a new desk one day. He'd seen a listing for it in the local paper and had picked it up for me so I have a new space to work and study. And also write. I haven't written anything new since Mom's death, but eventually, I'd like to begin again.

I can see that Dad meant what he said to me, about wanting to be here for me and take care of me. I haven't exactly doubted him, but I'd never seen it play out either. So far, he's kept his word.

Even though I'm not part of the public school system anymore, Dad has built us an unofficial "spring break." It feels a bit too soon to be thinking about going somewhere, but I think we both need it. We've been stuck in this place for far too long, and without Mom here, things aren't quite the same. They aren't the same at all. Dad keeps trying his hand at new recipes, which end in failure, and we end up ordering food. I miss cooking, but it reminds me too much of her. I simply can't right now. Maybe someday, but not today.

It's two p.m. in the afternoon when Dad mentions going somewhere again, and this time I don't make untimely jokes, I listen. I'm ready for a break as much as he is. He could tell me we are going to spend a week at a farm and I'd say okay. Anywhere but here. The house feels hollow and lifeless without her, and we both sense that. It'll probably feel the same as soon as we return, but at least we get a break from here for a little while.

"So, when are we leaving?" I ask, closing my laptop on the kitchen table. I've been working here today and have completed all my assignments.

"Next weekend has a spot open, but they fill up fast, so we will need to reserve our place today."

Wow that soon, huh?

"Where are we going?" I ask, busying myself with gathering up my spread of supplies along the table. I've got a notebook, a calculator, a dictionary, and my laptop.

"Uh, I was thinking maybe we'd go to Sally's," he says.

I instantly stop what I'm doing and stare up at him. I blink a few times before I get that he's not joking. He's being serious right now.

"Sally's... as in Sally's in the Park?" I ask, incredulous.

He nods. "Yep, that's it. I know what you're thinking right now. Don't give me that look, P."

If he thinks we are spending a long weekend or even a week at that state park, he's lost his mind. I've changed my mind. If that's where he wants to go, I'm better off staying here—alone. *I'll come in and kiss you goodnight when I get home, okay? I need some time alone.* My mother's voice rings in my ears. I close my eyes and will her presence away from me.

"That was Mom's place," I say quietly, fidgeting with a peeling piece of paint on the edge of the table.

"I know... and that's why I think it'd be special if we went there. We've never camped there before, only the day camps. Come on, it would be a great way to honor her memory, while also trying to make some new ones."

I know he means well, but really. Any place else. Say the word and I'll go. Anywhere else. Please.

"I don't want to go there, Dad. Sorry," I say, avoiding a glance at the hurt look I know is in his eyes. I'm not trying to be mean. I don't want to hurt his feelings, but it's obvious that is exactly what I'm doing.

"Okay..." he says, defeat laced in his voice.

I don't mean to crush his spirit, but I also don't want to be in the very place that screams her name. I'm trying to do the very opposite.

"Remember last summer when Mom and I went to California?" I ask.

He lifts an eyebrow at me, unsure of where I'm going with this.

"Yes, of course. Why?"

"Well, I never really asked you, but does Mom have a sister that lives there?"

He stares at me blankly, as if I'm speaking a foreign language. Maybe I am. I could be speaking in tongues for all I know.

"What? You're asking me if Mom has a sister?"

"Yes."

"Uhhh, well I don't know. She never mentioned anyone living there."

I've asked before, but Mom always avoided the topic and changed the subject. It seems like a lifetime ago now. While we're here I may as well ask now.

"What happened to Mom's family, Dad? I mean, she never talked about them, but she had one right?"

"Of course. Everybody does. I never met them. She did mention having siblings once, but not any of their names. When she'd gotten pregnant in college, dropped out, and married her college professor her family removed her name from their family entirely. They were ashamed of her behavior and wanted nothing to do with her. Or me. They were ashamed she'd chosen *me.* She was pretty much on her own the moment we got together. So, she may have a sister, but I've never met her. I was never given a chance to meet anyone from her family. That's something I'll carry with me forever."

His eyes look down as he says this, and I want to reach out and grab his hand, to let him know that I don't resent him for it. I understand him better because of it. But I don't move.

"Then what did she tell you we were doing in Cali the whole time?" I ask, truly curious and also trying to steer the conversation somewhere lighter.

"Oh." He chuckles.

I haven't heard him laugh in ages. I'd almost forgotten what it sounded like. I wished he'd do it more often.

"She said she was taking you to the beach so you could finally get some sunshine and wind in your hair." He smiles at me, tears in his eyes at the memory. It had only been last summer, but we both remember it like it happened yesterday.

This time it's my turn to laugh. I seriously can't with that woman, my mother—always keeping us on our toes. Always wondering what is coming next.

"Well, did you get a chance to do that?" he asks me.

I smile back and nod my head. "Well, I don't know what she was doing, but yes, I got plenty of sunshine and wind in my hair. Mom was off with somebody that might have been her sister. But I guess we'll never really know."

"No, I guess we won't." He agrees.

"You know what, you're right. Let's go to Sally's. That would have meant a lot to her," I say, meaning it.

"Really? Because if you would rather go someplace else—" For the first time in what feels like forever, his dull-gray eyes shimmer with something I'd almost forgotten... hope.

I don't let him finish. "No, Dad. It's perfect. I'll get started making a list of all the items we are going to need. It's going to be great."

And for the first time in weeks, I believe that. Of course, I miss Mom. I miss her so bad that every time I think of her—smell her around the house or see something of hers lying around as though she's just out on one of her errands and will be home soon—my chest throbs with an ache so deep that sometimes I worry it's possible for my heart to have split into two pieces. It's not an ache that will go away. It might fade with time, but I'm not convinced that it ever will.

I am looking forward to spending some time with Dad. I wish it could have happened more. Happened sooner. When we were still a whole family. But we never really were whole to begin with, were we? I've quickly learned that if something happens *eventually* that is better than never happening at all—and here we are. At the end of the day, sometimes little girls still need their daddies.

45

Now: March 14th

I t's a Friday evening, and Wendy has been here the last hour and a half running through everything with me one last time before my big book release. Well, I like to tell her it's *our* big release because she does a ton of work behind the scenes. She helps bring the magic of the story to life. I couldn't have gotten this far without her.

The last book of *The Honey Sisters* trilogy officially releases a week from tomorrow. It's been a long journey, and I can't believe it's finally coming to an end. I haven't started working on anything else yet. I might even be taking a small break, but I haven't decided yet. We'll see.

The series is based on some of the silly adventures me and my mom used to go on. Like all the times we'd play hooky during school, and that time she drove us out to California to meet a sister I'm not sure was her sister after all. My story is fictionalized following a set of three sisters who grew up apart and through different and crazy circumstances they were brought back together. Each story is written from a different sister's point of view. Honey is their last name, and by the end, they all decide to start a honey business together on a farm they'd grown up on during some part of their lives. It's a beautiful story that I poured my heart and soul into, and I'm finally ready to share it with the rest of the world.

Not that long ago, a local filmmaker, who partners with somebody in LA, expressed interest in my trilogy and offered me a studio deal if I ever wanted to turn this into something big, like a TV show. I didn't exactly decline, but I haven't said yes yet, either. I need time to decide. Luckily, it's somebody Wendy and I both know and it'll be easy to get back in touch with them if I ever decide that's something I want to pursue. Let's see how this last book kicks off first and go from there.

"Have you thought any more about it?" Wendy asks me now. We are sitting on the floor by the couch in the living room.

My thoughts must have wandered off because I missed what she asked me.

"Thought about what?" I ask absentmindedly as I flip through the pages of my novel. The proof copy came in about a month ago. Wendy surprised me with a special edition copy of my novel before its release date, and I'm holding it in my hands for the first time. I can't stop turning it over and flipping through the pages. Needless to say, it might be my favorite book yet. Anytime a new release of mine hits the shelves, it automatically becomes my new favorite. Not to mention, it's also a bit of a distraction.

"About signing again at Books and Beyond. They want you to come back, Nicki. I mean Phoenix. Sorry, I'm still getting used to calling you by your real name," she says, blushing.

Oh, right. That. The thought of doing another signing terrifies me. Then another idea strikes me.

"Actually, I think I'd like to do it somewhere else," I say, setting my book down in my lap and looking over at her. She's sitting with her legs crossed and a binder in her lap. She's always been over-the-top organized when it comes to everything, and I'm super grateful.

"Oh, yeah? Where's that?" she questions, curious.

"At G&G," I say with a straight face. The idea just came to me, but I've decided to run with it for the moment. See what she thinks. And by the funny look on her face, she can't tell if I'm serious or not.

"I'm serious, I think it would be the perfect place to do my next book signing. Not during group, of course. Those meetings are special, and I wouldn't want to stomp over that. But I think if they are invited, it might be something cool for them." Her eyes meet mine and she nods, understanding but slightly skeptical.

She leans over and gives my knee a soft squeeze. "I am still so proud of you for what you did last time you were there. That was so brave, and I don't think I could have done it. I wouldn't have. I would have walked out before I'd been able to get any words out."

She lost her mom at a young age to cancer, and while it's not the same as what happened to mine, she knows what it feels like to grow up without a mom.

"Thank you," I say quietly. "I wanted to. A few times. Walk out. But I didn't. That's the thing about being brave. It's pushing through, especially when everything in you is screaming the opposite. I'm glad I didn't."

At this, she wiggles her eyebrows, and I don't know where she's about to steer us, but it can't be good. There's a mischievous gleam in her eyes.

"And then you met up with a certain someone..." She playfully hits my arm like we are teenagers gossiping about boys.

I *feel* like a teenager again, remembering the times I'd done this very thing with my mom. I smile at the familiar memory.

"Yes, I did," I say.

"How's that going, by the way? I meant to ask." She leans back into the couch and grabs a blanket from nearby, wrapping it around herself.

"Really well, I think. It's been almost a month. Can you believe it?"

"No, I can't. That's amazing. He seems good for you," she says.

"Yeah, thanks. I think so too. We are taking things slow, but we're both okay with that since neither of us has much experience when it comes to dating and relationships. Honestly, he's one of the most patient people I've ever met."

"Yeah, it sure seems that way. Good for you. You deserve this."

"You think so?" I ask. For the longest time, I convinced myself of the opposite. I never thought I'd be capable of loving somebody else. If I was lucky enough to find somebody, I didn't think they'd stick around. It's still fairly early and things can change, but we are taking things day by day, moment by moment, and seeing where that takes us.

"I know so. It just feels right. Like this could be it." She's always been the more optimistic out of the two of us, and I hope she's right.

"I sure hope so. He's coming with me to apartment shop tomorrow."

"Oh? Is he really?" She's doing that crazy eyebrow thing at me again. Stop it.

"It's not like that. He hasn't asked me to move in with him yet." I feel my cheeks turn pink.

"No? Darn," she says, casually pretending to check her nails.

"He offered to help me look around. He knows of some good apartment complexes and helped arrange appointments for me. Plus, he doesn't mind chauffeuring me around."

"Oh, alright. But as soon as you get the keys I want to help you move in and get all set up. I think this is a really big step for you, and I want to be there any way that I can. You're a good friend, don't sell yourself short."

Friend. I do sell myself short, too often. She's the best. She's turning me into a mushball. Any second I'm going to melt at our feet.

"Thank you. That's kind of you, Wendy."

"Of course, I'm more than happy to help. The girls would love to come too. They are really big into decorating their rooms right now."

I laugh at this. I'm sure they are.

"Good luck tomorrow. I know it's tough picking out a new place, especially knowing that it's not a part of your mom's story. But I think you've been living in her shadow for far too long now, and it's time you start living yours."

She's right. I know she is. I've been living on my own for years, but not really. This isn't the same. It's time I do this for myself.

"You're right. It's been time for a long time, but I finally feel ready to take this leap."

"I'm so freaking proud of you," she says, her eyes blurring.

"Come here," I offer, holding out both of my arms to her.

We embrace and wipe our eyes as we draw back.

"I think the G&G location is a great idea. But it is a little last minute and I'll need to contact them ASAP to see if they can help make this happen."

I have all the confidence in the world that she will, and even if it doesn't work out that's okay too. I know with Wendy on my side everything will turn out perfect, no matter what.

46

Then: July 12th, 17 years ago
"Girls' Trip"

Mom never mentions anything about her upbringing. She told me once that both of her parents were deceased and she's never mentioned any siblings, cousins, or anyone. When I was younger I'd ask why she doesn't like to talk about her past, and she usually responded with big arm circles in the air, waving me and my questions away. *We don't need to live in the past, silly. We are living in the present. The past doesn't matter.*

I'm not so sure that's the truth though. The past shapes everything we are. For better or worse. Sometimes I feel like I know her better than anyone. After all, she's the only real friend I've ever had. But when it comes to something simple, like if we were similar as kids, I wouldn't have a clue. Because my mom only lives in forward motion, never looking back.

I can't recall the last time we took a vacation. We've never ventured too far outside of our cozy town, Atlas Creek. Except for the few hiking trips we've made. But they are always day trips, never overnight stays. Some could say my parents shelter me, and maybe that's true. But I've never resented them for it. I'm a bit of a homebody myself. I don't mind though.

So, on a Saturday morning in early July, when Mom tells me over IHOP pancakes that we are packing our bags when we get home to drive all the way to California, I nearly choke. She can't be serious. Only, she one thousand percent is. Dad can't go, just us girls.

Girls' Day. For real this time.

She's in one of her playful moods, and I don't want to burst her bubble, but I need to know more about what exactly she's planning for us. We've never even driven out of the state, and why California?

After we finish our breakfast and hurry home, she immediately follows me into my room. She's never in my room, and yet here she is going through my closet, tossing shirt after shirt at me to stuff inside my suitcase. A lump sits in my stomach, and I can't help but feel like maybe this isn't such a good idea.

"Mom... why are we doing this?" I tread carefully as I slowly fold the shirts she's tossing at me, making no move to add them into my suitcase, yet.

She throws another shirt into the air and I catch it. She laughs in return. "Really, P? We've always dreamed of going somewhere like this together, just you and me. It's going to be so much fun. It'll be warm and sunny, and we can spend all day at the beach. The *beach!* Can you imagine it?"

This time she turns around and faces me. Hands on her hips. "Don't tell me you don't want to go?" She challenges me.

I know better than to challenge her when she's like this. Yet I can't push away the nagging feeling inside. I feel it in my very soul.

I sigh and set another folded shirt aside. "We've never gone anywhere that far before, and I hate to leave Dad behind... Are you sure he can't come along too?" What I should also be asking is if

Dad knows the details of Mom's plans for this trip, because so far she hasn't given me much—which is typical, but still.

"Fine, P. Don't go. I'm still going though. My bags are already packed. I was only trying to help, but if you don't like the idea, then stay here." She throws her hands in the air and starts to walk out of my room.

Panic suddenly seizes me. She has been a little on edge the last couple of days. I can't quite put my finger on it, yet she seems jumpy and quick to make decisions. Like right now. Sometimes she disappears during the day for hours, and to be frank, I don't know that I can fully trust her judgment.

This time she'll be gone for at least three weeks... I can't let her do this on her own. I'm afraid if I let her go this time—she won't come back. I can't let that happen. I leap off my bed, some of the folded shirts crashing to the ground, and I throw my arms around her. We rarely touch, but this time I do. I hug her, tears welling in my eyes, and I don't let her go.

"Mom, I want to go. I'll go with you," I whisper into her soft hair that smells of vanilla and honey. She wraps her arms around me softly and kisses the top of my head. She doesn't say anything else, but she doesn't have to. We are going to California for three weeks. Without Dad. But at least she won't be alone. Neither of us will be.

I was shocked when Dad said we could go. He didn't put up a fight, but he made sure I had my phone with me. I'm a fifteen-year-old girl, of course I wouldn't go anywhere without my phone. I don't text a ton, but I made a few friends towards the end of the school year that I message here and there. Dad hugged me goodbye and reminded me that he would be no more than a phone call away.

TURNS out Mom has a sister who has been living in Cali for the past seven years. They just reconnected (no idea how) and she invited us to come stay with her. I am excited to meet my aunt. We have a family after all. Who knew?

I can't help but wonder if this aunt, who is a stranger to me, isn't a stranger to Mom too. Maybe she's the reason for Mom disappearing. Mom would never admit anything outright though. She would just deny, deny, deny.

My aunt lives within walking distance of the beach, so that's nice. She's shorter than my mom and has lighter hair and eyes. Her name is Margaret, but she insists I call her Margie. If I knew better, I'd say they weren't sisters at all. But I don't know that for a fact, and I don't want to ruin this trip for either one of them. I can't squash Mom's "Girl Trip," even though when she'd said that I'd assumed it meant *us*. Not some long-lost sister she's never once mentioned before.

Who knows, maybe Mom is telling the truth about her. Maybe this doesn't have to make sense. Maybe it just is. Mom doesn't go into details about her past, and maybe Margie is part of that past. For the sake of this trip, I won't question it. Sister or not, in the end, it doesn't matter that much. As long as it makes Mom happy coming here, I'm on board with it.

Margie, my "aunt," cooks for us the first two nights, and then something unexpected happens. Mom wakes me up early on the third morning to announce that she and her sister are going into town for the day. She doesn't ask me to tag along but says there is plenty of food in the kitchen, TV I can watch, or I can spend the day at the beach. She tells me not to wait around for them, that they will probably return late. The awful feeling in my stomach returns, but I just nod and say okay. What else can I do? Beg her to let me tag along? Maybe, but I don't.

I find leftover lobster mac in the fridge and reheat it for lunch. I decide to spend my day at the beach. I bring along a journal and a novel. I read for two hours straight and then start working on a story until sunset. I head back to my aunt's beach house, but it's empty. I don't know what time they return, I'm already asleep.

The next morning Mom greets me the same way. This time they are checking out antique shops and shopping in local stores. She promises to buy me something and bring it back for me but again doesn't extend the invitation.

I can't help but be a little disappointed, but I don't mind the solitude. It's nothing I'm not used to, besides I enjoy listening to the sound of the waves crashing along the shore.

It goes on like this for the rest of the vacation. Mom had said we'd be here for three weeks, and miraculously, she kept her word. Three weeks to the day, we start the long drive back home. She came home with all sorts of new things. Totes full of books, paintings, and small pieces of furniture she is able to stuff into her small car.

Music blaring over the speakers, windows cracked, she yells over to me from the driver's seat, "Did you have a wonderful time in Cali, Sweet P?"

I can hardly hear her, but instead of reaching for the volume dial, I shout back, "Yeah, it was nice."

"Nice," she repeats.

I can't tell if my lack of embellishment has upset her.

"I enjoyed the beach, Mom," I try again.

"It was nice, wasn't it?" she says more to herself than to me, and that seems to satisfy her. She leans back in her seat. I think for her this has honestly been a dream vacation. In her eyes, she'd done nothing wrong.

The next time we stop and fill up with gas she asks me to drive for a while so she can rest. I say okay and drive for five hours straight while she sleeps the entire time. This trip was far from perfect, but I am glad I came. Because at least this way, I know she's coming home with me.

Now: March 15th

I end the call and shake my head. Wendy had sent an email to Sam, the director at Grieve and Grow, with details about my upcoming book release. We hadn't heard anything back this morning, and by noon I'd decided to give her a call. Sometimes all it takes is a simple person-to-person conversation. Only this time, it hadn't worked out.

"I can't believe she said no," I say to Denver who had been close enough to hear the entire thing, even though I hadn't had it on speaker. We have spent most of the morning looking at various apartments in the neighborhood. I've been taking notes at each new place we visit so that, when I go home later, I can make a pros and cons list. Mom's lists have helped me narrow down some really tough decisions.

I walked outside to the backyard patio of the current place so I could make this call, and now I wish I'd been paying more attention to the landlord sharing details about the property instead.

He comes up beside me and gently rubs my shoulder. "I'm surprised she did. Did she say why?"

I sigh and sit down on one of the steps. The house is built on a hill and the backyard rolls down at a slope. Probably not the best for young kids running around, but I don't have to consider that prospect for a while. But it's not entirely crazy to think about. My maternal clock is ticking, and I'm not even married yet. I know myself though. Whatever place I land on, I'll want to stay there for as long as possible. I need a place I can feel steady in. A place I'll want to claim as home long-term.

Placing each arm against my legs, I rest my head in my hands, eyes closed. I sense Denver sitting down next to me, and he continues rubbing soft, soothing circles along my back.

"Yeah, she said it has to do with their confidentiality policy. She doesn't feel right inviting the public into a private space. Which I guess makes sense. I'm just bummed."

"Hmm, yeah I hadn't thought of that either. I'm sorry. But hey, I'm sure we'll figure it out," he says, trying to reassure me.

I open my eyes and stare off into the distance. My book comes out next Saturday, so finding somewhere now is going to be nearly impossible. I may as well forget it. It isn't meant to happen.

"Hey," his voice, deep and pure, reaches me, luring me in. Tugging me to him. I look over at him. His deep, sea-green eyes hold steadfast to mine and I let them.

"It's going to be okay. We'll figure this out," he repeats.

I know he means well and I appreciate that, but I just don't see how it can happen at this point. Maybe I shouldn't have been so quick to write off Books and Beyond. I had one bad experience, but that doesn't mean a second signing would be bad too. There is always room for second chances.

I know what it means to be on the other side of second chances—I'd given plenty of those to my mom. And then to my dad, after he'd come clean with me about his affair and we'd talked about everything. Most people I found it easy to give second chances to; giving them to myself was a different story. One I was still writing.

"I don't know... it's only a week away." I sigh, defeated.

"Leave it to me, okay?" he offers.

It's too much to ask of him, I couldn't do that. I shake my head. "No, I can't ask that of you. That's too much weight for you to carry."

He tucks a piece of hair behind my ear. It sends a wave of goosebumps all over my body, and I shiver.

"Believe me, this is nothing. I've carried way more than this." I know exactly what he's talking about. Tears instantly prick my eyes, and I pull my gaze away from him. He gently tugs my chin back towards him. As if to say, *Look at me.*

"We both have. We both have carried so much weight. And we had to carry that weight alone. But we're not alone any longer, and this is nothing. I want to do this for you. Let me help you, Phoenix."

"Why do you care so much?" I ask, my voice breaking. Doubt is creeping in. Don't let it...

"Because..." he says, still holding me close to him, "I care about *you.* Don't you get that by now? I want *you,* Phoenix."

"Nobody besides family has ever wanted me... besides Wendy of course, but she doesn't exactly count—" I start.

He shakes his head. *No?*

"I want you."

"But surely not all—"

He doesn't let me finish. "All. Of. You."

WE DIDN'T RIP off each other's clothes in the middle of the back patio with the realtor standing right inside, but I'm sure it crossed both our minds. It's not a conversation we've had yet, but that's okay. I'm not exactly ready for that. I'm a virgin and need to work up to the bigger stuff. Obviously, he's no virgin. He's been married and has a daughter that he's raised most of her life, but I'm not sure where he stands in that department. I haven't been brave enough to talk to him about it yet, but I'm sure it'll come up at some point.

We have done some heavy making out and touching, but we aren't in any rush when it comes to each other. I think we both waited what feels like a lifetime to find one another, and so we're willing to spend the rest of this one discovering what it means to be with one another. When I'm with him everything just feels *right*.

I do still question myself from time to time, but I am getting better. More confidence, less self-deprecation. I am a work in progress, and so is he. Although, I haven't found many flaws about Denver yet. Except that he says he snores. I have yet to witness that, but we'll see how I feel about it then.

Later, after we finish looking at all that we're going to look at for the afternoon, we are both starving. We end up at a local burger joint and order burgers. I play it safe with the black bean veggie burger and a side of curly fries, while he orders a bleu cheese burger with a fried egg. Maybe after we've been dating for a little longer I'll brave eating the double-stacked BBQ Queen burger that I've heard is a fan favorite at this place.

While we wait for our food, he asks me what I thought about the places we'd seen today. I'd taken pictures in each, except for one. We'd both walked in, said a quick "nope," and walked out. Needless to say, we didn't need to see the rest. The place had reeked of cigarette smoke and the carpet and walls were stained badly. The place hadn't been well-cared for at all and would need more TLC than I was willing to give.

"So, what did you think? Any for sures? Any maybes? Any you

can cross off your list?" he asks as he takes a sip from his Diet Dr Pepper.

"Definitely some maybes, and I think there might be a few I'm nixing as well. The one we both walked out of is certainly crossed off the list, and I think there may have been one other. But I think I'm mixing them up in my head, and I'll have to look back through all the pictures later."

It was a lot of fun doing this with him. I'd been nervous to go with him at first, but he stood back and let me look without pressing his opinions on me. He wanted this to be my decision, and I'm glad he respected that.

"That's fair. I could see you living in just about any one of them. There is, however, another option..." he says, a sly smile spreading across his face.

What's he talking about? We've seen all the ones we had in mind for today. I don't have anything else scheduled.

"Another option?" I ask innocently, obviously not getting where he's heading with this. My stomach pinches with nerves.

"Yeah, my place. Move in with me," he says so casually that I nearly spit out the drink I was about to swallow.

He wants me to do what? He can't possibly be serious. Everything about him says he is one hundred percent serious right now. I set my drink back down on the table and lean a little closer to him. "What did you just say?"

"Move in with me."

Wow, he said it again. He isn't joking. But what about Marvel? Has he already discussed this with her? We've spent all morning looking at place after place, why hasn't he asked me sooner? How long has he considered this as an option for us?

As if he can read my thoughts he answers me, "Marvel was the one that suggested the idea to me first."

"You're kidding." I deadpan.

"Absolutely not. I'd told her we were apartment hunting today, and she asked why you wouldn't move in with us already. She wouldn't joke about something like that. We discussed it and thought it'd be a great idea, on all accounts."

He's so sure of this. I wish I had his kind of confidence, but I don't. I've never lived with anyone else before, and I'm not sure I'm ready for that yet. We just got back into a relationship, I don't want to mess it up now by bringing all my baggage to his front door. I shake my head.

"I'm sorry, but I don't think so. At least not right now," I say, dropping my gaze.

"Tell me why. I want to at least hear your reasons. Give me your pros and cons list of why you shouldn't move in with us," he says matter-of-factly.

Okay, that's how he wants it. I'll shoot him straight then. Wait, what are my reasons?

"Um, okay. Well, con: We haven't been dating for that long and this is all still so new to me. I'm not sure that I'm ready for that step yet." It's the truth at least.

He nods. "Okay, that one's fair. Continue."

"Hmm. Con: I don't cook anymore."

"That's fine, I enjoy cooking and I've been teaching Marvel more and more. So you're covered there. Next."

I try to hide my smile from him. I'm enjoying this little game we're playing but don't want to let him in on my little secret. I keep going.

"I don't have a car, and I don't drive. I'm pretty inconvenient. I have to be driven everywhere and that can get pretty tiresome," I offer. Surely that will stop him in his tracks. But do I want it to stop him?

"Nice try. You'd be living with two people who can drive. Marvel's a great driver, believe it or not. Plus, I'd still help you get around if you were living alone. Living here makes it more convenient. So this is really a pro instead of a con." He chuckles at this and I smile. He's good.

"Okay," he says, taking another drink, "Now for the pros. Go."

"Pro: I like you, and it'd be nice waking up to you every morning." I blush as I say this.

He doesn't say anything, so I keep going.

"I've never felt so drawn to someone before and it feels like I've known you for a long time. It doesn't feel like we met only a couple of months ago. It feels like I've known you forever. I know that probably sounds crazy."

He shakes his head. "No, I don't think it does. Anything else?"

"I can be real with you. I can fully be myself around you. You take me as I am and don't try to change me. You accept my flaws, and there are many, but you know them and you came back for me."

"I won't run again, Phoenix. I'm here to stay," he says, and I believe it with all of my heart.

"I know, and that's the other thing. For the longest time, I ran away from love, safety, and comfort because I didn't believe that it was something I could have or ever deserved. I still didn't think I deserved any of those things when I first met you. But little by little, you've melted my icy exterior and found my heart. I even tried to run away from you. I didn't know what any of this was or what any of it meant, and it terrified me. And when I get scared, I run. I don't want to run away anymore." Especially not from *him*.

"Then choose to stay. Stay with me," he pleads, reaching across the table for my hands.

There's that word again. *Stay.* A word that has echoed in my life like a heartbeat. An anthem I've had on repeat ever since the day I lost my mom. Maybe this time my head will actually listen to what my heart is telling me. The song it's been trying to sing for sixteen years now.

Our food hasn't come yet, so I reach for his hands in return. We both hold on tightly, not wanting to let the other go.

"I need time to consider the possibility of moving in with you, but it's not because I don't want to. I just need to think it through," I say.

"Okay, take your time."

"Thank you."

We both say each other's names at the same time again, like we've done once before.

"You first." He laughs.

"No, you." I laugh back.

"Phoenix... I'm in love with you. I love you."

I am so taken aback by this that I find myself at a loss for words. But not *those* words. I never, in a million years, expected to hear them again. And to hear them coming from his mouth. For me. He loves *me*.

"I love you back," I whisper across the table to this man, and I mean it with my whole heart.

We sit there grinning at each other.

"What were you going to say?" he asks.

"Nothing that significant." I grin.

"Like what?"

"Just that I hope our food shows up soon because my stomach is about to start growling."

He smiles. I can't get over his smile. His gorgeous, white-as-snow, perfect teeth. With lips I'm dying to kiss again.

Right on cue, our waitress arrives at our table with two steaming hot plates full of food. We look at each other across the table and smile. I can't remember ever feeling this happy, except when I'd been with my mom.

Denver said he was in love with me. Maybe God has forgiven my sins after all. Maybe I will finally get my happy ending.

Then: March 15th, 16 years ago

The drive from Atlas Creek to the state park is a solid two-hour drive. I pass the time by reading a book I'd started a few days ago, while Dad keeps his eyes steady on the road.

I haven't gotten behind the wheel since Mom's death. I can't face it. It almost feels worse than the terrible sin I've committed. Dad and I haven't been going to church as often as we used to, and I'm starting to wonder if God forgives all sins, especially mine and Mom's.

She'd taken her own life, but I'd taken somebody else's. Hers had been on purpose, while mine was an accident. Still, I had been behind the wheel when I was in no right mind to be driving. As part of my punishment, for as long as I have left on this earth, I don't think I should be behind the wheel.

It might seem a little extreme, but I don't think so. I haven't said any of this to Dad, of course. He can tell something is eating away at me, and the front bumper on Mom's car has a dent. For weeks all I'd thought I'd hit was the mailbox in front of the house. Until that awful article came out that told me a different story. A twelve-year-old girl named Genny had been killed in a hit-and-run, and if anyone knew anything they were to come to the local police station right away.

I felt sick about what I'd done. At first, I didn't think it could have possibly been me. I'd heard the car scrape loudly against metal, and when I'd gathered the courage to walk past the house weeks later, the mailbox was gone. I was sure that was all the damage I'd caused.

But when I later read that someone at that very address had been killed in a car accident, I experienced an entirely different sense of dread. *Surely, I didn't read that right. It could have been somebody else that same day right?* But you know how sometimes you just get that horrible sensation in your gut and it won't go away no matter what you do? It was that very thing that would start to eat at me from that day forward. Something I couldn't erase, and something I couldn't forgive.

Something so dark and tragic that my brain couldn't even hold onto the memory of it—just tiny fragments of the whole picture.

All kinds of thoughts raced through my head. *Should I tell someone? Who, Dad? What would he do? Would he blame me and leave me alone like Mom had? Would I spend the rest of my life in a jail cell, all because I'd been grieving the loss of my mother?* I'm sixteen years old. A sixteen-year-old that just lost her best friend, her mother. And now the only family I'm left with is my dad, who takes good care of me but isn't someone who's exactly been there for me growing up. Now he has no choice.

Maybe I don't deserve anything and should be rotting the rest of my life away in jail. But that thought doesn't make me feel any better. It makes me feel a whole lot worse. The least I can do is leave flowers or something for the girl who went to be with my mother. This might be weird to think about, but maybe they are in a better place together. Maybe she's already forgiven me for taking her out of this world too soon.

I am so unbelievably sorry. I can't say it enough to mean anything. But I am. I will be sorry for the pain I've caused the rest of my life.

SALLY'S IS BUSIER than I thought it would be. We arrive around lunchtime and eat at our favorite spot on the patio that overlooks the lake. It's still just as beautiful as I remember it being. After we finish our burgers and fries, we get checked in and start setting up camp. By camp, I mean old-school camping. It feels a little strange without Mom here, but maybe she's here anyway. I feel her in most places I go.

We have all of our food packed in coolers with tons of ice, and Dad's trunk is filled with all the necessities. We are only staying here for three nights. It's a brief getaway, but I'm looking forward to it. We've both been suffocating in our house and need to breathe the fresh mountain air again. It's early spring and the earth is starting to bloom.

The air is crisp but as soon as we get all set up, Dad makes a fire. We sit around it and cook hotdogs and marshmallows. Later he makes me some hot chocolate and we drink our hot drinks underneath the stars. It's a beautiful night, and I can't help but think about Mom again. Always. I wonder how long she will be a constant in my thoughts. Some days it's super painful, and I can't cope with it. And then other times, on a night like this, it brings me peace, knowing that she can invade my thoughts without it feeling invasive.

"Dad?" I say, sitting next to him in my camping fold-out chair, with my legs out-stretched toward the fire for warmth.

"Yes, Sweet P?" he asks, poking at the fire. He is constantly poking and prodding at the flames. I know you can't just sit here and enjoy the fire, somebody has to put in all the effort, and I'm thankful that it's him and not me. I find it a little funny because he's always so still and calm, and right now he's like a child that can't leave something alone.

"Is it hard for you when you think about Mom?" I ask gently. Holding onto my mug in between both hands, keeping them warm.

He doesn't look over at me, keeping his focus solely on the fire, but he's thinking it over. Mom rarely thought before she spoke, I like that Dad takes his time before answering.

"Yes, especially at night. It's why I haven't been sleeping great, and I'm sure you've probably noticed that I've been sleeping on the couch for now. Eventually, I'll make my way back in there, but it's too much right now, and I can't do it. Does that make any sense?" he asks.

I understand it completely, because after all, I had found her first.

"Yeah, it's hardest for me in the mornings. When I wake up it hits me all over again. Sometimes it takes several tries before I finally convince myself that the day has any significance at all. I know that sounds dark and depressing, but it's true. And then when hunger finally hits me, I have to go into the kitchen and that's where I remember her the most. Always singing, always dancing, always whipping up something delicious.

"I can't walk in there and not want to burst out in song. I feel like I can still smell the syrup from the pancakes she'd always make me for my birthday every year. Now, when I walk in there, I only feel her absence. I feel the empty spaces that she's isn't. And sometimes I have to walk back out because it's too much and I can't handle it. So yeah, I get it," I say, surprised by the depth of our conversation so far. But in a good way.

He takes a break from playing with the fire and leans back in his chair. This is usually the time of year he shaves his beard. But he hasn't yet and it's the longest I've ever seen it. He looks even older than he is, and sitting here now with the mountains fading into the background he looks like a true mountain man. I stifle a laugh but instead, it flies free, escaping in full force.

He looks over at me, wondering what in the world could be funny right now. Here we are talking about how painful it's been without Mom in the picture, and I'm sitting here laughing. What is wrong with me?

I can't help it. Laughs are bubbling out of me now like a cackling hyena. A smile cracks over Dad's face and a small chuckle falls out.

"What's so funny? What are you laughing at?"

"Y-you." I giggle. I cover my mouth in an attempt to hush myself, but it's no use. I'm turning hysterical. Fits of laughter are bellowing out of me.

"Me?" he asks, laughing and pointing to himself.

"Yes. You!" I double over. I can't stop.

"What did I do? Or say?"

"N-nothing."

"Doesn't sound like nothing."

I get myself together briefly, out of breath from laughing so hard. Man, that feels good. I feel like I just ran a marathon and my lungs are trying to keep up as I catch my breath. Eventually, my breathing returns to a normal speed. Whew.

"What was all that about?" he asks again, still smiling.

Ah, it's so good to see him smile. I'd almost forgotten what it looked like. I don't remember the last time I'd laughed like that, or if I ever had. It felt *good*.

"Nothing really, but your beard makes you look like you live out here in the wilderness." I grin.

He reaches up and strokes his beard, and then nods at me as though he agrees. "I think you might be right. Should I shave it?"

"No, I like it. It suits you somehow," I say, honestly.

"Hmm. I don't think I'm going to be going off the grid anytime soon though," he teases.

"Oh yeah, I wasn't expecting that." I joke.

"But maybe someday?"

"Sure, if you want to," I offer, not sure if he's serious or pulling my leg. Either way, if anyone could figure it out, he could.

"Well, I think I'm happy here for now. I'm glad we're doing this. Thanks for agreeing to come out here. I know none of this has been easy," he says, sincerely.

I finish off what's left in my mug and set it down in the grass beside me. "Me too, Dad. Really."

We're quiet for a while, simply watching the heavens and enjoying each other's company.

"One last thing," I say.

"Sure."

"Do you think we'll ever be happy again?"

He pauses for another moment, contemplating just how to answer that. *Don't ever be afraid to ask the hard things*, Mom once told me.

"Right away? No. Tomorrow or the next day? Probably not. Eventually? Yeah. I believe one day we will be happy again. I'll miss her forever, but that doesn't mean I can't ever be happy again," he starts, and then adds, "I am happy when I'm with you."

I smile and spend the rest of the evening watching the flames dance until we let them fall away. When the last ember fades to black I head off to bed. I end up sleeping the best night I've slept in months.

Now: March 22nd

The final piece of *The Honey Sisters* is officially being released today. The full title is *The Honey Sisters, The Journey Rediscovered.* I first started writing this series two years ago. I've come out with a few others in between because I wanted to make sure that I did this story justice. After the first one had been a hit, it was the confidence boost I needed to keep going.

This one's for you, Mom.

Denver wasn't lying when he said he wanted to make this day happen for me. Wendy had politely turned down the bookstore's offer to have the signing there and told me she had something better in mind.

At the time, I didn't have a clue what she meant. All I knew was that Wendy and Denver had something up their sleeves, and I was to be no part of it. They'd wanted to plan the whole thing themselves and surprise me. Well, fortunately for them, I am no good at guessing, and after the third or fourth failed attempt, I gave up. I'd find out what they were up to soon enough.

It's a little nerve-wracking leaving something completely in the hands of somebody else. But if there's anyone I can put my trust in, it's the two of them. I'm thankful we didn't have to cancel the event entirely. I would have been fine doing a virtual "launch" party of sorts, but this is better. Way better.

Denver is driving with Wendy in the passenger seat and me in the backseat next to Marvel. Everyone is giddy because everyone knows what the surprise is but me. Even Dad was sworn into secrecy and is on his way with Deb.

It's a long car ride, and it feels like we are driving forever. When we are getting closer, I'm instructed to close my eyes and promise not to peek. Marvel covers my eyes with the palm of her hand for good measure. Just to make sure I'm not trying to cheat. I wouldn't dare ruin their surprise.

"ONE, TWO, THREE, OPEN!" they yell at the same time. Slowly I open my eyes, and Marvel removes her hand from my face. I roll down my window and my mouth drops wide open at the sight before me.

We are entering the gates of a state park. I recognize the gates immediately and tears instantly well in my eyes. I can't believe they brought me *here*. I haven't been here in ages, but I remember this place clearly. This is where Dad and I used to come every year for our camping trips after Mom's passing. Eventually, as I got older and started writing more, and Dad took over the accounting firm and got busier, we stopped coming as often. Until finally, we stopped coming at all. I couldn't tell you the last time we'd set up camp here in Mom's memory. It has been too long.

I hear something as we start to pass through the gates, and I realize it sounds a bit like people chanting. What are they saying? Surely, I'm not hearing them right. Lined up on both sides of the entrance to the park are rows and rows of people. Some are holding signs, some are holding up copies of my books, and others are jumping up and down, excited to see us. To see *me.* There has to be hundreds of people here. We drive through slowly, and I force myself to wave to them out the window, tears blurring my vision. They all came here to see me and support my new book? I cannot believe it. It's too much.

They are chanting my name, over and over. But it's not *Nicki! Nicki! Nicki!* like I would have expected to hear. No, it's something entirely new. Something I wasn't even sure my fans would have accepted, yet here they are chanting my name—the one my mother had given me at birth. *Phoenix! Phoenix! Phoenix!* I bring a hand over to my mouth in awe. I'm fighting tears and an ugly sob that wants to escape from my lungs. I feel a small arm wrap around my shoulders and pull me close as she whispers, "You did it, you really did it."

I guess I did. Wow.

I can't get over the fact that Denver and Wendy planned all of this. I have no idea how many people are here right now, but they are still pouring in by the hundreds. More than I could have ever imagined. They brought me to one of my mom's favorite places, Sally's in the Park.

They have tables lined up with each novel in my series, plus a few others I've written in the more recent years for sale. The crowd has been patiently waiting for me to arrive and to officially announce the launch of my new book. I'm still in shock.

"Hello, and good afternoon. Um, wow. I can say with one hundred percent certainty that when my writing team told me they were planning something big, I wasn't expecting this," I say nervously into the microphone Wendy just handed me. I look over at my best friend, and she's beaming from ear to ear. She takes a bow and blows me a kiss. She's ridiculous, but I wouldn't change a thing about her. I give a little wave to Janie, my publisher, who is standing off to the side. She has tears in her eyes and gives me a thumbs up. I couldn't have gotten this far without either of them. I have an amazing team.

"As you all know, the last book in *The Honey Sisters* officially releases in just a moment, and you all get the *first* sneak peek into my latest novel."

Loud cheers and claps erupt from the crowd. Denver is standing off to the side with his hands on his daughter's shoulders, next to my Dad and his girlfriend, Deb, who couldn't look more proud to be here right now. It means more than they will ever know to have all of them here with me now.

"We will cut the ribbon and open the lines up for book sales and autographs in a moment, but I have to make a quick announcement first."

A soft murmur goes through the crowd, wondering what kind of announcement I'm about to make. I have decided to go through with the LA film team, but won't be making that announcement until a few months from now, just to make sure everything is up and running first.

This is something even bigger. Something I've debated doing for a while, but finally decided to go for it. If I don't do it now, it may not happen until years from now, or maybe not ever.

I take a deep breath and exhale. I can do this.

I start telling the crowd about my mom. It reminds me of the day, not that long ago, when I told a group of strangers my story at one of the G&G meetings. The one I had no idea that Denver was listening to. But he'd been there the whole time. I plan to start attending regularly now. I feel like it could be good for me. I didn't think it would ever be a place I could fit in, but I'm starting to make a few connections, and Denver's offered to continue going with me. It's a huge step for both of us.

By the time I finish talking about my mom, several people are either sniffling, wiping their eyes, or even blowing their noses. I glance over at Dad and his eyes are filled with tears, but they aren't tears of sadness this time. They are tears filled with love at remembering who she was. And for loving her despite all her flaws. None of us are perfect.

I motion to Wendy, and she walks over to me and hands me something. I tuck it behind my back for a moment before pulling it out into view.

"Sixteen years ago, my mother gave me her most prized possession—her journal. It had been filled with poems she'd written over the years. I've read over them countless times, so many times in fact, that I've memorized several. Some of her writing is dark. She mentions wanting to die, thoughts of death, and often feeling like she was suffocating. My mother was many things, but I had no idea she'd felt this way. For her birthday, I'd spent weeks typing all of her poems and binding them into book form. I never had the chance to give them to her. And it broke my heart. I lost my love of writing for a long time."

I look down at the book in my hands and hold it out for everyone to see. It's a hardback cover that is dark green like the worn journal she'd given me, and on the front of the cover, etched in a shimmery gold, is a picture of a phoenix, rising through the flames. Underneath the bird is the title I've chosen for her collection, along with her name.

"Until one day," I began again, "Writing gave me new wings. It brought me hope in my darkest nights. It allowed me to get up again and start my new beginning. Hence, the title of the book my mother wrote, in her honor, *New Beginnings.*"

Applause immediately takes over the crowd. Many are cheering, some are still wiping their eyes, and I don't realize I'm crying and smiling until someone's arms wrap around my shoulders. I know without looking who it is. I know, without a doubt, that he is not only standing here to support me today but quite possibly forever. I never thought in a million years that I would ever deserve someone like him. And yet here he is, standing by my side. For me and with me. I've never loved someone the way that I love him. I can only pray that he feels the same way. He kisses the top of my head and in that moment, I *know*.

I just do.

WE END up selling out of all of my books. The moment the ribbon has been officially cut, the people come streaming in by the hundreds. It is insane. Denver, Marvel, Dad, and Deb are all at a table, working. I'm at a table with Wendy and her two daughters signing all the books after people purchased them from the other lines. We work quickly and sell out within hours of opening. I've never experienced something more exciting in my life. Copies of my mom's poetry book sold the quickest.

I had countless people thank me for sharing my story and say how they could relate to my pain. Some had also lost a parent in some terrible tragedy. I laughed and cried with strangers, and swapped memories with others. The afternoon quickly turns into evening, and by the time the sun is setting, people are finally starting to leave. This has seriously been the best day. If only Mom could have been here for it—maybe in some ways she was. I felt her in the gentle breeze and the whispering of the trees between the mountains. Her very aroma was somewhere in the air, honey, and vanilla... *Mom*. She had been here, I sensed it.

Dad finds me after and gives me one of his bear hugs. "I love you so much, Phoenix. You're an amazing writer and an even more amazing daughter. I am so proud, and your mother would have been too. I remember that night you first showed her journal to me and told me your idea for her birthday. Sixteen years, and I still remember. And because of what you've done with your mother's precious gift... others can remember her too. You are incredible, and it's a huge blessing to be your dad."

He pulls away before we can start crying again, and I thank him and Deb both for coming. I'm really glad that they have each other, he's needed someone by his side ever since Mom left. It's nice that we have both finally found that person.

Before Wendy drives back home with her family, she gives me a final hug and we both lose it. I can't help it, she's been here with me through it all. She's stuck around the longest. I can't believe she's put up with me for so long, but I'm forever grateful that she has.

Denver is the last to come up to me. He's got one last surprise for me. I just can't with this guy. How could he possibly do one more thing tonight that he hasn't already done? This day has been nothing shy of amazing. I can't stop replaying today's events in my head.

"Okay, seriously, what is it now? You all have done *more* than enough today," I say, making sure to emphasize the word more.

"You'll see." And this time he places a hand over my eyes and walks me a little ways away from where we'd held today's event. Marvel got a ride home with Wendy, so I have no idea what this is about. I try to pull his hand away, and he finally lets me.

When I open them I gasp. A full camping scene unfolds before my eyes. There's a tent set up with tiny twinkling lights wrapped all the way around it so it glows in the darkening night sky. There's a fire burning and two chairs set up right next to it. I cannot believe it. Denver did all of this?

"You did this? Are you camping here tonight?" I ask, shocked. I can't believe he did this. He is full of surprises today.

"Your dad helped me set everything up when people started to leave. He's the one who told me what this place has meant to you and helped make it all happen. He loves you, you know."

I do know. I should have never once doubted his love for me, even during the years he had a funny way of showing it, but this speaks volumes to me. This kind of love reaches higher than the mountaintops.

"And correction. *We* are camping here tonight." He grins, winking at me as he motions for me to sit in one of the camping chairs.

I raise an eyebrow at him in question. Is he being serious right now? It sure looks that way.

"Oh, are we now? You've decided this?"

"Only if you want me to, Phoenix. You say the word and I will."

I don't even need to hesitate. I am in love with him. I don't want to let him out of my sight for a single moment. I want to spend the rest of my days with him, just like this. Through the valleys and the mountaintops. Because this is our story—our new beginning.

"Stay here with me tonight, Denver."

"Just tonight?" he questions, teasing me.

I scoot my chair closer to his so that our legs are touching. I lay my head upon his shoulder and our fingers weave together.

"Forever, if you'll let me," I say quietly into the night air.

"I will love you until the day I die, Phoenix Larrs. Let's live out our forever."

And so we begin.

Then: April 1st, 15 years ago

It's been one year and one month since Mom passed. Passed is too gentle of a term for what she did, but it sounds less aggressive than saying my mom killed herself a year ago. Not that anyone is asking me this, but if it ever comes up in conversation I'll probably say that she left and leave it at that. It's part of the truth without having to dive deep into all of the whys about what she did. I'll never understand her *why*.

After our camping trip last spring, we agreed to make it a yearly tradition. It wouldn't necessarily need to be in the same spot, but why not? Why fix what's not broken? And it turned out to be a great trip. Dad and I bonded over s'mores and day hikes over nearby trails. Nothing too strenuous, but just right for both of us. We'd return to camp after hours of walking through rocky terrain and sometimes, before the sun disappeared below the horizon, I'd dip myself in the creek for a quick rinse. The water had been freezing, but it'd been the perfect shock to my system. It made me feel *alive*.

We're already planning for our yearly trip next month when it's a little warmer.

As soon as we'd returned home, Dad kept his word and dropped me off at the library each day, as promised. I'd spent the morning pouring over my assignments and finished my school-work for the day by lunchtime. Dad went into a private study room somewhere else in the library with his laptop and got work done there. I think we both enjoy the quiet space of the library, knowing that we don't have to be stuck at home all day.

I start setting an alarm and waking up early each morning. Dad sometimes still attempts new recipes whenever he gets an itch to cook something, but it isn't long before we both conclude that it isn't doing either of us any favors. Before long, we start making our own meals. Sometimes for breakfast, I'll have a bowl of yogurt with cinnamon granola, or avocado spread on toast with salt and pepper. Lunch is often salad, soup, or a sandwich. Dinner is often something I can easily pop into the microwave. I miss Mom's home-cooked meals, but I still can't force myself to make any of them. Maybe someday, but not today.

Monday through Friday we head to the library and are the first to arrive as soon as they open at nine a.m. We both work until noon, and then I allow myself to wander through the bookshelves. Since we've been coming to the library more often, I've started reading again. I read book after book. The more books I read, the more I'm itching to start writing again. The ideas are there, but I haven't let any come to life on paper. I've waved them away, as though they are pesky bugs I want to get rid of—but they are getting harder to ignore.

One day after finishing up my assignments, I turn to a blank page in my notebook and start to write. I plan to jot down ideas for a story that has been replaying in my head for the past few weeks, but my pen has a different plan instead. Funny how that happens sometimes.

What came out wasn't a story at all, but a poem. A poem that flows out of me effortlessly. I don't think I've ever written poetry before, that was Mom's thing, not mine. I read the words I've just written, and then I read them again.

I walk up to the front desk and show it to the librarian. She is an older lady with thick, black-rimmed glasses, and she's reading a large novel at her desk when she glances up at me from over the top of her lenses. It always weirds me out when people do that.

"Can I help you, dear?" she asks me politely.

I don't say anything but hand her my writing. She adjusts her glasses and peers down at the paper. She takes a moment to read through it and looks up at me.

"This is good. Did you write this?"

I'm beaming. But maybe she is supposed to say that sort of thing. "I did, thank you."

"*Really* good. In fact, you should join our writing club. We meet on Fridays at four o'clock. It's only an hour and there's snacks."

A writing group? I don't know... I don't know if I'm ready for that sort of thing. I've enjoyed coming here before other people arrive. It's not busy during the weekdays since most other people my age are at school, and other adults are working. We mostly have the whole place to ourselves. I don't know about sharing this poem with a group of people.

She must read my nervous expression as she softens her gaze and hands my poem back to me.

"No pressure, of course, but it's a great tool if you want to improve your writing. Sometimes we have authors come in and do talks, and sometimes we offer different writing courses. If it's something you're passionate about you should come check it out."

She reaches somewhere below her desk and pulls out a flier, handing it to me.

I thank her and quietly walk back to where I've been working and pack up my things. Maybe I will go. It won't hurt anything to go at least once and see what it's all about.

FRIDAY AFTERNOONS HAVE QUICKLY BECOME my favorite. I always bring something new that I've written. Whether it's a short story or ideas for one that I want to run by the group, I always make sure to have something I can offer. It's not a large group, there are never more than six people in attendance each week. I'm not sure how many have signed up, but at least four or five come every week.

Surprisingly, I'm the youngest aspiring writer in the group. I tell them I'm thinking of getting my degree in creative writing and literature. Several who are currently in college or graduated years ago have online colleges they recommend to me. I start applying to all of them right away.

Friday afternoons have become my new safe haven. I already spend most of my days here, but coming here with a group of like-minded people has never felt so refreshing. I didn't say much the first couple of meetings, but ever since then I've connected in a way, a year ago, I would never have imagined.

I ended up graduating early. I worked all through the summer and didn't take any breaks except for our one camping trip. On weekends we never do much, I usually save those for reading and writing. During the week I was back into go-mode.

My old school, Atlas High, reached out to me and asked if I would like to walk with my class next month, but I declined. It isn't a bad school or anything, but it isn't a place I have any desire to return to, even if it is to walk across the stage and be handed an official diploma. The online school I graduated from partners with my school for students who have dropped out or, due to certain life circumstances, need a break from the on-campus education style. Everyone in school knew about what happened last February. It'd been one of the smartest decisions for me personally not going back to the public school system.

For the first couple of weeks, students I'd barely said one word to were suddenly texting me about how sorry they were for my loss. A few even had the nerve to ask how she had ended her life. I thanked a few of the ones I felt were sincere, but after the news became "old news," not one of them continued talking to me. It was as though they had wanted to be a part of the gossip and when it died down, they had already moved on.

I can't fault them for it too much, I'd probably have done the same thing. Because they didn't know what it was like. They hadn't lost their mom in such a tragic, terrible way. To them, it was another name in the paper, another name on a tombstone they would have forgotten by tomorrow.

They probably already have.

I haven't heard back from any of the colleges I've applied to yet, but it's still probably a bit early. I turned seventeen earlier this school year and have recently started working on my first novel. It's going to be a murder mystery that takes place in the course of one evening. The murder happens around midnight and the story starts ten hours earlier that day and counts down until the big moment when "it" happens. I haven't reached that point yet, but I'm close.

Dad has mostly kept busy with his work. I asked him if he got a new job, and he said it was the same one but he was able to do most of it from home. When I asked him what he'd meant by "most," he shrugged and said it meant that once a month or so he'd have to go into the main office downtown. But not like the crazy hours he used to work.

As odd as our relationship can be at times, it is slowly and surely getting better. I am thankful for him being here. I'm not sure what our day-to-day would look like if I'd stayed in public school and he'd continued commuting and working long hours. Our lives would look a lot different, and I try not to dwell on it too much. Rather, I want to be grateful for how things are. As grateful as I can be anyway.

Even though we've had a year without Mom, it still feels like she left us yesterday. I still see her and hear her in everything. But already, most days, it's not as painful. Like when I'm lost in my writing, or wrapped up in a book I'm trying to finish, or talking about book things with some of my new writing friends at the library.

Those are the few times I'm allowed to escape. Escape the gaping hole she's left inside my heart. Escape the pain when I'm lying there at night tossing and turning because I miss her so much it's unbearable. She will never wrap her warm arms around me and hug me close to her beating heart. I will never hear her laugh echo through the walls of this house. I will never sing and dance with her to our favorite 90s bands in the kitchen, cooking our favorite meals together.

She will never drag me to therapy again. She will never show up unannounced and demand her presence like she often would. She will never whisk me away on another one of her adventures. We will never get to play our favorite game of Christmas Shopping List. She never did let me win.

Some days I write all of these things down. I write lists of all the things I loved about my mother and another list of all the things that drove me wild. Once, on a really bad day, I'd spent a solid hour coming up with a list of things, only to shred them all to pieces by the time I finished. I immediately regretted it and tried to rewrite as many of the items as I could remember. Dad had walked into my room to find me madly scribbling a new list on a ripped-out sheet of paper, sobbing.

He walked over to me, without saying a word, and wrapped his arms around me tightly. He didn't let go until I stopped crying.

And then he kissed me on the top of my head, something Mom used to do on some of our best days together. The gesture made me cry even more, and even then he didn't let me go. His arms wrapped back around me and we stayed that way for what felt like a lifetime.

I never imagined needing my dad in this way until now. And now, for as many days as we are given on this earth together, I never want to let him go.

Stay, stay, stay.

EPILOGUE

Now: Valentine's Day, 1 year later

For the longest time, I've dreaded this day. This day only brings back memories that are too painful to recall, and every year I have to relive this nightmare. The nightmare of losing my mother.

Today, that all changes. After I released my mom's book, *New Beginnings,* along with mine, things did not slow down one bit. Denver and I spent the rest of the weekend at Sally's. On the last day, as we were getting everything all packed up, Denver was zipping up our sleeping bags on the ground when he looked up at me with a goofy grin on his face. What was he up to now? Turns out, he wasn't just zipping up our sleeping bags, he was down on one knee getting ready to propose to me. Oh. *Ohhh.*

I said yes. A thousand times, yes.

By the end of the month, we moved in together. I decided it was time, and I was as ready as I was ever going to be. Denver was sweet, of course, and said we could take things slow. None of this is slow, but he's cute for saying it anyway.

A month after *that,* I started gathering all of my mom's best recipes together, and a cookbook in her name will be coming out as soon as we return from our honeymoon. It took some digging to gather enough recipes to fill a book, but it's finally ready. With much-appreciated help from Wendy, Dad, Denver, and Marvel. Marvel created all of the illustrations in the book, and did a spectacular job—I have high hopes for that kid! Speaking of...

Shortly after our engagement, Marvel offered to take me out for a drive. My first time behind the wheel since the accident seventeen years ago. We decided to take it slow. Every Friday after she's done at school, she swings home and I hop into the driver's seat. I have to admit it was weird at first. So far, thankfully, there has only been a couple of times where I flat-out panicked and she had to talk me through it. She is really good at that.

But she agreed that I should start small. So every drive I pick one place to take us to. It's typically within a twenty or thirty-mile radius, and then I drive us back home. Any other day of the week when Denver is with us, he always takes the wheel. But I love that Marvel and I get this special one-on-one time together. Just me and her. *Just us girls.*

Baby steps. Sometimes that's all it takes. There's also been another minor change in the last year. Seeing the joy that Marvel and Denver have together creating something in the kitchen, has uncovered a newfound passion when it comes to cooking and baking. Every Saturday night Dad and Deb join us for a home-cooked meal. Neither of them cook much, that hasn't changed, but they always bring something along. Denver and Marvel have both enjoyed getting to try new recipes that my mom had created from scratch, and make into something that we'd all enjoy as a family again years after she passed.

Today, we are getting married. This is technically our second Valentine's together, but last year's doesn't count. I had just told him the news about his sister, and it'd been too much too soon for both of us. I wouldn't say things are perfect, but fairly close. Especially since he wants to marry me.

Things progressed a bit quicker after we got engaged, but we wanted to wait a little bit before picking a date and making it official. Marvel has been amazing too. From the moment we met when I passed out at her first book signing, to the time I blacked out practically in her arms—she's been there for me. She accepts me into their family without question or apprehension. She loves fiercely, and so does her dad.

For the last seventeen years, this day has haunted me. Haunted both of us. Denver with the anniversary of his sister's death, and me with my mom's. Today, we are going to change that. We aren't erasing the past or blocking out their memories. We are doing the opposite. We are bringing back love and hope to this day. This day will no longer be remembered only as a day of tragic loss, but a day of rebirth, new life, and a new beginning.

Marvel was born on this day seventeen years ago. For most of her life, her birthday lived in the dark shadows of her father's tragedy. But not anymore. It was Marvel who had surprised me one day by asking if we would pick this day as our wedding day. At first, I'd wondered why in the world she would have chosen today of all three-hundred-sixty-five days in a year—but she'd wanted it to be this one. Today.

Not a day sooner and not a day later. Now.

So, here we are moments away from saying *I do.*

If someone had asked my sixteen-year-old self if I pictured this very day now seventeen years into the future, I would have said no. Absolutely not.

But today, I can see it clearly. I have found my silver lining. I chose to rise from the ashes, rather than remain stuck on the ground. I stopped running from the pain of my past and embraced my new wings. Now, I'm soaring.

There's also one little thing I haven't mentioned to anyone

yet. I just found out a week ago. There's a tiny bundle of life growing inside of me, and before too long, I am going to be a mom.

We had planned on waiting a little longer, but what can I say? I love everything about this man, and we couldn't wait a moment longer to share that strong connection. He is amazing, and I can't wait to tell him the news. Our news.

It's too soon to say if it's a boy or a girl, but I'm betting it's going to be a girl. And I've even jotted down a pros and cons list. Silly, I know, but I can't help it. I think I've narrowed it down between two names. If it's a boy, I want to name him Matty Jo Marks. Matt is my dad's name, and Jo is short for Jolene, my mom's. But if it's a girl, I know exactly what I want to name her. *God, if you're listening.*

I would name my baby girl after the two people in our lives we both loved and lost. The name would not only be in their honor but provide a new legacy for her to live out. She wouldn't be tied down by a name, no, she would claim it and live. Live because her life has meaning, purpose, and hope. Live because God has given her the very air that she breathes.

I can't stop thinking about Denver, the man I am going to marry. I don't deserve his love, yet he gives it to me freely, without cost or reserve. I want to share the rest of my life with this person —how quickly he's become *my* favorite person. I can't wait to see where life takes us. Because I know no matter what kinds of twists and turns life has to throw our way, he will be there by my side. He will be there to *stay*.

I look at myself in the mirror. Marvel is curling my hair, and for a moment I don't see my reflection staring back at me, I see my mother's. Shiny, copper eyes, like a new penny. Sparkling and bright, the way hers used to light up. I'll never forget the way her entire face would light up when she was happy to see me. Today, I'll remember that side of my mother.

Tears form in my eyes, and I quickly blink them away. I've

dreamed about this day for ages, written about it in countless novels, and it's finally coming true in my own story.

Baby girl, if you get the chance to read this someday... I hope you know how much you are already loved. My sweet little girl, my sweet *Genesis Jo.* This is for you. Go and live out your dreams, like I am living out mine.

"NEW BEGINNINGS"
PHOENIX JO MARKS

I'D BEEN LOST
BROKEN DOWN
BY LIFE'S CRUEL HANDS.

I COULDN'T WALK
ON SOLID GROUND
INSTEAD, I RAN.

I HID MYSELF AWAY
I WASN'T WORTHY
DIDN'T DESERVE TO BE LOVED.

YOU CAME WITH SCARS
WRITTEN ON YOUR HEART
OUR STORIES COLLIDED.

THE OLD BECAME NEW
PAST WOUNDS BEGAN TO HEAL
FROM A LOVE THAT WAS REAL.

TOGETHER WE CREATED
A NEW STORY
THIS WOULD BE OUR NEW BEGINNING.

TWO BROKEN PEOPLE
IN NEED OF MENDING
LOVE HAS MADE A WAY.

TRIGGER WARNING

Contains Spoilers

There are elements in this story that can be triggering to some, and I want to try and be sensitive to that. If you are easily triggered by events such as the following, this story may not be for you. While this novel is fictional and not based on real events, it touches heavy subjects such as: suicide, severe depression, manic episodes, mania, panic attacks, parent/sibling death, and car accidents.

You know what you can handle, your mental health matters.

AUTHOR'S NOTE

I couldn't quite tell you exactly how I came up with this story. As most stories do, it just came to me one day. It quite literally is a "lightbulb" moment. But it goes a little deeper than that. I love to dip my toes in different genres. My first self-published piece was my poetry collection back in 2022. This past year in 2024, I released my debut mystery novel, and now in 2025, I'm publishing my first standalone romance novel.

Like some movie actors stick with similar roles, some authors do the same thing. And I think that is great. If you've found your niche, then why mess with that, right? I don't think I have just one niche. I read all genres, and therefore I write all genres. Okay, you will probably never get horror, sports romance, or fantasy from me... sorry to burst any bubbles! But the second the tiny spark of this story ignited, I immediately had to run with it. I could not let it go, and I became obsessed. I hope the same happens for you!

I love books that bring me to tears. Okay, "almost tears" because, as many of you know, I have a hardened heart when it comes to reading and getting emotional. BUT, I love heartbreaking stories that have Happily Ever Afters (HEAs). Thus, the birth of Genesis. I had a few goals when I started this. One: If I could bring out some of those strong emotions through something I wrote, I did something right. Doesn't even have to be crying, but I want you to feel something when you read this.

Two: I want to break your heart for the things that break mine, and then put them together again. I want you to fall in love with my characters and root for them to succeed by the end. I want you to laugh when they laugh and cry when they cry. If I accomplished any one of those things, then my goals have been met.

Also, I realize Denver and Phoenix's story contains some heavy material. That was fully intentional. Even though it is fictionalized, I want readers to be able to relate to their pain. We all have lost somebody we love, whether that be a grandparent, a parent, or a close friend. We have all lost, and we have all gained.

We have hurt and ached over things in this life that have beaten and broken us down. I get that. I've been there too. And while this story walks through that pain and trauma, I also want readers to know that there is hope. There is light on the other side of their darkest night, and by the end, Phoenix and Denver both realize that. They find each other and despite everything that they have experienced, love still finds a way.

If anything else, I want readers to take away that message. Despite what has happened in Phoenix and Denver's pasts, as long as they are still breathing, their life isn't over. Their story isn't over yet. Don't think of this as the end, but a new beginning. You too, can begin again.

Never give up hope. You are not alone.

In crisis and need someone to talk to? Text HOME to 741741 to speak with a Crisis Counselor today. Or visit crisistextline.org.

JOLENE'S RECIPES

Butterscotch Maple Pancakes

Ingredients

<u>Butterscotch Sauce:</u>
½ cup unsalted butter
½ cup dark brown sugar (packed down)
1 cup of heavy cream
½ tsp kosher salt
2 tsp vanilla extract
1 tbsp whiskey (optional)

<u>Pancake Batter:</u>
1 ½ cup of all-purpose flour
1 ½ tsp baking powder
3/4 tsp baking soda
1/4 tsp salt
2 large eggs
1 cup of buttermilk
1 cup of butterscotch sauce

3 TBSP UNSALTED BUTTER (MELTED + COOLED)
MAPLE SYRUP (A GIVEN!)

How to Make the Magic Sauce!

IN A MEDIUM SAUCEPAN, MELT THE BUTTER OVER MEDIUM HEAT.

ADD BROWN SUGAR + STIR TO COMBINE. BRING TO A BOIL THEN REDUCE HEAT TO A SLOW AND STEADY BOIL. STIR FREQUENTLY AROUND 2-3 MINUTES (BEST ENJOYED TO A CLASSIC 90's TUNE TO HELP PASS THE TIME!)

CAREFULLY ADD IN THE HEAVY CREAM + SALT; STIR TO COMBINE. RETURN MIXTURE TO A BOIL FOR ANOTHER 3-4 MINS, STIRRING FREQUENTLY.

REMOVE BUTTERSCOTCH SAUCE FROM HEAT + STIR IN VANILLA EXTRACT (AND WHISKEY) AND LET THAT BABY REST.

*SAVE A LITTLE BONUS SAUCE FOR THE END, YOU'LL THANK ME LATER!

How to Make the Perfect Pancakes:

IN A LARGE BOWL MIX TOGETHER FLOUR, BAKING POWDER, BAKING SODA, + SALT. SET ASIDE.

IN A MEDIUM BOWL WHISK TOGETHER EGGS, BUTTER-MILK, BUTTERSCOTCH SAUCE, + MELTED BUTTER.

ADD WET MIXTURE TO DRY + STIR TOGETHER, MIXING WELL. *DO NOT OVERMIX OR YOU WILL HAVE LUMPY HOTCAKES! WHOMP, WHOMP!*

HEAT GRIDDLE/SKILLET TO MEDIUM HEAT. COAT WITH BUTTER GENEROUSLY + LADLE 1/3 CUP OF THE BATTER ONTO THE GRIDDLE FOR EACH PANCAKE.

COOK UNTIL THE EDGES ARE GOLDEN + BUBBLY (ABOUT 2-3 MINS... ABOUT THE TIME TO LISTEN TO ANOTHER JAM). FLIP THAT BABY + COOK ANOTHER 2-3 MINS ON THE OTHER SIDE (YOU KNOW WHAT TO DO!)

Top with softened butter, REAL maple syrup + a bonus drizzle of the magic sauce you made earlier.

Enjoy!!

Mama's Meatloaf

Ingredients:

2 lbs. ground beef
2 eggs
1 ½ cup bread crumbs
3/4 cup chili sauce
2 tbsp "W-Sauce" aka Worcestershire

The Easy Part!
Get your tunes on of course. Now, you're ready to go!
Combine beef, eggs, and bread crumbs.
Mix chili sauce + W-sauce and set aside.
Place the meat mixture into a loaf pan. Toss in not one, but two pinches of salt for extra flavor.
Pour sauce over the top.
Bake for 1 hour at 350°. Serves 6.

Apple Crumble Muffins

Ingredients:

<u>But First, Muffins!</u>
2 1/4 cup of flour
1 1/2 cup of brown sugar, packed
1 tsp baking soda
1/2 tsp salt
1 tsp cinnamon
1 tsp nutmeg
1 egg
1 cup of buttermilk
1/2 cup of butter, melted
1 tsp vanilla extract
2 cups of apples, diced (leave the peeling on, you'll thank me later!)

<u>Muffin Top-pings (Get it?)</u>
1/2 cup of brown sugar
1/2 cup of pecans, chopped
1/3 cup of flour
1 tsp of cinnamon
2 tbsp of butter, melted

<u>Now, for the fun part!</u>
Preheat the oven to 375°.
Combine dry ingredients into a large bowl.
Add wet ingredients together. Do your very best not to overmix
Add apples and gently stir in until coated.
Place the mixture into the muffin pan, scooping about 2/3 full into each cup on the pan. That's about 3 tbsp full each if you want to be exact. I just like to throw some in and hope for the best!

In a small bowl combine topping ingredients.
Coat everything in butter.
Cover muffins with the topping. Yum!
Bake in the oven for 25-30 minutes.

ABOUT THE AUTHOR

Delon Nicole Starkey is an author from Ohio. She lives there with her husband and two beautiful children. She's passionate about her faith, family, friendships, and writing. You'll catch her sneaking off to local coffee shops as often as she can.

LET'S CONNECT!

Instagram: author.delonnicole
Facebook: Delon Nicole (author)
Goodreads: Delon Nicole
Website: www.delonnicole.com

Your Feedback Matters!
Please leave a review on Goodreads or Amazon!